LIGHT O' THE MORNING
The Story of an Irish Girl

by

L. T. Meade

Double 9
BOOKS

LIGHT O' THE MORNING
The Story of an Irish Girl
by L. T. Meade

ISBN: 978-93-59396-01-9

Published by

DOUBLE 9 BOOKS
2/13-B, Ansari Road
Daryaganj, New Delhi – 110002
info@double9books.com
www.double9books.com
Tel. 011-40042856

ABOUT THE AUTHOR

Elizabeth Thomasina Meade Smith (1844–1914), a prolific author of novels for girls, used the pen name L. T. Meade. She was the daughter of Rev. R. T. Meade of Nohoval, County Cork, and was born in Bandon, Ireland. In September 1879, she wed Alfred Toulmin Smith after relocating to London. In her lifetime, she wrote over 280 volumes, starting when she was just 17 years old. She was so productive that eleven new books with her name on them appeared in the first few years after her passing. She was most recognized for her young adult novels, the most well-known of which was A World of Girls, which was released in 1886. 37,000 copies of A World of Girls were sold, and it had a significant impact on novels about girls' schools written in the 20th century. She did, however, also write "sentimental" and "sensational" tales, religious tales, historical novels, journeys, romances, and mysteries, some of which had male co-authors. Meade was a pioneer club member and a feminist. Meade wrote The Cleverest Woman in England, a novel based on the life of women's rights activist and Pioneer Club founder Emily Langton Massingberd (1847–1897), after her passing in 1898.

CONTENTS

CHAPTER I
NORA

"Why, then, Miss Nora—"

"Yes, Hannah?"

"You didn't see the masther going this way, miss?"

"What do you mean, Hannah? Father is never at home at this hour."

"I thought maybe—" said Hannah. She spoke in a dubious voice, backing a little away.

Hannah was a small, squat woman, of a truly Irish type. Her nose was celestial, her mouth wide, her eyes dark, and sparkling with fun. She was dressed in a short, coarse serge petticoat, with what is called a bedgown over it; the bedgown was made of striped calico, yellow and red, and was tied in at the waist with a broad band of the same. Hannah's hair was strongly inclined to gray, and her humorous face was covered with a perfect network of wrinkles. She showed a gleam of snowy teeth now, as she looked full at the young girl whom she was addressing.

"Ah, then, Miss Nora," she said, "it's I that am sorry for yez."

Before Nora O'Shanaghgan could utter a word Hannah had turned on her heel.

"Come back, Hannah," said Nora in an imperious voice.

"Presently, darlint; it's the childer I hear calling me. Coming, Mike asthore, coming."

The squat little figure flew down a side walk which led to a paddock: beyond the paddock was a turnstile, and at the farther end of an adjacent field a cabin made of mud, with one tiny window and a thatched roof. Hannah was making for the cabin with rapid, waddling strides. Nora stood in the middle of the broad sweep which led up to the front door of the old house.

Castle O'Shanaghgan was a typical Irish home of the ancient régime. The house, a great square pile, was roomy and spacious; it had innumerable staircases, and long passages through which the wind shrieked on stormy nights, and a great castellated tower at its north end. This tower was in ruins, and had been given up a long time ago to the exclusive tenancy of the bats, the owls, and rats so large and fierce that the very dogs were afraid of them. In the tower at night the neighbors affirmed that they heard shrieks and ghostly noises; and Nora, whose bedroom was nearest to it, rejoiced much in the distinction of having twice heard the O'Shanaghgan Banshee keening outside her window. Nora was a slender, tall, and very graceful girl of about seventeen, and her face was as typical of the true, somewhat wild, Irish beauty as Hannah Croneen's was the reverse.

In the southwest of Ireland there are traces of Spanish as well as Celtic blood in many of its women; and Nora's quantities of thick, soft, intensely black hair must have come to her from a Spanish ancestor. So also did the delicately marked black brows and the black lashes to her dark and very lovely blue eyes; but the clear complexion, the cheeks with the tenderest bloom on them, the softly dimpled lips red as coral, and the little teeth white as pearls were true Irish characteristics.

Nora waited for a moment after Hannah had left her, then, shading her eyes from the westerly sun by one hand, she turned slowly and went into the house.

"Where is mother, Pegeen?" she said to a rough-looking, somewhat slatternly servant who was crossing the hall.

"In the north parlor, Miss Nora."

"Come along, then, Creena; come along, Cushla," said the girl, addressing two handsome black Pomeranians who rushed to meet her. The dogs leaped up at her with expressions of rapture, and girl and dogs careered with a wild dance across the great, broad hall in the direction of the north parlor. Nora opened the door with a somewhat noisy bang, the dogs precipitated themselves into the room, and she followed.

"Ah, then, mother dear! and have I disturbed you?" she said.

A pale-faced lady, who was lying full-length on a very old and hard sofa, rose with a querulous expression on her face when Nora entered.

"I wish someone would teach you thoughtfulness," she said; "you are the most tiresome girl in the world. I have been two hours trying to get a wink of sleep, and just when I succeed you come in and wake me."

"It's sorry I am to my heart's core," said Nora. She went up to her mother, dropped on one knee, and looked with her rosy face into the worn and faded one of the elder woman. "Here I am, mammy," she said again, "your own little Nora; let me sit with you a bit—may I?"

Mrs. O'Shanaghgan smiled faintly. She looked all over the girl's slim figure, and finally her eyes rested on the laughing, lovely face. Then a cloud crossed her forehead, and her eyes became dim with tears.

"Have you heard the last thing, Nora?"

"There are so many last things, mother," said Nora.

"But the very last. Your father has to pay back the money which Squire Murphy of Cronane lent him. It is the queerest thing; but the mortgagee means to foreclose, as he calls it, within three months if that money is not paid in full. I know well what it means."

Nora smiled. She took her mother's hand in hers, and began to stroke it gently.

"I suppose," she said, "it means this. It means that we must part with a little more of the beloved land, every sod of which I love. We certainly do seem to be getting poorer and poorer; but never mind—nothing will ever alter the fact that—"

"That what, child?"

"That we O'Shanaghgans are the proudest and oldest family in the county, and that there is scarcely an Englishman across the water who would not give all he possesses to change places with us."

"You talk like a silly child," said Mrs. O'Shanaghgan; "and please remember that I am English."

"Oh, mummy, I am so sorry!" said the girl. She laid her soft head down on the sofa, pressing it against her mother's shoulder.

"I cannot think of you as English," she said. "You have lived here all, all my life. You belong to father, and you belong to Terence and me—what have you to do with the cold English?"

"I remember a time," said Mrs. O'Shanaghgan, "when I thought Ireland the most desolate and God-forsaken place on the earth. It is true I have become accustomed to it now. But, Nora, if you only could realize what my old home was really like."

"I don't want to realize any home different from this," said the girl, a cloud shading her bright eyes for the moment.

"You are silly and prejudiced," said Mrs. O'Shanaghgan. "It is a great trial to me to have a daughter so unsympathetic."

"Oh, mummy! I don't mean to be unsympathetic. There now, we are quite cozy together. Tell me one of the old stories; I do so love to listen."

The frown cleared from Mrs. O'Shanaghgan's forehead, and the peevish lines went out of her face. She began to talk with animation and excitement. Nora knew exactly what she was going to say. She had heard the story so often; but, although she had heard it hundreds and thousands of times, she was never tired of listening to the history of a trim life of which she knew absolutely nothing. The orderly, well-dressed servants, the punctual meals, the good and abundant food, the nice dresses, the parties, the solid education, the discipline so foreign to her own existence, all—all held their proper fascination. But although she listened with delight to these stories of a bygone time, she never envied her mother those periods of prosperity. Such a life would have been a prison to her; so she thought, although she never spoke her thought aloud.

Mrs. O'Shanaghgan began the old tale to-night, telling it with a little more *verve* even than usual. She ended at last with a sigh.

"Oh, the beautiful old times!" she said.

"But you didn't know father then," answered Nora, a frown coming to her brows, and an angry feeling for a moment visiting her warm heart. "You didn't have father, nor Nora, nor Terry."

"Of course not, darling, and you make up for much; but, Nora dear, although I love my husband and my children, I hate this country. I hate it!"

"Don't, mother," said Nora, with a look of pain. She started to her feet. At that moment loud, strong steps were heard in the hall; a hearty voice exclaimed:

"Where's Light o' the Morning? Where have you hidden yourself, witch?"

"It's father," said Nora. She said the words with a sort of gasp of rejoicing, and the next moment had dashed out of the room.

CHAPTER II
"SOME MORE OF THE LAND MUST GO"

Squire O'Shanaghgan was a tall, powerfully built man, with deep-set eyes and rugged, overhanging brows; his hair was of a grizzled gray, very thick and abundant; he had a shaggy beard, too, and a long overhanging mustache. He entered the north parlor still more noisily than Nora had done. The dogs yelped with delight, and flung themselves upon him.

"Down, Creena! down, Cushla!" he said. "Ah, then, Nora, they are as bewitching as yourself, little woman. What beauties they are growing, to be sure!"

"I reared them," said Nora. "I am proud of them both. At one time I thought Creena could not live; but look at her now—her coat as black as jet, and so silky."

"Shut the door, won't you, Patrick?" said his wife.

"Bless me! I forgot," said the Squire. He crossed the room, and, with an effort after quietness, closed the door with one foot; then he seated himself by his wife's side.

"Better, Eileen?" he said, looking at her anxiously.

"I wish you would not call me Eileen," she said. "I hate to have my name Irishized."

The Squire's eyes filled with suppressed fun.

"Ah, but you are half-Irish, whether you like it or not," he said. "Is not she, colleen? Bless me, what a day it has turned out! We are getting summer weather at last. What do you say to going for a drive, Eileen—Ellen, I mean? Black Bess is eating her head off in the stables. I want to go as far as Murphy's place, and you might as well come with me."

"And I too?" said Nora.

"To be sure, child. Why not? You run round to the stables, Norrie, and give the order."

Nora instantly left the room, the dogs following her.

"What ails her?" said the Squire, looking at his wife.

"Ails her, Pat? Nothing that I know of."

"Then you know very little," was his answer. "I never see that sort of anxious frown between the colleen's brows without knowing there's mischief in the wind. Somebody has been worrying her, and I won't have it." He put down his great hand with a thump on the nearest table.

"Don't, Pat. You quite shatter my nerves."

"Bless you and your nerves, Ellen. I want to give them all possible consideration; but I won't have Light o' the Morning worried."

"You'll spoil that girl; you'll rue it yet."

"Bless her heart! I couldn't spoil her; she's unspoilable. Did you ever see a sweeter bit of a thing, sound to the core, through and through?"

"Sweet or not," said the mother, "she has got to learn her lesson of life; and it is no good to be too tender with her; she wants a little bracing."

"You have been trying that on—eh?"

"Well, not exactly, Pat; but you cannot expect me to keep all our troubles to ourselves. There's that mortgage, you know."

"Bother the mortgage!" said the Squire. "Why do you harp on things the way you do? I'll manage it right enough. I am going round to see Dan Murphy now; he won't be hard on an old friend."

"Yes; but have you not to pay up?"

"Some day, I suppose."

"Now listen, Patrick. Do be reasonable. Whenever I speak of money you fight shy of the subject."

"I don't—I don't," said the Squire restlessly; "but I am dead tired. I have had a ride of thirty miles; I want my tea. Where is Nora? Do you mind my calling her? She'll order Pegeen to bring the tea here."

"No; I won't have it. We'll have tea in the dining room presently. I thought you objected to afternoon tea."

"So I do, as a rule; but I am mighty dhry—thirsty, I mean, Ellen. Well, all the better; I'll get more to drink in the dining room. Order the tea as soon as you please."

"Ring the bell, Patrick."

The Squire strode to the mantelpiece, pulled a bell-cord which hung from the ceiling, a distant bell was heard ringing in noisy fashion, and a moment afterward Pegeen put in her head.

"Come right in, Margaret," said her mistress.

"Aw! then, I'm sorry, ma'am, I forgot," said the girl. She came in, hiding both her hands under her apron.

Mrs. O'Shanaghgan uttered an impatient sigh.

"It is impossible to train these creatures," she said under her breath. Aloud, she gave her order in quiet, impassive tones:

"Tea as soon as possible in the west parlor, and sound the gong when it is ready."

"Why, then, wasn't I getting it?" said Pegeen. She left the room, leaving the door wide open.

"Just like them," said Mrs. O'Shanaghgan. "When you want the door open they invariably shut it, and when you want it shut they leave it open."

"They do that in England too, as far as I can tell," said the Squire, with a slightly nettled tone in his voice.

"Well, now, Patrick, while we have a few moments to ourselves, I want to know what you mean to do about that ten thousand pounds?"

"I am sure, Ellen, it is more than I can tell you."

"You will have to pay it, you know."

"I suppose so, some day. I'll speak to Dan to-night. He is the last man to be hard on a chap."

"Some more of the land must go," said the wife in a fretful tone. "Our rent-roll will be still smaller. There will be still less money to educate Terence. I had set my heart on his going to Cambridge or Oxford. You quite forget that he is eighteen now."

"Cambridge or Oxford!" said the Squire. "Not a bit of it. My son shall either go to Old Trinity or he does without a university education. Cambridge or Oxford indeed! You forget, Ellen, that the lad is my son as well as yours."

"I don't; but he is half an Englishman, three parts an Englishman, whatever his fatherhood," said the Squire's wife in a tone of triumph.

"Well, well! he is Terence O'Shanaghgan, for all that, and he will inherit this old place some day."

"Much there will be for him to inherit."

Eager steps were heard on the gravel, and the next instant Nora entered by the open window.

"I have given the order," she said; "Angus will have the trap round in a quarter of an hour."

"That's right, my girl; you didn't let time drag," said her father.

"Angus wants you and mother to be quite ready, for he says Black Bess is nearly off her head with spirit. Now, then, mother, shall I go upstairs and bring down your things?"

"I don't mind if you do, Nora; my back aches a good bit."

"We'll put the air-cushion in the trap," said the Squire, who, notwithstanding her fine-lady airs, had a great respect and admiration for his wife. "We'll make you right cozy, Ellen, and a rattle through the air will do you a sight of good."

"May I drive, father?" said Nora.

"You, little one? Suppose you bring Black Bess down on her knees? That horse is worth three hundred pounds, if she's worth a penny."

"Do you think I would?" said the girl reproachfully. "Now, dad, that is about the cruelest word you have said to your Nora for many a day."

"Come and give me a hug, colleen," said the Squire.

Nora ran to him, clasped her arms round his neck, and kissed him once or twice. He had moved away to the other end of the room, and now he looked her full in the face.

"You are fretting about something?"

"Not I—not I," said the girl; but she flushed.

"Listen to me, colleen," said the Squire; "if it is that bit of a mortgage, you get it right out of your head. It's not going to worry *me*. I am going this very evening to have a talk with Dan."

"Oh, if it is Dan Murphy you owe it to," said the girl.

"Ah, he's all right; he's the right sort; a chip of the old block—eh? He wouldn't be hard on a brother in adversity?"

"He wouldn't if he could help it," said Nora; but the cloud had not left her sensitive face. Then, seeing that father looked at her with intense anxiety, she made a valiant effort.

"Of course, I believe in you," she said; "and, indeed, what does the loss of money matter while we are together?"

"Right you are! right you are!" said the Squire, with a laugh. He clapped her on the shoulder. "Trust Light o' the Morning to look at things in the right direction," he said.

CHAPTER III
THE WILD MURPHYS

Terence made his appearance at the tea table. In every respect he was a contrast to Nora. He was very good-looking—strikingly handsome, in fact; tall, with a graceful elegance of deportment which was in striking contrast to the burly figure of the old Squire. His face was of a nut-brown hue; his eyes dark and piercing; his features straight. Young as he was, there were the first indications of a black silky mustache on his short upper lip, and his clustering black curls grew in a high ridge off a lofty brow. Terence had the somewhat languid air which more or less characterized all his mother's movements. He was devoted to her, and took his seat now by her side. She laid her very thin and slender hand on his arm. He did not respond by look or movement to the gesture of affection; but had a very close observer been present he would have noticed that he drew his chair about the tenth of an inch nearer to hers.

Nora and her father at the other end of the table were chattering volubly. Nora's face was all smiles; every vestige of that little cloud which had sat between her dark brows a few moments before had vanished. Her blue eyes were sparkling with fun.

The Squire made brilliant sally after sally, to which she responded with all an Irish girl's aptitude for repartee.

Terence and his mother conversed in low tones.

"Yes, mother," he was saying, "I had a letter from Uncle George this morning; he wants me to go next week. Do you think you can manage?"

"How long will you be away, Terence?"

"I don't know; a couple of months, perhaps."

"How much money will it cost?"

"I shall want an evening suit, and a new dress-suit, and something for everyday. These things are disgraceful," said the lad, just glancing at the frayed coat-sleeve, beneath which showed a linen cuff of immaculate whiteness.

Terence was always the personification of fastidiousness in his dress, and for this trait in his character alone Mrs. O'Shanaghgan adored him.

"You shall have it," she said—"somehow."

"Well, I must reply tonight," he continued. "Shall I ask the governor, or will you?"

"We won't worry him, Terry; I can manage."

He looked at her a little anxiously.

"You are not going to sell any more of them?" he said.

"There is a gold chain and that diamond ring; I never wear either. I would fifty times rather think that you were enjoying yourself with my relations in England. You are fitted to grace any society. Do not say another word, my boy."

"You are the very best and noblest mother in the world," said the lad with enthusiasm.

Meanwhile, Nora and her father continued their gay conversation.

"We will take a basket with us," said Nora, "and Bridget shall give me a couple of dozen more of those little brown eggs. Mrs. Perch shall have a brood of chicks if I can manage it."

"Trust the girleen for that," said the Squire, and then they rose from table.

"Ellen," he continued, addressing his wife, "have you and Terence done colloguing together? for I hear Black Bess coming to the front door."

"Oh, hasten, mother; hasten!" said Nora. "The mare won't stand waiting; she is so fresh she is just ready to fly."

The next few moments witnessed a scene of considerable bustle. Mrs. O'Shanaghgan, with all her English nerves, had plenty of pluck, and would scorn to show even a vestige of fear before the hangers-on, as she called the numerous ragged urchins who appeared from every quarter on each imaginable occasion. Although she was shaking from head to foot with absolute terror at the thought of a drive behind Black Bess, she stepped into her seat in the tall dog-cart without a remark. The mare fidgeted and half reared.

"Whoa! whoa! Black Bess, my beauty!" said the Squire. The groom, a bright-faced lad, with a wisp of yellow hair falling over his forehead, held firmly to the reins. Nora jumped up beside her mother.

"Are you going to drive?" asked that lady.

"Yes, mummy; you know I can. Whoa, Black Bess! it's me," said the girl. She took the reins in her capable little hands; the Squire sprang up behind, and Black Bess flew down the avenue as if on the wings of the wind.

Mrs. O'Shanaghgan gave one hurried pant of suppressed anguish, and then sat perfectly still, her lips set, her hands tightly locked together. She endured these drives almost daily, but had never yet got accustomed to them. Nora, on the contrary, as they spun through the air, felt her spirits rising; the hot young blood coursed through her veins, and her eyes blazed with fun and happiness. She looked back at her father, who nodded to her briefly.

"That's it, Nora; keep her well in. Now that we are going uphill you can give her her head a bit. Whoa, Black Bess! Whoa!"

The mare, after her first wild canter, settled into a more jog-trot gait, and the dog-cart did not sway so violently from side to side. They were soon careering along a wide, well-made road, which ran for many miles along the top of some high cliffs. Below them, at their feet, the wild Atlantic waves curled and burst in innumerable fountains of spray; the roar of the waves came up to their ears, and the breath of the salt breeze, the freshest and most invigorating in the world, fanned their cheeks. Even Mrs. O'Shanaghgan felt her heart beating less wildly, and ventured to put a question or two to Nora with regard to the clucking hen, Mrs. Perch.

"I have not forgotten the basket, mammy," said the girl; "and Hannah will put the eggs under the hen tonight."

"I am quite certain that Hannah mismanaged the last brood," said Mrs. O'Shanaghgan; "but everything goes wrong at the Castle just now."

"Oh, mother, hush! he will hear," said Nora.

"It is just like you, Nora; you wish to keep——"

"Oh, come, now," said the Squire; "I hear the grumbles beginning. No grumbles when we are having our ride—eh, Ellen? I want you to come back with a hearty appetite for dinner, and a hearty inclination to sleep tonight."

They drove faster and faster. Occasionally Nora touched the mare the faintest little flick with the end of her long whip. The creature responded to her touch as though girl and horse were one.

At last they drew up outside a dilapidated gate, one hinge of which was off. The Squire jumped down from his seat, came round, and held the horse's head.

"Whoa! whoa!" he said. "Hullo, you, Mike! Why aren't you in your place? Come and open the gate this minute, lad."

A small boy, with bare feet and ragged trousers, came hurrying, head over heels, down the road. Mrs. O'Shanaghgan shuddered and shut her eyes. The gate was swung open. Nora led the mare skillfully round a somewhat sharp corner, and the next instant they were dashing with headlong speed up a steep avenue. It was neglected; weeds grew all over it, and the adjacent meadows were scarcely distinguishable from the avenue itself.

The Squire ran after the dog-cart, and leaped up while the mare was going at full speed.

"Well done, father!" called back Nora.

"Heaven preserve us!" thought Mrs. O'Shanaghgan, who still sat speechless, and as if made of iron.

At last they reached a long, rambling old house, with many small windows, interspersed with a few of enormous dimensions. These were called parliament windows, and had been put into many houses of that period in order to avoid the window-tax. Most of the windows were open, and out of some of them ragged towels were drying in the evening breeze. About half a dozen dogs, most of which were of mongrel breed, rushed forward at the sound of the wheels, barking vociferously. Nora, with a dexterous touch of her hand, drew the mare up just in front of the mansion, and then sprang lightly to her feet.'

"Now, mother, shall I help you down?"

"You had better find out first if Mrs. Murphy is in," said the Squire's wife.

A ragged urchin, such as seemed to abound like mushrooms in the place, came and held the reins close to the horse's mouth. The creature stood trembling from the violence of her exertions, and pouring down moisture at every pore. "She wants to be well rubbed down," said the Squire. "She doesn't get half exercise enough; this will never do. What if I have to make money on her, and she is spoiled?"

The low words which came to his lips were not heard by anyone; there was a frown, very like Nora's own, between his brows. The next moment a small man, with reddish hair, in a very shabby suit of half-worn tweed, appeared on the steps of the front door.

"Hullo, O'Shanaghgan, is that yourself?" he called out. "How are you, Mrs. O'Shanaghgan? Right glad to see you. You'll step inside—won't you? I believe the wife is somewhere round. Neil, my man, go and look for the missus. Tell her that Madam O'Shanaghgan is here, and the Squire. Well, Nora, I suppose you are wanting a chat with Bridget? You won't find her indoors this fine evening."

"Where is she, Mr. Murphy?" asked the girl. "I do want to have a talk with her."

"Ah! what's the basket for?"

"I want her to give me some of the pretty brown eggs."

"Well, go right down there by the sea-path, and you'll find her, as likely as not."

"Very well," answered Nora. Slinging her basket on her arm, she started for her walk. As soon as she was out of sight she began to run. Presently she stopped and began whistling "The Wearing of the Green," which was responded to in a moment by another voice, sweet as that of a blackbird. She looked to right and left, and presently saw a pair of laughing black eyes looking down at her from beneath the shelter of a huge oak tree.

"Here I am. Will you climb up?" said the voice of Bridget Murphy.

"Give me a hand, and I'll be up with you in a moment," said Nora. She tossed her basket on the ground; a very firm, little brown hand was extended; and the next moment the girls were seated side by side on a stout branch of the tree.

"Well, and what has brought you along here?" said Bridget.

"I came with father and mother in the dog-cart," replied Nora. "Father let me drive Black Bess. I had a jolly time; but she did pull a bit—my wrists are quite stiff."

"I am glad you have come," said the other girl. "I was having a concert all by myself. I can imitate the thrush, the blackbird, and most of the birds round here. Shall I do the thrush for you?"

Before Nora could speak she began imitating the full liquid notes of the bird to perfection.

"I declare you have a genius for it," said Nora. "But how are you yourself, Biddy?"

"What should ail me?" replied Biddy. "I never had a care nor a worry nor a trouble yet; the day is long, and my heart is light. I am at peace, and I never had an ache in my body yet. But what is up with you, Nora alannah?"

"It's that mortgage, you know," said Nora, dropping her voice. "What is your father going to do?"

"Oh, the mortgage," said Bridget. "Mr. Morgan came down from Dublin yesterday; he and father had a long talk. I don't know. I believe there's worry in the air, and when there is I always steer clear of it."

"Your father, you mean?"

"I can't tell you; don't question me. I am glad you have come. Can't you stay for the night?"

"No, I can't. I must go back with father and mother. The fact is this, Bridget, I believe your father would do anything in the world for you."

"I suppose he would. What do you want to coax out of me now? Oh, Nora alannah! don't let us talk of worries. Come down to the sea with me—won't you? I have found the most lovely cave. I mean to explore it with lanterns. You go into the cave, and you can walk in nearly half a mile; and then it takes a sudden turn to the right, and they say there's an entrance into another cave, and just beyond that there's a ghost supposed to be. Some people say it is the home of the O'Shanaghgans' Banshee; but whatever it is, I mean to see all about it."

"Do you mean the Sea-Nymphs' Cave?" said Nora. "But you can only get to that by crossing the bay."

"Yes. Well, I am going tomorrow night; the moon is at the full. You will come over and go with me—won't you?"

"Oh! I wish I could."

"But why can't you? Don't let us worry about fathers and mothers. We're a pair of girls, and must have our own larks. There's Neil and there's Mike; they will get the boat all ready, and we can start off for the cave just when the tide is high; we can only get in then. We'll run the boat in as far as it will go, and we'll see what we'll see. You will come—won't you, Nora?"

"I should like it of all things in the world," said Nora.

"Well, why not? You can come over tomorrow afternoon, and stay the night here. Just say that I have asked you."

"But mother does not much like my sleeping out."

"You mean that she does not like you to sleep at the house of the wild Murphys—that's what you mean, Nora. Then, get away; I don't want to force my company on you. I am as good as any other girl in Ireland; I have the blood of the old Irish kings in my veins; but if you are too proud to come, why——"

"I am not, and you know it," said Nora; "but mother is an Englishwoman, and she thinks we are all a little rough, you and I into the bargain. All the same, I'll come to-morrow. I do want to explore that cave. Yes, I'll come if you give me a proper invitation before mother."

"Oh, mercy me!" said the girl, "must I go back to the house? I am so precious shabby, and your lady-mother has got such piercing eyes. But there, we can smuggle in the back way. I'll go up to my room and put on my bits of finery. Bedad! but I look as handsome as the best when I am dressed up. Come along, Nora; we'll get in the back way, and I'll give the invitation in proper style."

CHAPTER IV
THE INVITATION

Bridget and Nora began to climb up a very steep and narrow winding path. It was nothing more than a grass path in the midst of a lot of rock and underwood, but the girls were like young chamois, and leaped over such obstacles with the lightness of fawns. Presently they arrived at the back entrance of Cronane, the Murphys' decidedly dilapidated residence. They had to cross a courtyard covered with rough cobbles and in a sad state of neglect and mess. Some pigs were wallowing in the mire in one corner, and a rough pony was tethered to a post not far off; he was endeavoring, with painful insistence, to reach a clump of hay which was sticking out of a hayrick a foot or two away. Nora, seeing his wistful eyes, sprang forward, pulled a great handful of the hay, and held it to his mouth. The little creature almost whinnied with delight.

"There you are," said Bridget. "What right have you to give our hay to that pony?"

"Oh, nonsense," said Nora; "the heart in him was starving." She flung her arms round the pony's neck, pressed a kiss on his forehead, and continued to cross the yard with Biddy. Two or three ragged urchins soon impeded their path; one of them was the redoubtable Neil, the other Mike.

"Is it to-morrow night you want the boat, Miss Biddy?" said Neil.

Bridget dropped her voice to a whisper.

"Look here, Neil," she said, "mum's the word; you are not to let it out to a soul. You and Mike shall come with us, and Miss Nora is coming too."

Neil cast a bashful and admiring glance at handsome Nora, as she stood very erect by Biddy's side.

"All right, miss," he said.

"At ten o'clock," said Bridget; "have the boat in the cove then, and we'll be down there and ready."

"But they say, miss, that the Banshee is out on the nights when the moon is at the full."

"The O'Shanaghgans' Banshee," said Biddy, glancing at Nora, whose face did not change a muscle, although the brightness and wistfulness in her eyes were abundantly visible. She was saying to herself:

"I would give all the world to speak to the Banshee alone—to ask her to get father out of his difficulty."

She was half-ashamed of these thoughts, although she knew and almost gloried in the fact that she was superstitious to her heart's core.

She and Biddy soon entered the house by the back entrance, and ran up some carpetless stairs to Biddy's own room. This was a huge bedroom, carpetless and nearly bare. A little camp-bed stood in one corner, covered by a colored counterpane; there was a strip of carpet beside the bed, and another tiny strip by a wooden washhand-stand. The two great parliament windows were destitute of any curtain or even blind; they stared blankly out across the lovely summer landscape as hideous as windows could be.

It was a perfect summer's evening; but even now the old frames rattled and shook, and gave some idea of how they would behave were a storm abroad.

Biddy, who was quite accustomed to her room and never dreamed that any maiden could sleep in a more luxurious chamber, crossed it to where a huge wooden wardrobe stood. She unlocked the door, and took from its depths a pale-blue skirt trimmed with quantities of dirty pink flounces.

"Oh, you are not going to put *that* on," said Nora, whose own training had made her sensitive to incongruity in dress.

"Yes, I am," said Biddy. "How can I see your lady-mother in this style of thing?"

She went and stood in front of Nora with her arms akimbo.

"Look," she said, "my frock has a rent from here to here, and this petticoat is none of the best, and my stockings—well, I know it is my own fault, but I *won't* darn them, and there is a great hole just above the heel. Now, this skirt will hide all blemishes."

"But what will your mother say?"

"Bless her!" said Biddy, "she won't even notice. Here, let's whip on the dress."

She hastily divested herself of her ragged cotton skirt, and put on the pale blue with the dirty silk flounces.

"What are you looking so grave for?" she said, glancing up at Nora. "I declare you're too stately for anything, Nora O'Shanaghgan! You stand there, and I know you criticise me."

"No; I love you too much," replied Nora. "You are Biddy Murphy, one of my greatest friends."

"Ah, it's sweet to hear her," said Biddy.

"But, all the same," continued Nora, "I don't like that dress, and it's terribly unsuitable. You don't look ladylike in it."

"Ladylike, and I with the blood of——"

"Oh, don't begin that," said Nora; "every time I see you you mention that fact. I have not the slightest doubt that the old kings were ruffians, and dressed abominably."

"If you dare," said Biddy. She rushed up to the bed, dragged out her pillow, and held it in a warlike attitude. "Another word about my ancestors, and this will be at your devoted head!" she cried.

Nora burst into a merry laugh.

"There, now, that's better," said Biddy. She dropped the pillow and proceeded with her toilet. The dirty skirt with its tawdry flounces was surmounted by a bodice of the same material, equally unsuitable.

Biddy brushed out her mop of jet-black hair, which grew in thick curls all over her head and stood out like a mop round her shoulders. She was a plain girl, with small, very black eyes, a turned-up nose, and a wide mouth; but there was an irresistible expression of drollery in her face, and when she laughed, showing her milk-white teeth, there were people who even thought her attractive. Nora really loved her, although the two, standing side by side, were, as far as appearances were concerned, as the poles asunder.

"Now, come along," said Biddy. "I know I look perfectly charming. Oh, what a sweet, sweet blue it is, and these ducky little flounces! It was Aunt Mary O'Flannagan sent me this dress at Christmas. She wore it at a fancy ball, and said it might suit me. It does, down to the ground. Let me drop a courtesy to you, Nora O'Shanaghgan. Oh, how proper we look! But I don't care! Now I'm not afraid to face anyone—why, the old kings would have been proud of me. Come along—do."

She caught Nora's hand; they dashed down the wide, carpetless stairs, crossed a huge hall, and entered a room which was known as the drawing room at Cronane. It was an enormous apartment, but bore the same traces of neglect and dirt which the whole of the rest of the house testified to. The paper on the walls was moldy in patches, and in one or two places it had detached itself from the wall and fell in great sheets to the ground. One loose piece of paper was tacked up with two or three huge tacks, and bulged out, swaying with the slightest breeze. The carpet, which covered the entire floor, was worn threadbare; but, to make up for these defects, there were cabinets of the rarest and most exquisite old china, some of the pieces being worth fabulous sums. Vases of the same china adorned the tall marble mantelpiece, and stood on brackets here and there about the room. There were also some exquisite and wonderfully carved oak, a Queen Anne sofa, and several spindle-legged chairs. An old spinet stood in a distant window, and the drab moreen curtains had once been handsome.

Standing on the hearth, with his elbow resting on the marble mantelpiece close to a unique vase of antique design, stood Squire O'Shanaghgan. He was talking in pleasant and genial tones to Mrs. Murphy, a podgy little woman, with a great likeness to Biddy.

Mrs. Murphy wore a black alpaca dress and a little three-cornered knitted shawl across her shoulders. She had gray hair, which curled tightly like her daughter's; on top of it was a cap formed of rusty black velvet and equally rusty black lace. She looked much excited at the advent of the Squire, and her cheeks testified to the fact by the brightness of their color.

Mr. Murphy was doing penance opposite to Mrs. O'Shanaghgan. He was dreadfully afraid of that stately lady, and was glancing nervously round at his wife and the Squire from moment to moment.

"Yes, madam," he was saying, "it's turnips we are going to plant in that field just yonder. We have had a very good crop of hay too. It is a fine season, and the potatoes promise to be a sight for sore eyes."

"I hate the very name of that root," said Mrs. O'Shanaghgan in her most drawling tones.

"Why, then, ma'am, you don't say so," answered Murphy; "it seems hard on the poor things that keep us all going. The potheen and the potatoes—what would Ireland be without 'em? Glory be to goodness, it's quite awful to hear you abusing the potato, ma'am."

"I am English, you know," said Mrs. O'Shanaghgan.

On this scene Nora and Biddy entered. Mr. Murphy glanced with intense relief at his daughter. Mrs. O'Shanaghgan slightly raised her brows. It was the faintest of movements, but the superciliousness of the action smote upon Nora, who colored painfully.

Biddy, taking her courage in her hand, went straight up to the august lady.

"How do you do?" she said.

Mrs. O'Shanaghgan extended her hand with a limp action.

"Oh, dear!" panted Biddy.

"What is up, my dear Bridget?" said her mother, turning round and looking at her daughter. "Oh, to goodness, what have you put that on for? It's your very best Sunday-go-to-meeting dress, and you won't have another, I can tell you, for six months."

"There now, mother, hush, do," said Biddy. "I have put it on for a purpose. Why, then, it's sweet I want to make myself, and I believe it's sweet I look. Oh, there's the mirror; let me gaze at myself."

She crossed the room, and stood in front of a long glass, examining her unsuitable dress from the front and side; and then, being thoroughly satisfied with the elegance of appearance, she went back and stood in front of Mrs. O'Shanaghgan.

"It's a request I want to make of you, ma'am," she said.

"Well, Biddy, I will listen to it if you will ask me properly," said Mrs. O'Shanaghgan.

"Yes, to be sure," said Biddy. "How shall I say it?"

"Speak quietly, my dear."

"Yes, Biddy, I do wish you would take pattern by Nora, and by Mrs. O'Shanaghgan," said Mrs. Murphy, who in her heart of hearts envied Mrs. O'Shanaghgan's icy manners, and thought them the most perfect in all the world. She was in mortal fear of this good lady, even more terrified of her than her husband was.

"Well, Biddy," said Mrs. O'Shanaghgan.

"May Nora come and spend tomorrow night here?"

"No," was on Mrs. O'Shanaghgan's lips; but just then the Squire came forward.

"To be sure she may; it will do her a sight of good. The child hardly ever goes from home."

Mrs. O'Shanaghgan raised displeased eyes to her husband's face.

"Girls of Nora's age ought to stay at home," she said.

"Yes, to be sure, to be sure," said the Squire; "and we would miss her awfully if she was away from us; but a day or two off duty—eh, madam?" He glanced at his wife.

"You have your answer, Biddy," said Mrs. O'Shanaghgan; "her father wishes Nora to accept your invitation. She may stay away for one night—no longer."

Biddy winked broadly round at Nora.

"Now, then," she said, "come along." She seized her friend by the arm, and whisked her out of the room.

"It was the dress that did it," she said; "it is the loveliest garment in all the world. Come along now, and let's take it off. I want to gather those eggs for you."

She ran upstairs again, followed by Nora. The dress was disposed of in the large wooden wardrobe, the old torn frock readjusted on Biddy's stout form, and the girls went out into the lovely summer air. The eggs which Nora required were put into the little basket, and in half an hour the O'Shanaghgans' party were returning at full speed to Castle O'Shanaghgan. Nora glanced once into her father's face, and her heart gave a great leap. Her high spirits left her as if by magic; she felt a lump in her throat, and during the rest of the drive hardly spoke.

The Squire, on the contrary, talked incessantly. He talked more than ever after Nora had looked at him. He slapped his wife on the shoulder, and complimented her on her bravery. Nora's driving was the very best in all the world; she was a born whip; she had no fear in her; she was his own colleen, the Light o' the Morning, the dearest, sweetest soul on earth.

Mrs. O'Shanaghan replied very briefly and coldly to her husband's excited words. She treated them with what she imagined the contempt they deserved; but Nora was neither elated just then by her father's praise nor chilled by her mother's demeanor. Every thought of her heart, every nerve in her highly strung frame, was concentrated on one fact alone—she had surprised a look, a look on the Squire's face, which told her that his heart was broken.

CHAPTER V
"I AM ASHAMED OF YOU"

It was late that same evening, and the household at the Castle had all retired to rest. Nora was in her own room. This room was not furnished according to an English girl's fancy. It was plain and bare, but, compared to Biddy Murphy's chamber, it was a room of comfort and even luxury. A neat carpet covered the floor, there were white dimity curtains to the windows, and the little bed in its distant recess looked neat and comfortable. It is true that the washhand-stand was wooden, and the basin and jug of the plainest type; but Mrs. O'Shanaghgan herself saw that Nora had at least what she considered the necessaries of life. She had a neat hanging-press for her dresses, and a pretty chest of drawers, which her mother herself had saved up her pin-money to buy for her.

Nora now stood by one of the open windows, her thick and very long black hair hanging in a rippling mass over her neck and shoulders. Suddenly, as she bent out of the window, the faint, very faint perfume of a cigar came up on the night air. She sniffed excitedly for a moment, and then, bending a little more forward, said in a low tone:

"Is that you, Terry?"

"Yes—why don't you go to bed?" was the somewhat ungracious response.

"I am not sleepy. May I come down and join you?"

"No."

"Will you come up and join me?"

The answer was about to be "No"; there was a moment's hesitation, then Nora's voice said pleadingly, "Ah, do now, Terry; I want to say something so badly."

"But if anybody hears?"

"They can't hear. Father and mother's room is at the other end of the house."

"All right; don't say any more; you'll wake people with that chatter of yours. I'm coming."

In a couple of minutes there was a knock at Nora's door. She flew to open it, and Terence came in.

"What do you want?" he said.

"To talk to you; I have got something to say. Come over and sit by the window."

Terence obeyed.

"The first thing to do is to put out that light," said Nora. She ran to the dressing table, and before her brother could prevent her had extinguist.ed the candle.

"Now, then, there is the dear old lady moon to look down upon us, and nothing else can see us."

"Why don't you go to bed, Nora? Hannah would say that you are losing your beauty-sleep sitting up at this, hour."

"As if anything about me mattered just now," said Nora.

"Why, what's up?"

"The old thing, Terry; you must know what's up."

"What old thing? I am sure I can't guess."

"Well, then, if you can't you ought. Father is in a peck of trouble—a peck of trouble."

Nora's voice broke and trembled. Terence, who disliked a scene beyond anything, fidgeted restlessly. He leaned out of the window, and dropped his cigar ash on the ground beneath.

"And you are his only son and the heir to Castle O'Shanaghgan."

"The heir to a pack of ruins," said the boy impatiently.

"Terry, you don't deserve to be father's son. How dare you speak like that of the—the beloved old place?"

"Come, come, Nora, if you are going into heroics I think I'll be off to bed," said Terence, yawning.

"No, you won't; you must listen. I have got something most important to say."

"Well, then, I will give you five minutes; not another moment. I know you, Nora; you always exaggerate things. You are an Irishwoman to your backbone."

"I am, and I glory in the fact."

"You ought to be ashamed to glory in it. Don't you want to have anything to do with mother and her relations?"

"I love my mother, but I am glad I don't take after her," said Nora; "yes, I am glad."

The moon shone on the two young faces, and Nora looked up at her brother; he put on a supercilious smile, and folded his arms across his broad chest.

"Yes," she replied; "and I should like to shake you for looking like that. I am glad I am Irish through and through and *through*. Would I give my warm heart and my enthusiasm for your coldness and deliberation?"

"Good gracious, Nora, what a little ignorant thing you are! Do you suppose no Englishman has enthusiasm?"

"We'll drop the subject," said Nora. "It is one I won't talk of; it puts me into such a boiling rage to see you sitting like that."

Terence did not speak at all for a moment; then he said quietly:

"What is this thing that you have got to tell me? The five minutes are nearly up, you know."

"Oh, bother your five minutes! I cannot tell you in five minutes. When my heart is scalded with unshed tears, how can I measure time by *minutes*? It has to do with father; it is worse than anything that has ever gone before."

"What is it, Norrie?" Her brother's tone had suddenly become gentle. He laid his hand for a moment on her arm; the gentleness of the tone, the unexpected sweetness of the touch overcame Nora; she flung her arms passionately round his neck.

"Oh, and you are the only brother I have got!" she sobbed; "and I could love you—I could love you like anything. Can't you be sympathetic? Can't you be sweet? Can't you be dear?"

"Oh, come, come!" said Terence, struggling to release himself from Nora's entwining arms; "I am not made like you, you know; but I am not a bad chap at heart. Now, what is it?"

"I will try and tell you."

"And for goodness' sake don't look so sorrowfully at me, Nora; we can talk, and we can act and do good deeds, without giving ourselves away. I hate girls who wear their hearts on their sleeves."

"Oh! you will *never* understand," said Nora, starting back again; all her burst of feeling turned in upon herself. "I can't imagine how you are father's son," she began. But then she stopped, waited for a moment, and then said quietly, "There is a fresh mortgage, and it is for a very big sum."

"Oh, is that all?" said Terence. "I have heard of mortgages all my life; it seems to be the fashion at O'Shanaghgan to mortgage to any extent. There is nothing in that; father will give up a little more of the land."

"How much land do you think is left?"

"I am sure I can't say; not much, I presume."

"It is my impression," said Nora—"I am not sure; but it is my impression—that there is *nothing* left to meet this big thing but the—the—the land on which"—her voice broke—"Terry, the land on which the house stands."

"Really, Nora, you are so melodramatic. I don't know how you can know anything of this."

"I only guess. Mother is very unhappy."

"Mother? Is she?"

"Ah, I have touched you there! But anyhow, father is in worse trouble than he has been yet; I never, *never* saw him look as he did tonight."

"As if looks mattered."

"The look I saw tonight does matter," said Nora. "We were coming home from Cronane, and I was driving."

"It is madness to let you drive Black Bess," interrupted Terence. "I wonder my father risks spoiling one of his most valuable horses."

"Oh, nonsense, Terry; I can drive as well as you, and better, thanks," replied Nora, much nettled, for her excellent driving was one of the few things she was proud of. "Well, I turned round, and I saw father's face, and, oh! it was just as if someone had stabbed me through the heart. You know, or perhaps you don't, that the last big loan came from Squire Murphy."

"Old Dan Murphy; then we are as safe as we can be," said Terence, rising and whistling. "You really did make me feel uncomfortable, you have such a queer way; but if it is Dan Murphy, he will give father any amount of time. Why, they are the best of friends."

"Well, father went to see him on the subject—I happen to know that—and I don't think he has given him time. There is something wrong, anyhow—I don't know what; but there *is* something very wrong, and I mean to find out tomorrow."

"Nora, if I were you I wouldn't interfere. You are only a young girl, and these kind of things are quite out of your province. Father has pulled along ever since you and I were born. Most Irish gentlemen are poor in these days. How can they help it? The whole country is going to ruin; there is no proper trade; there is no proper system anywhere. The tenants are allowed to pay their rent just as they please— —"

"As if we could harry them," said inconsistent Nora. "The poor dears, with their tiny cots and their hard, hard times. I'd rather eat dry bread all my days than press one of them."

"If these are your silly views, you must expect our father to be badly off, and the property to go to the dogs, and everything to come to an end," said the brother in a discontented tone. "But there, I say once more that you have exaggerated in this matter; there is nothing more wrong than there has been since I can remember. I am glad I am going to England; I am glad I am going to be out of it all for a bit."

"You going to England—you, Terry?"

"Yes. Don't you know? Our Uncle George Hartrick has asked me to stay with him, and I am going."

"And you can go? You can leave us just now?"

"Why, of course; there will be fewer mouths to feed. It's a good thing every way."

"But Uncle George is a rich man?"

"What of that?"

"I mean he lives in a big place, and has heaps and heaps of money," said Nora.

"So much the better."

"You cannot go to him *shabby*. What are you going to do for dress?"

"Mother will manage that."

"Mother!" Nora leaped up from the window-ledge and stood facing her brother. "You have spoken to mother?"

"Of course I have. Dear me, Nora, you are getting to be quite an unpleasant sort of girl."

"You have spoken to mother," repeated Nora, "and she has promised to help you? How will she do it?"

Terence moved restlessly.

"I suppose she knows herself how she will do it."

"And you will let her?" said Nora—"you, a man, will let her? You know she has no money; you know she has nothing but her little trinkets, and you allow her to sell those to give you pleasure? Oh, I am ashamed of you! I am sorry you are my brother. How can you do it?"

"Look here, Nora, I won't be scolded by you. After all, I am your elder, and you are bound, at any rate, to show me decent outward respect. If you only mean to talk humbug of this sort I am off to bed."

Terence rose from his place on the window-ledge, and, without glancing at Nora, left the room. When he did so she clasped her hands high above her head, and sat for a moment looking out into the night. Her face was quivering, but no tears rose to her wide-open eyes. After a moment she turned, and began very slowly to undress.

"I will see the Banshee tomorrow, if it is possible," she whispered under her breath. "If ruin can be averted, it shall be. I don't mind leaving the place; I don't mind starving. I don't mind *anything* but that look on father's face. But father's heart shall not be broken; not while Nora O'Shanaghgan is in the world."

CHAPTER VI
THE CAVE OF THE BANSHEE

At ten o'clock on the following evening two eager excited girls might have been seen stealing down a narrow path which led to Murphy's Cove. Murphy's Cove was a charming little semicircular bay which ran rather deeply into the land. The sand here was of that silvery sheen which, at low tide, shone like burnished silver. The cove was noted for its wonderful shells, producing many cowries and long shells called pointers.

In the days of her early youth Nora had explored the treasures of this cove, and had secured a valuable collection of shells, as well as very rare seaweeds, which she had carefully dried. Her mother had shown her how to make seaweeds and shells into baskets, and many of these amateur productions adorned the walls of Nora's bedroom.

All the charm of these things had passed away, however; the time had come when she no longer cared to gather shells or collect seaweeds. She felt that she was turning very fast into a woman. She had all an Irish girl's high spirits; but she had, added to these, a peculiarly warm and sensitive heart. When those she loved were happy, no one in all the world was happier than Nora O'Shanaghgan; but when any gloom fell on the home-circle, then Nora suffered far more than anyone gave her credit for.

She had passed an anxious day at home, watching her father intently, afraid to question him, and only darting glances at him when she thought he was not looking. The Squire, however, seemed cheerful enough, plodding over his land, or arranging about the horses, or doing the thousand-and-one small things which occupied his life.

Mrs. O'Shanaghgan seemed to have forgotten all about the mortgage, and was eagerly discussing ways and means with Terence. Terence avoided Nora's eyes, and rode off early in the evening to see the nearest tailor. It was not likely that this individual could make a fitting suit for the young heir to O'Shanaghgan; but the boy must have something to travel in, and Mrs. O'Shanaghgan gave implicit directions as to the London tailor whom he was to visit as soon as he reached the Metropolis.

"For you are to look your best, and never to forget that you are my son," was her rejoinder; and Terence forgot all about Nora's words on the previous evening. He was to start in two days' time. Even Nora became excited over his trip and in her mother's account of her Uncle Hartrick.

"I wish you were going, Nora," said the mother. "I should be proud of you. Of course you are a little rough colt; but you could be trained;" and then she looked with sudden admiration at her handsome daughter.

"She has a face in a thousand," she thought, "and she is absolutely unconscious of her beauty."

At five o'clock Nora had started off in the pony-trap to visit her friend Biddy. The trap had been brought back by one of the numerous gossoons who abounded all over O'Shanaghgan, and Biddy and Nora had a few hours before the great secret expedition was to take place. And now the time had come. The girls had put on thick serge petticoats, short jackets, and little tight-fitting caps on their heads. There was always a breeze blowing round that extreme corner of the Atlantic. Never did the finest summer day find the waves calm there. Nora and Biddy had been accustomed to these waves since their earliest girlhood, and were not the least afraid. They stood now waiting in the little cove, and looking round wonderingly for the appearance of Mike and Neil upon the scene. They were to bring the boat with them. The girls were to wade through the surf to get into it, and Biddy was stooping down to take off her shoes and stockings for the purpose.

"Dear, dear!" she cried. "Do you see that ugly bank of clouds just behind the moon? I hope my lady moon is not going to hide herself; we can do nothing in the cave if we have not light."

"But the cave is dark, surely?"

"Yes. But don't you know there is a break in the cliffs above, just in the center? And it is down there the moon sends its shafts when it is at the full; it is there the Banshee will meet us, if we are to see her at all. The shafts from the moon will only enter the cave at midnight. I have counted the times, and I know everything."

"I want to see the Banshee so badly," said Nora.

"You won't be frightened, then, Nora?"

"Frightened? No. Not of our own Banshee."

"They say," began Biddy, "that if you see a spirit, and come face to face with it, you are good for—"

"What?" said Nora.

"If you hold out during the year you have seen the spirit, you are good to live for another ten; but during that first year you are in extreme danger of dying. If you escape that fate, however, and are whole and sound, you will be quite safe to live for ten more years. They say nothing can send you out of the world; not sickness, nor accidents, nor fire, nor water; but the second year you are liable to an accident, and the year after to a misfortune; then in the fourth year your luck turns—in the fourth year you find gold, in the fifth year health, in the sixth year beauty. Oh, I would give anything to be beautiful!"

"You are very well as you are, Biddy."

"Very well as I am? What nonsense! Look at my turned-up nose." Here Biddy pressed her finger on the feature in question.

"It looks very racy," answered Nora.

"Bedad, then, it does that," replied Biddy. "I believe I got it sound and safe from one of the old——"

"You needn't go on," cried Nora. "I know what you are going to say."

"And why shouldn't I say it? You would be proud enough to be descended from——"

"Oh, I have a very fine descent of my own," answered Nora, with spirit.

"Now, if I was like you," began Biddy, "wouldn't I be proud, just? But dear, dear! there never were two Irish girls farther asunder as far as appearance goes. See here, let me describe myself, feature by feature. Oh, here's a clear pool. I can get a glimpse of myself in it. You come and look in too, Nora. Now, then, we can see ourselves. Oh, holy poker! it's cruel the difference between us. Here's my forehead low and bumpy, and my little nose, scarcely any of it, and what there is turned right up to the sky; and my wide mouth, and my little eyes, and my hair just standing straight up as rakish as you please. And look at you, with your elegant features and your—oh, but it's genteel you are!—and I love you, Nora alannah; I love you, and am not a bit jealous of you."

Here the impulsive girl threw her arms round her friend's neck and kissed her.

"All the same," she added, "I wish those clouds were not coming up. It has been so precious hot all day that I should not be the least surprised if we had a thunderstorm."

"A thunderstorm while we are in the cave would be magnificent," said Nora.

"Does anything ever frighten you, Nora?"

"I don't think anything in nature could frighten me; but there are some things I am frightened at."

"What? Do tell me. I should like to know."

"You'll keep it a secret—won't you, Biddy?"

"To be sure I will. When did I ever blaze out anything you told me? If I am plain, I am faithful."

"Well, I am afraid of *pain*," said Nora.

"Pain! You? But I have seen you scratch yourself ever so deep and not so much as wink; and I mind that time when you twisted your ankle and you didn't even pretend you were hurt."

"Oh, it is not that sort of pain. I am terrified of pain when it affects those I love. But there! don't ask me any more. Here are the boys; we'll jump into the boat and be off. Why, it is half-past ten, and it will take half-an-hour's good rowing to cross the bay, and then we have to enter the cave and——"

"I don't like those clouds," said Biddy. "I wonder if it is safe to go."

"Safe?" said Nora. "We must go. Mother won't allow me to spend another night here, and I shall lose my chance. I am determined to speak to the Banshee or die in the attempt."

The splash of oars was now distinctly audible, and the next moment a four-oared gig swiftly turned the little promontory and shot with a rapid movement into the bay.

"Why," said Biddy, running forward, "who's in the boat?"

A lad and a man now stood upright and motioned to the girls.

"Where's Neil?" said Biddy.

"Neil could not come, Miss Biddy, so I'm taking his place," said the deep voice of a powerful-looking man. He had a black beard down to his waist, flashing black eyes, a turned-up nose, and a low forehead. A more bull-dog and ferocious-looking individual it would be hard to find. Biddy, however, knew him; he was Neil's father—Andy Neil, as he was called. He was known to be a lawless and ferocious man, and was very much dreaded by most of the neighbors around. Neither Nora nor Biddy, however, felt any reason to fear him and Nora said almost cheerfully:

"As we are to have such a stiff row, it is just as well to have a man in the boat."

"Faix, now, young ladies, come along, and don't keep me waiting," said Andy, rising and brandishing one of his oars in a threatening way. "There's a storm coming on, and I want to be out of this afore it overtakes us. Oh, glory be to goodness, there's a flash of lightning!"

There came a flash on the edge of the horizon, lighting up the thick bank of rapidly approaching clouds.

"Nora, had we better go tonight?" said Biddy. She had as little fear as her friend, but even she did not contemplate with pleasure a wild storm in the midst of the Atlantic.

The man Neil looked gravely round.

"Och! good luck to ye now, young ladies; don't be kaping me waiting after the botheration of coming to fetch yez. Come along, and be quick about it."

"To be sure," said Nora. She splashed bravely into the surf, for the boat could not quite reach the shore. The waves reached high above her pretty, rosy ankles as she stepped into the boat.

Biddy followed in her wake; and then Nora, producing a rough towel, began to dry her feet. Both girls put on their shoes and stockings again in absolute silence.

Neil had now faced the boat seaward, and with great sweeps with a pair of sculls was taking it out to sea. The tide was in their favor, and they went at a rapid rate. The man did not speak at all, and his face was in complete shadow. Nora breathed hard in suppressed excitement and delight. Biddy crouched at the bottom of the boat and watched the clouds as they came up.

"I wish I hadn't come," she muttered once or twice.

The boy Mike sat at the stern. The two girls had nothing whatever to do.

"Shall I take an oar, Andy?" said Nora at last.

"You, miss?"

"I can take a pair of oars and help you," said the girl.

"If it plazes you, miss." The man hastily stepped to the back of the boat. Nora took her place, and soon they were going at greater speed than ever. She was a splendid oarswoman, and feathered her oars in the most approved fashion.

In less than the prescribed half-hour they reached the entrance to the great cave.

They were safe. A hollow, booming noise greeted them as they came close. Andy bent forward and gave Nora a brief direction.

"Ship your oars now, miss. Aisy now; aisy now. Now, then, I'll take one pull; pull your left oar again. Now, here we are."

He spoke with animation. Nora obeyed him implicitly. They entered the shadow of the cave, and the next instant found themselves in complete darkness. The boat bobbed up and down on the restless water, and just at that instant a flash of vivid lightning illuminated all the outside water, followed by a crashing roar of thunder.

"The storm is on us; but, thank the Almighty, we're safe," said Mike, with a little sob. "I wish to goodness we hadn't come, all the same."

"And so do I," said Biddy; "it is perfectly awful being in a cave like this. What shall we do?"

"Do!" said Neil. "Hould your tongues and stay aisy. Faix, it's the Almighty is having a bit of a talk; you stay quiet and listen."

The four oars were shipped now, and the boat swayed restlessly up and down.

"Aren't we going any farther?" said Nora.

"Not while this storm lasts. Oh, for goodness' sake, Nora, do stay quiet," said Biddy.

Andy now produced out of his pocket a box of matches and a candle. He struck a match, applied it to the candle, and the next moment a feeble flame shot up. It was comparatively calm within the cave.

"There! that will light us a bit," said Andy. "The storm won't last long. It's well we got into shelter. Now, then, we'll do fine."

"You don't think," said Biddy, in a terrified tone, "that the cave will be be crashed in?"

"Glory be to Heaven, no, miss—we have cheated the storm coming here." The man smiled as he spoke, showing bits of broken teeth. His words were gentle enough, but his whole appearance was more like that of a wild beast than a man. Nora looked full at him. The candle lit up her pale face; her dark-blue eyes were full of courage; a lock of her black hair had got loose in the exertion of rowing, and had fallen partly over her shoulder and neck. "Faix, then, you might be the Banshee herself," said Andy, bending forward and looking at her attentively.

"If the moon comes out again we may see the Banshee," whispered Nora. "Can we not go farther into the cave? Time is flying." She took her watch from her pocket and looked at the hour. It was already past eleven o'clock.

"The storm will be over in good time," said the man. "Do you want to get the gleam of moonlight in the crack of the inner cave? Is that what you're afther, missy?"

"Yes," said Nora.

"Well, you stay quiet; you'll reach it right enough."

"Nora wants to see the Banshee, Andy," called out Biddy. "Oh, what a flash! It nearly blinded me."

"The rain will soon be on us, and then the worst of the storm will be past," said the man.

Mike uttered a scream; the lightning was now forked and intensely blue. It flashed into every cranny in the cave, showing the barnacles on the roof, the little bits of fern, the strange stalactites. After the flash had passed, the darkness which followed was so intense that the light of the dim candle could scarcely be seen. Presently the rain thundered down upon the bare rock above with a tremendous sound; there were great hailstones; the thunder became less frequent, the lightning less vivid. In a little more than half an hour the fierce storm had swept on to other quarters.

"Now, then, we can go forward," said Andy. He took up his oars. "You had best stay quiet, missies; just sit there in the bottom of the boat, and let me push ahead."

"Then I will hold the candle," said Nora.

"Right you are, miss."

She took it into her cold fingers. Her heart was beating high with suppressed excitement; she had never felt a keener pleasure in her life. If only she might see the Banshee, and implore the spirit's intercession for the fortunes of her house!

The man rowed on carefully, winding round corners and avoiding many dangers. At last they came bump upon some rocks.

"Now, then," he said, "we can't go a step farther."

"But we must," said Nora. "We have not reached the chasm in the rock. We must."

"We dare not, miss; the boat hasn't water enough to float her."

"Well, then, I shall wade there. How far on is the chasm?"

"Oh, Nora! Nora! you won't be so mad as to go alone?" called out Biddy.

"I shan't be a scrap afraid," said Nora.

"But there's water up to your knees; you dare not do it," said Biddy.

"Yes, I dare; and the tide is going down—is it not?"

"It will be down a good bit in half an hour," said the man, "and we'll be stranded here as like as not. These are bad rocks when the tide is low; we must turn and get out of this, miss, in a quarter of an hour at the farthest."

"Oh, I could just do it in a quarter of an hour," said Nora.

She jumped up, and the next moment had sprung out of the boat into the water, which nearly reached up to her knees.

"Oh, Nora! Nora! you'll be lost; you'll slip and fall in that awful darkness, and we'll never see you again," said Biddy, with a cry of terror.

"No, no; let her go," said Andy. "There ain't no fear, miss; you have but to go straight on, holding your candle and avoiding the rocks to your left, and you'll come to the opening. Be as quick as you can, Miss Nora; be as quick as you can."

His voice had a queer note in it. Nora gave him a look of gratitude, and proceeded on her dangerous journey. Her one fear was that the candle might go out; the flame flickered as the air got less good; the hot grease scalded her fingers; but suddenly a breeze of fresher air reached her, and warned her that she was approaching the aperture. There came a little puff of wind, and the next moment the brave girl found herself in total darkness. The candle had gone out. Just at that instant she heard, or fancied she heard, a splash behind her in the water. There was nothing for it now but to go forward. She resolved not to be terrified. Perhaps it was a water-rat; perhaps it was the Banshee. Her heart beat high; still she had no fear. She was going to plead for her father. What girl would be terrified with such a cause in view? She walked slowly and carefully on, and at last the fresher air was followed by a welcome gleam of light; she was approaching the opening. The next moment she had found it. She stood nearly up to her knees in the water; the shaft of moonlight was piercing down into the cave. Nora went and stood in the moonlight. The hole at the top was little more than a foot in width; there was a chasm, a jagged chasm, through which the light came. She could see a bit of cloudless sky, and the cold moonlight fell all over her.

"Oh, Banshee!—Lady Spirit who belongs to our house, come and speak to me," cried the girl. "Come from your home in the rock and give me a word of comfort. A dark time is near, and we implore your help. Come, come, Banshee—it is the O'Shanaghgans who want you. It is Nora O'Shanaghgan who calls you now."

The sound of a laugh came from the darkness behind her, and the next instant the startled girl saw the big form of Andy Neil approaching.

"Don't you be frightened, Miss Nora," he said. "I aint the Banshee, but I am as good. Faix, now, I want to say something to you. I have come here for the purpose. There! don't be frightened. I won't hurt ye—not I; but I want yez to promise me something."

"What is that?" said Nora.

"I have come here for the purpose. She aint no good." He indicated with a motion of his thumb the distant form of Biddy within the dark recess of the cave.

"Does Miss Murphy know you have followed me?" said Nora.

"No, she don't know it; she's in the dark. There's the little lad Mike will look after her. She won't do nothing until we go back."

"Oh, I did want to see the Banshee!"

"The Banshee may come or not," said the man; "but I have my message to yez, and it is this: If you don't get Squire O'Shanaghgan to let me keep my little bit of land, and to see that I aint evicted, why, I'll—you're a bonny lass, you're as purty a young lady as I ever set eyes on, but I'll drownd yez, deep down here in this hole. No one will ever know; they'll think you has fallen and got drowned without no help from me. Yes, I'll do it—yes, I will—unless you promises that Squire O'Shanaghgan shan't evict me. If I go out, why, you goes out first. Now, you'll do it; you'll swear that you'll do it? You'll leave no stone unturned. You'll get 'em to leave me my cabin where I was born, and the childer was born, and where the wife died, or I'll drownd yez deep down here in the Banshee's hole. Look!" said the man as the moon nickered on a deep pool of water; "they say there is no bottom to it. Just one shlip, and over you goes, and nobody will ever see Nora O'Shanaghgan again."

"I'm not going to be frightened; you wouldn't do it, Andy," said the girl.

"Wouldn't I just? You think that I'd be afraid?"

"I don't think so. I am sure you are afraid of nothing."

"Then why shouldn't I do it?"

"Because you wouldn't be so bad, not to an innocent girl who never harmed you."

"Oh! wouldn't I just? Ain't I a-stharving, and aint the childer stharving, and why should they turn us out of our bit of a cabin? Swear you'll do it; swear you won't have me evicted; you has got to promise."

"*I* wouldn't evict you—never, never!" said Nora. "Oh, never!" she added, tears, not of fright, but of pity, filling her eyes. "But how can I control my father?"

"That's for you to see to, missy; I must go back now, or we'll none of us leave this cave alive. But you'll just shlip into that water, and you'll never be heard of again unless you promises. I'll go back; they none of 'em will know I followed yez. You'll be drowned here in the deep pool, and I'll go back to the boat, or you promises and we both goes back."

"But, Andy, what am I to promise?"

"That you won't have me evicted. You say solemn here: 'Andrew Neil, I would rather die myself or have my tongue cut out, and may the Holy Mother cast me from her presence forever, and may the evil spirits take me, if I don't save you, Andy.' You has to say that."

"No, I won't," said Nora with sudden spirit. "I am not afraid. I'll do my very, very best for you; but I won't say words like those."

The man looked at her attentively.

"I was a little frightened at first," continued Nora; "but I am not now. I would rather you pushed me into that pool, I would rather sink and die, than take an awful vow like that. I won't take it. I'll do my very best to save you, but I won't make a vow."

"Faix, then, miss, it's you that has the courage; but now if I let yez off this time, will ye do yer best?"

"Yes, I'll do my best."

"If yer don't, bonny as you are, and the light of somebody's eyes, you'll go out of the world. But, come, I trust yez, and we must be turning back."

The man took the matches from his pocket, struck one, and lit the candle. Then, Andy going in front of Nora, they both turned in the direction where the boat was waiting for them.

CHAPTER VII
THE MURPHYS

It was between two and three in the morning when the girls found themselves back again in the desolate mansion of Cronane. Biddy had left a window open; they had easily got in by it and gone up to Biddy's big room on the first floor. They were to sleep together in Biddy's small bed. Personally, discomforts did not affect them; they had never been accustomed to luxury, and rather liked the sense of hardship than otherwise.

"I brought up a bit of supper beforehand," said Biddy. "I am real hungry. What do you say to cold bacon and taters—eh? I went down to the larder and got a good few early this morning. I put them in the cupboard in a brown bowl with a plate over it. You're hungry—aren't you, Norrie?"

"No, not very," answered Nora.

"What's come to you, you're so quiet? You have lost all your spirit. I thought we would have a real rollicking time over our supper, laughing and talking, and telling our adventures. Oh! it was awful in that cave; and when you were away talking to the lady Banshee I did have a time of it. I thought that awful Andy was going to murder me. I had a sort of feeling that he was getting closer and closer, and I clutched hold of little Mike. I think he was a bit surprised; I'll give him a penny to-morrow, poor gossoon. But aren't you hungry, and won't you laugh, and shan't we have a jolly spree?"

"Oh, I shall be very glad to eat something," said Nora; "and I am a little cold, too. I took a chill standing so long in that icy water."

"Oh, dear, oh, dear! it's the rheumatics you'll be getting, and then you'll lose your beautiful straight figure. I must rub your legs. There, sit on the bed and I'll begin."

Nora submitted to Biddy's ministrations. The room was lit by a small dip candle, which was placed in an old tin candlestick on the mantelpiece.

"Dear, dear! the light will be coming in no time, and we can quench the glim then," said Biddy. "I've got to be careful about candles. We're precious short of everything at Cronane just now. We're as poor as church mice; it's horrid to be so desperately poor as that. But, hurrah for the cold taters and bacon! We'll have a right good meal. That will warm you up; and I have a little potheen in a black bottle, too. I'll put some water to it and you shall have a drink."

"I never touch it," said Nora, shuddering.

"But you must tonight, or you'll catch your death of cold. There, the best thing you can do is to get right into bed. Why, you're shivering, and your teeth are chattering. It's a fine state Mrs. O'Shanaghgan will be in tomorrow when you go back to her."

"I must not get ill, Biddy; that would never do," said Nora, pulling herself together with an effort. "Yes, I'll get into bed; and I'll take a little of your potheen—very, very weak, if you'll mix it for me—and I'll have some of the bacon and potatoes. Oh! I would eat anything rather than be ill. I never was really ill in my life; but now, of all times, it would never do."

"Well, then, here you go. Tumble into bed. I'll pile the blankets on you. Now, isn't that better?"

Biddy bustled, intent on hospitality. She propped Nora up with pillows, pulled a great rug over her shoulders, and heaped on more and more blankets, which she pulled expeditiously from under the bed. "They always stay here in the summer," said Biddy. "That's to keep them aired; and now they're coming in very handy. You have got four doubled on you now; that makes eight. I should think you'd soon be warm enough."

"I expect I shall soon be too hot," said Nora; "but this is very nice."

She sipped the potheen, ate a little bacon and cold potatoes, and presently declared herself well again.

"Oh, I am perfectly all right!" she said; "it was coming home in the boat in my wet things. I wish I had taken a pair of sculls again; then I wouldn't even have been cold."

"Now you'll tell me," said Biddy, who sat on the edge of the bed munching great chunks of bacon and eating her cold potatoes with extreme relish. "Oh! it's hungry I am; but I want to hear all about the lady Banshee. Did she come? Did you see her, Nora?"

"No, she didn't come," said Nora very shortly.

"Didn't come? But they say she never fails when the moon is at the full. She rises up out of that pool—the bottomless pool it is called—and she floats over the water and waves her hand. It's awful to see her if you don't belong to her; but to those who belong to her she is tender and sweet, like a mother, they say; and her breath is like honey, and her kiss the sweetest you ever got in all your life. You mean to say you didn't see her? Why, Nora, what has come to you? You're trembling again."

"I cannot tell you, Biddy; don't ask me any more. I didn't see the Banshee. It was very, very cold standing up to my knees in the water. I suppose I did wrong to go; but that's done and over now. Oh, I am so tired and sleepy! Do get into bed, Biddy, and let us have what little rest we can."

Early the next morning Nora returned to O'Shanaghgan. All trace of ill effects had vanished under Biddy's prompt treatment. She had lain under her eight blankets until she found them intolerable, had then tossed most of them off, and fallen into deep slumber. In the morning she looked much as usual; but no entreaties on the part of Biddy, joined in very heartily by Squire Murphy and also by Mrs. Murphy, could induce her to prolong her visit.

"It's a message I'll take over myself to your father if you'll but stay, Nora," said the Squire.

"No, no; I must really go home," answered Nora.

"It's too fine you are for us, Nora, and that's the truth; and don't go for to be denying it," said Mrs. Murphy.

"No; I hope I may never be too fine for my real friends," said Nora a little sadly. "I must go back. I believe I am wanted at home."

"You're a very conceited colleen; there's no girl that can't be spared from home sometimes," said Mrs. Murphy. "I thought you would help Biddy and me to pick black currants. There are quarts and quarts of 'em in the garden, and the maids can't do it by themselves, poor things. Well, Biddy, you have got to help me today."

"Oh, mammy, I just can't," answered Biddy. "I'm due down at the shore, and I want to go a bit of the way back with Nora. You can't expect me to help you today, mammy."

"There she is, Nora—there she is!" exclaimed the good lady, her face growing red and her eyes flashing fire; "not a bit of good, not worth her keep, I tell her. Why shouldn't she stay at home and help her mother? Do you hear me, Squire Murphy? Give your orders to the girl; tell her to stay at home and help her mother."

"Ah, don't be bothering me," said Squire Murphy. "It's out I'm going now. I have enough on my own shoulders without attending to the tittle-tattle of women."

He rose from the table, and the next moment had left the room.

"Dear, dear! there are bad times ahead for poor Old Ireland," said Mrs. Murphy. "Children don't obey their parents; husbands don't respect their wives; it's a queer state of the country. When I was young, and lived at my own home in Tipperary, we had full and plenty. There was a bite and a sup for every stranger who came to the door, and no one talked of money, nor thought of it neither. The land yielded a good crop, and the potatoes—oh, dear! oh, dear! that was before the famine. The famine brought us a lot of bad luck, that it did."

"But the potatoes have been much better the last few years, and this year they say we're going to have a splendid crop," said Nora. "But I must go now, Mrs. Murphy. Thank you so much for asking me."

"You're looking a bit pale; but you're a beautiful girl," said the good woman admiringly. "I'd give a lot if Biddy could change places with you—that is, in appearance, I mean. She's not a credit to anybody, with her bumpy forehead and her cocked nose, and her rude ways to her mother."

"Mammy, I really cannot help the way I am made," said Biddy; "and as to staying in this lovely day picking black currants and making jam, and staining my fingers, it's not to be thought of. Come along out, Nora. If you must be off back to O'Shanaghgan, I mean to claim the last few moments of your stay here."

The girls spent the morning together, and early in the afternoon Nora returned to O'Shanaghgan. Terence met her as she was driving down the avenue.

"How late you are!" he said; "and you have got great black shadows under your eyes. You know, of course, that I have to catch the early train in the morning?"

"To be sure I do, Terry; and it is for that very reason I have come back so punctually. I want to pack your things my own self."

"Ah, that's a good girl. You'll find most of them laid out on the bed. Be sure you see that all my handkerchiefs are there—two dozen—and all marked with my initials."

"I never knew you had so many."

"Yes; mother gave me a dozen at Christmas, and I have not used them yet. I shall want every bit of decent clothing I possess for my visit to my rich Uncle Hartrick."

"How is mother, Terence?"

"Mother? Quite well, I suppose; she is fretting a bit at my going; you'll have to comfort her. The place is very rough for her just now."

"I don't see that it is any rougher than it has ever been," said Nora a little fiercely. "You're always running down the place, Terry."

"Well, I can't help it. I hate to see things going to the dogs," said the young man. He turned on his heel, called a small fox-terrier, who went by the name of Snap, to follow him, and went away in the direction of the shore.

Nora whipped up her pony and drove on to the house. Here she was greeted by her father. He was standing on the steps; and, coming down, he lifted her bodily out of the dog-cart, strained her to his heart, and looked full into her eyes.

"Ah, Light o' the Morning, I have missed you," he said, and gave a great sigh.

The girl nestled up close to him. She was trembling with excess of feeling.

"And I have missed you," she answered. "How is the mother?"

"I suppose she is all right, Nora; but there, upon my word, she does vex me sometimes. Take the horse to the stables, and don't stand staring there, Peter Jones." The Squire said these latter words on account of the fixed stare of a pair of bright black eyes like sloes in the head of the little chap who had brought the trap for Nora. He whipped up the pony, turned briskly round, and drove away.

"Come out for a bit with me round the grounds, Nora. It's vexed I am, sometimes; I feel I cannot stand things. I wish my lady would not have all those fine airs. But there, I have no right to talk against your mother to you, child; and of course she is your mother, and I am desperately proud of her. There never was her like for beauty and stateliness; but sometimes she tries me."

"Oh! I know, father; I know. But let's go round and look at the new calf and the colt. We can spare an hour—can we not?"

"Yes; come along quick, Nora," answered the Squire, all smiles and jokes once more. "The mother doesn't know you have come back, and we can have a pleasant hour to ourselves."

CHAPTER VIII
THE SQUIRE'S TROUBLE

Nora and her father went slowly down a shady walk, which led in the direction of the shore. Soon they found themselves in a hay-field. The crop here was not particularly good. The hay had been spoiled by rains, which had soaked down on the lands a fortnight ago. It was stunted in height, and in some parts had that impoverished appearance which is so painful to the heart of the good farmer.

Squire O'Shanaghgan, notwithstanding his somewhat careless ways, was really a capital farmer. He had the best interests of the land at heart, and did his utmost to get profit out of his many acres. He now shook his head over the hay-crop.

"It's just like all the rest, Norrie—everything going to ruin—the whole place going to the dogs; and yet—and yet, colleen, it's about the sweetest bit of earth in all God's world. I wouldn't give O'Shanaghgan for the grandest place in the whole of England; and I told your lady-mother so this morning."

"Why did you say it, father? Had mother been—"

"Oh, nothing, child—nothing; the old grumbles. But it's her way, poor dear; she can't help herself; she was born so. It's not to be expected that she who was brought up in that prim land over yonder, where everything is cut and dry, and no one ever thinks of managing anything but by the rule of three, would take to our wild ways. But there, Norrie, it's the freedom of the life that suits me; when I am up and away on Black Bess or on Monarch, I don't think there is a happier fellow in the world. But there, when I come face to face with money, why, I'm bothered—I'm bothered entirely, child."

"Father," said Nora, "won't you tell me what is worrying you?"

"How do you know I am worried about anything, colleen?"

"How do I know, father?" answered Nora a little playfully. She turned and faced him. "I know," she said; "that is enough; you are worried. What is it?"

The Squire looked at her attentively. He was much the taller of the two, and his furrowed face seemed to the girl, as she looked up at him, like a great rock rising above her. She was wont to sun herself in his smile, and to look to him always as a sure refuge in any perplexity. She did not love anyone in the whole world as she loved her father. His manliness appealed to her; his generous ways suited her; but, above all these things, he was her father; he was Irish to his backbone, and so was she.

"You must tell me," she said. "Something is troubling you, and Nora has to know."

"Ah, my Light o' the Morning! what would I do without you?" answered the Squire.

"Prove that you trust me," said Nora, "and tell me what worries you."

"Well, Nora, you cannot understand; and yet if you could it would be a relief to unburden my mind. But you know nothing about mortgages—do you, little woman?"

"More than you think," said Nora. "I am not a child—I am nearly seventeen; and I have not lived at O'Shanaghgan all my life for nothing. Of course we are poor! I don't know that I want to be rich."

"I'll tell you what I want," said the Squire; "I want to forget that there is such a thing as money. If it were not for money I would say to myself, 'There's not a better lot than mine.' What air we have here!" He opened his mouth and took in a great breath of the pure Atlantic breezes. "What a place it is! Look at the beauty of it! Look round, Norrie, and see for yourself; the mountains over there; and the water rolling up almost to our doors; and the grand roar of the waves in our ears; and those trees yonder; and this field with the sun on it; and the house, though it is a bit of a barrack, yet it is where my forebears were born. Oh, it's the best place on earth; it's O'Shanaghgan, and it's mine! There, Nora, there; I can't stand it!"

The Squire dashed his hand to his brow. Nora looked up at him; she was feeling the exposure and excitement of last night. Her pallor suddenly attracted his attention.

"Why, what's the matter with you, colleen?" he said. "Are you well—are you sure you're well?"

"Absolutely, perfectly well, father. Go on—tell me all."

"Well, you know, child, when I came in for the estate it was not to say free."

"What does that mean, father?"

"It was my father before me—your grandfather—the best hunter in the county. He could take his bottle of port and never turn a hair; and he rode to hounds! God bless you, Nora! I wish you could have seen your grandfather riding to hounds. It was a sight to remember. Well, he died—God bless him!—and there were difficulties. Before he died those difficulties began, and he mortgaged some of the outer fields and Knock Robin Farm—the best farm on the whole estate; but I didn't think anything of that. I thought I could redeem it; but somehow, child, somehow rents have been going down; the poor folk can't pay, and I'm the last to press them; and things have got worse and worse. I had a tight time of it five years ago; I was all but done for. It was partly the fact of the famine; we none of us ever got over that—none of us in this part of Ireland, and many of the people went away. Half the cabins were deserted. There's half a mile of 'em down yonder; every single one had a dead man or woman in it at the time of the famine, and now they're empty. Well of course, you know all about that?"

"Oh, yes, father; Hannah has told me of the famine many, many times."

"To be sure—to be sure; but it is a dark subject, and not fit for a pretty young thing like you. But there, let me go on. It was five years ago I mortgaged some of the place, a good bit, to my old friend Dan Murphy. He lent me ten thousand pounds—not a penny more, I assure you. It just tided me over, and I thought, of course, I'd pay him back, interest and all, by easy stages. It seemed so easy to mortgage the place to Murphy, and there was nothing else to be done."

The Squire had been walking slowly; now he stopped, dropped Nora's hand from his arm, and faced her.

"It seemed so easy to mortgage the land to Dan Murphy," he said, dropping his voice, "so very easy, and that money was so handy, and I thought—"

"Yes, father?" said Nora in a voice of fear. "You said these words before. Go on—it was so easy. Well?"

"Well, a month ago, child, I got a letter from Murphy's lawyer in Dublin, to say that the money must be paid up, or they would foreclose."

"Foreclose, father. What is that?"

"Take possession, child—take possession."

"A month ago you got that letter? They would take possession—possession of the land you have mortgaged. Does that mean that it would belong to Squire Murphy, father?"

"So I thought, my dear colleen, and I didn't fret much. The fact is, I put the letter in the fire and forgot it. It was only three days ago that I got another letter to know what I meant to do. I was given three months to pay in, and if I didn't pay up the whole ten thousand, with the five years' interest, they'd foreclose. I hadn't paid that, Nora; I hadn't paid a penny of it; and what with interest and compound interest, it mounted to a good round sum. Dan charged me six per cent, on the money; but there, you don't understand figures, child, and your pretty head shan't be worried. Anyhow, I was to pay it all up within the three months—I, who haven't even fifty pounds in the bank. It was a bit of a staggerer."

"I understand," said Nora; "and that was why you went the day before yesterday to see Squire Murphy. Of course, he'll give you time; though, now I come to think of it, he is very poor himself."

"He is that," said the Squire. "I don't blame him—not a bit."

"But what will you do, father?"

"I must think. It is a bit of a blow, my child, and I don't quite see my way. But I am sure to, before the time comes; and I have got three months."

"But won't he let you off, father? Must you really pay it in three months?"

"God help me, Norrie! I can't, not just now; but I will before the time comes."

"But what did he say, father? I don't understand."

"It's this, Nora. Ah, you have a wise little head on your shoulders, even though you are an Irish colleen. He said that he had sold my mortgage to another man, and had got money on it; and the other man—he is an Englishman, curse him!—and he wants the place, Nora, and he'll take it in lieu of the mortgage if I don't pay up in three months."

"The place," said Nora; "O'Shanaghgan—he wants O'Shanaghgan?"

"Yes, yes; that's it; he wants the land, and the old house."

"But he can't," said Nora. "You have not—oh! you have not mortgaged the house?"

"Bless you, Nora! it is I that have done it; the house that you were born in, and that my father, and father before him, and father before him again, were born in, and that I was born in—it goes, and the land goes, the lake yonder, all these fields, and the bit of the shore; all the bonny place goes in three months if we cannot pay the mortgage. It goes for an old song, and it breaks my heart, Nora."

"I understand," said Nora very gravely. She did not cry out; the tears pressed close to the back of her eyes, and scalded her with cruel pain; but she would not allow one of them to flow. She held her head very erect, and the color returned to her pale cheeks, and a new light shone in her dark-blue eyes.

"We'll manage somehow; we must," she said.

"I was thinking of that," said the Squire. "Of course we'll manage." He gave a great sigh, as if a load were lifted from his heart. "Of course we'll manage," he repeated; "and don't you tell your mother, for the life of you, child."

"Of course I will tell nothing until you give me leave. But how do you mean to manage?"

"I am thinking of going up to Dublin next week to see one or two old friends of mine; they are sure to help me at a pinch like this. They would never see Patrick O'Shanaghgan deprived of his acres. They know me too well; they know it would break my heart. I was thinking of going up next week."

"But why next week, father? You have only three months. Why do you put it off to next week?"

"Why, then, you're right, colleen; but it's a job I don't fancy."

"But you have got to do it, and you ought to do it at once."

"To be sure—to be sure."

"Take me with you, father; let us go tomorrow."

"But I have not got money for us both. I must go alone; and then your mother must not be left. There's Terence gallivanting off to England to visit his fine relations, and that will take a good bit. I had to give him ten pounds this morning, and there are only forty now left in the bank. Oh, plenty to tide us for a bit. We shan't want to eat much; and there's a good supply of fruit and vegetables on the land; and the poor folk will wait for their wages. Of course there will be more rents coming in, and we'll scrape along somehow. Don't you fret, colleen. I declare it's light as a feather my heart is since I told you the truth. You are a comfort to me, Norrie."

"Father," said Nora suddenly, "there's one thing I want to say."

"What is that, pet?"

"You know Andy Neil?"

"What! Andrew Neil—that scoundrel?" The Squire's brow grew very black. "Yes, yes. What about him? You have not seen him, have you?"

"Yes, father, I have."

"Over at Murphy's? He knew he dare not show his face here. Well, what about him, Nora?"

"This," said Nora, trembling very much; "he—he does not want you to evict him."

"He'll pay his rent, or he'll go," thundered the Squire. "No more of this at present. I can't be worried."

"But, oh, father! he—he can't pay it any more than you can pay the mortgage. Don't be cruel to him if you want to be dealt with mercifully yourself; it would be such bad luck."

"Good gracious, Nora, are you demented? The man pays his rent, or he goes. Not another word."

"Father, dear father!"

"Not another word. Go in and see your mother, or she'll be wondering what has happened to you. Yes, I'll go off to Dublin to-morrow. If Neil doesn't pay up his rent in a week, off he goes; it's men like Andrew Neil who are the scum of the earth. He has put my back up; and pay his rent he will, or out he goes."

CHAPTER IX
EDUCATION AND OTHER THINGS

The next day the Squire and Terence went off together. Mrs. O'Shanaghgan was very angry with her husband for going, as she expressed it, to amuse himself in Dublin. Dirty Dublin she was fond of calling the capital of Ireland.

"What do you want to go to Dirty Dublin for?" she said. "You'll spend a lot of money, and God knows we have little enough at the present moment."

"Oh, no, I won't, Ellen," he replied. "I'll be as careful as careful can be; the colleen can witness to that. There's a little inn on the banks of the Liffey where I'll put up; it is called the 'Green Dragon,' and it's a cozy, snug little place, where you can have your potheen and nobody be any the wiser."

"I declare, Patrick," said his lady, facing him, "you are becoming downright vulgar. I wish you wouldn't talk in that way. If you have no respect for yourself and your ancient family, you ought to remember your daughter."

"I'm sure I'm not doing the colleen any harm," said the Squire.

"That you never could, father," replied Nora, with a burst of enthusiasm.

Mrs. O'Shanaghgan surveyed her coldly.

"Go upstairs and help Terence to pack his things," she said; and Nora left the room.

The next day the travelers departed. As soon as they were gone Mrs. O'Shanaghgan sent for Nora to come and sit in the room with her.

"I have been thinking during the night how terribly neglected you are," she said; "you are not getting the education which a girl in your position ought to receive. You learn nothing now."

"Oh, mother, my education is supposed to be finished," answered Nora.

"Finished indeed!" said Mrs. O'Shanaghgan.

"Since Miss Freeman left I have had no governess; but I read a good bit alone. I am very fond of reading," answered Nora.

"Distasteful as it all is to me," said Mrs. O'Shanaghgan, "I must take you in hand myself. But I do wish your Uncle George would invite you over to stay with them at The Laurels. It will do Terence a wonderful lot of good; but you want it more, you are so unkempt and undignified. You would be a fairly nice-looking girl if any justice was done to you; but really the other day, when I saw you with that terrible young person Bridget Murphy, it gave my heart quite a pang. You scarcely looked a lady, you were laughing in such a vulgar way, and quite forgetting your deportment. Now, what I have been thinking is that we might spend some hours together daily, and I would mark out a course of instruction for you."

"Oh, mammy," answered Nora, "I should be very glad indeed to learn; you know I always hated having my education stopped, but father said—"

"I don't want to hear what your father said," interrupted Mrs. O'Shanaghgan.

"Oh, but, mother dear, I really must think of father, and I must respect what he says. He told me that my grandmother stopped her schooling at fourteen, and he said she was the grandest lady, and the finest and bonniest, in the country, and that no one could ever put her to shame; for, although she had not much learning to boast of, she had a smart answer for every single thing that was said to her. He said you never could catch her tripping in her words, never—never; and he thinks, mother," continued Nora, sparkling and blushing, "that I am a little like my grandmother. There is her miniature upstairs. I should like to be like her. Father did love her so very, very much."

"Of course, Nora, if those are your tastes, I have nothing further to say," answered Mrs. O'Shanaghgan; "but while you are under my roof and under my tuition, I shall insist on your doing a couple of hours' good reading daily."

"Very well, mother; I am quite agreeable."

"I suppose you have quite forgotten your music?"

"No, I remember it, and I should like to play very much indeed; but the old piano—you must know yourself, mother dear, that it is impossible to get any music out of it."

Mrs. O'Shanaghgan uttered a groan.

"We seem to be beset with difficulties at every step," she said. "It is such a mistake your father going to Dublin now, and throwing away his little capital. Has he said anything to you about the mortgage, by the way, Nora?"

Nora colored.

"A little," she answered in a low voice.

"Ah, I see—told it as a secret; so like the Irish, making mysteries about everything, and then blabbing them out the next minute. I don't want, my dear, to encroach upon your father's secrets, so don't be at all afraid. Now, bring down your Markham's History of England and Alison's History of Europe, and I will set you a task to prepare for me for to-morrow."

Nora went slowly out of the room. She hated Markham's History of England. She had read it five or six times, and knew it by heart. She detested George and Richard and Mary, and their conversations with their mother were simply loathsome to her. Alison's History, however, was tougher metal, and she thought she would enjoy a good stiff reading of it. She was a very intelligent girl, and with advantages would have done well.

She returned with the books. Her mother carelessly marked about twenty pages in each, told her to read them in the course of the day, and to come to her the next morning to be questioned.

"You can go now," she said. "I was very busy yesterday, and have a headache. I shall lie down and go to sleep."

"Shall I draw down the blind, mother?"

"Yes, please; and you can put that rug over me. Now, don't run shouting all over the house; try to remember you are a young lady. Really and truly, no one would suppose that you and Terence were brother and sister. He will do great credit to my brother George; he will be proud of such a handsome young fellow as his nephew."

Nora said nothing; having attended to her mother's comforts, she left the room. She went out into the sunshine. In her hand she carried the two books. Her first intention was to take them down to one end of the dilapidated garden and read them steadily. She was rather pleased than otherwise at her mother's sudden and unlooked-for solicitude with regard to her education. She thought it would be pleasant to learn even under her mother's rather peculiar method of tutelage; but, as she stood on the terrace looking across the exquisite summer scene, two of the dogs, Creena and Cushla, came into view. They rushed up to Nora with cries and barks of welcome. Down went the books on the gravel, and off ran the Irish girl, followed by the two barking dogs. A few moments later she was down on the shore. She had run out without her hat or parasol. What did that matter? The winds and sea-breezes had long ago taken their own sweet will on Nora's Irish complexion; they could not tan skin like hers, and had given up trying; they could only bring brighter roses into her cheeks and more sweetness into her dark-blue eyes. She forgot her troubles, as most Irish girls will when anything calls off their attention, and ran races with the dogs up and down the shore. Nora was laughing, and the dogs were barking and gamboling round her, when the stunted form of Hannah Croneen was seen approaching. Hannah wore her bedgown and her short blue serge petticoat; her legs and feet were bare; the breezes had caught up her short gray locks, and were tossing them wildly about. She looked very elfin and queer as she approached the girl.

"Why, then, Miss Nora, it's a word I want with you, a-colleen."

"Yes—what is it, Hannah?" answered Nora. She dropped her hands to her sides and turned her laughing, radiant face upon the little woman.

"Ah, then, it's a sight for sore eyes you are, Miss Nora. Why, it is a beauty you are, Miss Nora honey, and hondsomer and hondsomer you gets every time I see yez. It's the truth I'm a-telling yez, Miss Nora; it's the honest truth."

"I hope it is, Hannah, for it is very pleasant hearing," answered Nora. "Do I really get handsomer and handsomer? I must be a beauty like my grandmother."

"Ah, she was a lady to worship," replied Hannah, dropping a courtesy to the memory; "such ways as she had, and her eyes as blue and dark as the blessed night when the moon's at the full, just for all the world like your very own. Why, you're the mortal image of her; not a doubt of it, miss, not a doubt of it. But there, I want to say a word to yez, and we need not spend time talking about nothing but mere looks. Looks is passing, miss; they goes by and leaves yez withered up, and there are other things to think of this blessed morning."

"To be sure," answered Nora.

"And it's I that forgot to wish yez the top of the morning," continued the little woman. "I hear the masther and Masther Terry has gone to foreign parts—is it true, miss?"

"It is not true of my father," replied Nora; "he has only gone to Dublin."

"Ah, bless him! he's one in a thousand, is the Squire," said Hannah. "But what about the young masther, him with the handsome face and the ways?—aye, but he aint got your nice, bonny Irish ways, Miss Nora—no, that he aint."

"He has gone to England for a time to visit some of my mother's relations," replied Nora. "I am, sure it will do him a great deal of good, and dear mother is so pleased. Now, then, Hannah, what is it?"

Hannah went close to the girl and touched her on her arm.

"What about your promise to Andy Neil?" she asked.

"My promise to Andy Neil," said Nora, starting and turning pale. "How do you know about it?"

"A little bird told me," replied Hannah. "This is what it said: 'Find out if Miss Nora, the bonniest and handsomest young lady in the place, has kept her word to Andy.' Have you done it, Miss Nora? for it's word I have got to take the crayther, and this very night, too."

"Where?" said Nora. "Where are you going to meet him?"

"In the haunted glen, just by the Druid's Stone," replied the woman.

"At what hour?"

"Tin o'clock, deary. Aw, glory be to God! it's just when the clock strikes tin that he'll be waiting for me there."

"I have no message," said Nora.

"Are you sure, Miss Nora?"

"Quite sure."

"When will you have?"

"Never."

"Miss Nora, you don't mane it?"

"Yes, I do, Hannah. I have nothing to do with Andy Neil. I did what I could for him, but that little failed. You can tell him that if you like."

"But is it in earnest you are, Miss Nora? Do you mane to say that you'll let the poor crayther have the roof taken off his cabin? Do you mane it miss?"

"I wouldn't have the roof taken off his cabin," said Nora; "but father is away, and he is Andy's landlord, and Andy has done something to displease him. He had better come and talk to father himself. I kept my word, and spoke; but I couldn't do anything. Andy had better talk to father himself; I can do no more."

"You don't guess as it's black rage is in the crayther's heart, and that there's no crime he wouldn't stoop to," whispered Hannah in a low, awestruck voice.

"I can't help it, Hannah; I am not going to be frightened. Andy would not really injure me, not in cold blood."

"Oh, wouldn't he just? The man's heart is hot within him; it's the thought of the roof being taken off his cabin. I have come as his messenger.

You had best send some sort of message to keep him on the quiet for a bit. Don't you send a hard message of that sort, heart asthore; you'll do a sight of mischief if you do."

"I can only send him a true message," replied the girl.

"Whisht now, Miss Nora! You wouldn't come and see him yourself tonight by the Druid's Stone?"

Nora stood for a moment considering. She was not frightened; she had never known that quality. Even in the cave, when her danger was extreme, she had not succumbed to fear; it was impossible for her to feel it now, with the sunlight filling her eyes and the softest of summer breezes blowing against her cheeks. She looked full at Hannah.

"I won't go," she said shortly.

"Miss Nora, I wouldn't ask yez if I could help myself. It's bothered I am entirely, and frightened too. You'll come with me, Miss Nora—won't yez?"

"I will not come," answered Nora. "My mother is alone, and I cannot leave her; but I tell you what I will do. Just to show Andy that I am not afraid of him, when father returns I will come. Father will be back in a couple of days; when he returns I will speak to him once more about Andy, and I will bring Andy the message; and that is all I can promise. If that is all you want to say to me, Hannah, I will go home now, for mother is all alone."

Hannah stood with her little, squat figure silhouetted against the sky; she had placed both her arms akimbo, and was gazing at Nora with a half-comical, half-frightened glance.

"You're a beauty," she said, "and you has the courage of ten women. I'll tell Andy what you say; but, oh, glory! there's mischief in that man's eyes, or I'm much mistook."

"You can't frighten me," said Nora, with a laugh. "How are the children?"

"Oh, bless yez, they're as well and bonny as can be. Little Mike, he said he'd stand and wait till you passed by the gate, he's that took up with you, Miss Nora. You'd be conceited if you heard all he says about you."

Nora thrust her hand into her pocket.

"Here," she said, "is a bright halfpenny; give it to Mike, and tell him that Nora loves him very much. And now I am going home. Hannah, you'll remember my message to Andy, and please let him understand that he is not going to frighten me into doing anything I don't think right."

CHAPTER X
THE INVITATION

Squire O'Shanaghan came home in a couple of days. He entered the house in noisy fashion, and appeared to be quite cheerful. He had a great deal to say about Dublin, and talked much of his old friends during the evening that followed. Nora, however, try as she would, could never meet his eye, and she guessed, even before he told her, that his mission had been a failure. It was early the next morning that he gave her this information.

"I tried them, one and all, colleen," he said, "and never were fellows more taken aback. 'Is it you to lose your property, O'Shanaghgan?' they said. They wouldn't believe me at first."

"Well, father, and will they help?" said Nora.

"Bless you, they would if they could. There's not a better-natured man in the length and breadth of Ireland than Fin O'Hara; and as to John Fitzgerald, I believe he would take us all into his barrack of a house; but they can't help with money, Nora, because, bedad, they haven't got it. A man can't turn stones into money, even for his best and dearest friends."

"Then what is to be done, father?"

"Oh, I'll manage somehow," said Squire O'Shanaghgan; "and we have three months all but a week to turn round in. We'll manage by hook or by crook. Don't you fret your pretty little head. I wouldn't have a frown on the brow of my colleen for fifty O'Shanaghgans, and that's plain enough. I couldn't say more, could I?"

"No, father dear," answered Nora a little sadly.

"And tell me what you were doing while I was away," said the Squire. "Faith! I thought I could never get back fast enough, I seemed to pine so for you, colleen; you fit me down to the ground."

Nora began to relate the small occurrences which had taken place. The Squire laughed at Mrs. O'Shanaghgan's sudden desire that Nora should be an educated lady.

"I don't hold with these new fashions about women," he said; "and you are educated enough for me."

"But, father, I like to read, I like to learn," said the girl. "I am very, very anxious to improve myself. I may be good enough for you, dear father, for you love me with all my faults; but some day I may pine for the knowledge which I have not got."

"Eh! is it that way with you?" said the Squire, looking at her anxiously. "They say it's a sort of a craze now amongst women, the desire to beat us men on our own ground; it's very queer, and I don't understand it, and I am sorry if the craze has seized my girleen."

"Oh! never mind, father dear; I wouldn't fret you for all the learning in Christendom."

"And I wouldn't fret you for fifty estates like O'Shanaghgan," said the Squire, "so it strikes me we are both pretty equal in our sentiments." He patted her cheek, she linked her hand in his, and they walked together down one of the sunny meadows.

Nora thought of Neil, but determined not to trouble her father about him just then. Notwithstanding her cheerfulness, her own heart was very heavy. She possessed, with all her Irish ways, some of the common sense of her English ancestors, and knew from past experience that now there was no hope at all of saving the old acres and the old house unless something very unexpected turned up. She understood her father's character too well; he would be happy and contented until a week before the three months were up, and then he would break down utterly—go under, perhaps, forever. As to turning his back on the home of his ancestors and the acres which had come to him through a long line, Nora could not face such a possibility.

"It cannot be; something must happen to prevent it," she thought.

She thought and thought, and suddenly a daring idea came into her mind. All her life long her mother's relations had been brought up to her as the pink of propriety, the souls of wealth. Her uncle, George Hartrick, was, according to her mother, a wealthy man. Her mother had often described him. She had said that he had been very angry with her for marrying the Squire, but had confessed that at times he had been heard to say that the O'Shanaghgans were the proudest and oldest family in County Kerry, and that some day he would visit them on their own estate.

"I have prevented his ever coming, Nora," said Mrs. O'Shanaghgan; "it would be such a shock to him. He thinks we live in a castle such as English people live in, with suites of magnificent rooms, and crowds and crowds of respectably dressed servants, and that we have carriages and horses. I have kept up this delusion; he must never come over to see the nakedness of the land."

But now the fact that her Uncle George had never seen the nakedness of the land, and that he was attached to her mother, and proud of the fact that she had married an Irish gentleman of old descent, kept visiting Nora again and again. If she could only see him! If she could only beg of him to lend her father a little money just to avert the crowning disgrace of all— the O'Shanaghgans leaving their home because they could not afford to stop there, Nora thought, and the wild idea which had crept into her head gathered strength.

"There is nothing for it; something desperate must be done," she thought. "Father won't save himself, because he does not know how. He will just drift on until a week of the fatal day, and then he will have an illness. I cannot let father die; I cannot let his heart be broken. I, Nora, will do something."

So one day she locked herself in her room. She stayed there for a couple of hours, and when she came out again a letter was thrust into her pocket. Nora was not a good letter-writer, and this one had taken nearly two hours to produce. Tears had blotted its pages, and the paper on which it was written was of the poorest, but it was done at last. She put a stamp on it and ran downstairs. She went to Hannah's cabin. Standing in front of the cabin was her small admirer Mike. He was standing on his head with the full blaze of the sunlight all over him, his ragged trousers had slipped down almost to his knees, and his little brown bare legs and feet were twinkling in the sun. His bright sloe-black eyes were fixed on Nora as she approached.

"Come here, Mike," said the girl. Mike instantly obeyed, and gave a violent tug to one of his front locks by way of salutation. He then stood with his legs slightly apart, watching Nora.

"Mike, I want you to go a message for me."

"To be sure, miss," answered Mike.

"Take this letter to the post-office; put it yourself into the little slit in the wall. I will give you a penny when you have done it."

"Yes, miss," answered Mike.

"Here is the letter; thrust it into your pocket. Don't let anyone see it; it's a secret."

"A saycret, to be sure, miss," answered Mike.

"And you shall have your penny if you come up to the Castle tonight. Now good-by; run off at once and you will catch the mail."

"Yes, to be sure," said Mike. He winked at Nora, rolled his tongue in his cheek, and disappeared like a flash down the dusty road.

The next few days seemed to drag themselves somehow. Nora felt limp, and not in her usual spirits. The Squire was absent a good deal, too. He was riding all over the country trying to get a loan from his different friends. He was visiting one house after another. Some of the houses were neat and well-to-do, but most of them sadly required funds to put them in order. At every house Squire O'Shanaghgan received a hearty welcome, an invitation to dinner, and a bed for the night; but when he made his request the honest face that looked into his became sorrowful, the hands stole to the empty pockets, and refusals, accompanied by copious apologies, were the invariable result.

"There's no one in all the world I would help sooner, Pat, if I could," said Squire O'Grady; "but I have not got it, my man. I am as hard pressed as I can be myself. We don't get in the rents these times. Times are bad—very bad. God help us all! But if you are turned out, what an awful thing it will be! And your family the oldest in the place. You're welcome, every one of you, to come here. As long as I have a bite and sup, you and yours shall share it with me." And Squire Malone said the same thing, and so did the other squires. There was no lack of hospitality, no lack of good will, no lack of sorrow for poor Squire O'Shanaghgan's calamities; but funds to avert the blow were not forthcoming.

The Squire more and more avoided Nora's eyes; and Nora, who now had a secret of her own, and a hope which she would scarcely dare to confess even to herself, avoided looking at him.

Mrs. O'Shanaghgan was a little more fretful than usual. She forgot all about the lessons she had set her daughter in her laments over her absent son, over the tattered and disgraceful state of the Castle, and the ruin which seemed to engulf the family more and more.

Nora, meanwhile, was counting the days. She had made herself quite *au fait* with postal regulations during these hours of waiting. She knew exactly the very time when the letter would reach Mr. Hartrick in his luxurious home. She thought she would give him, perhaps, twelve hours, perhaps twenty-four, before he replied. She knew, then, how long the answer would take on its way. The night before she expected her letter she scarcely slept at all. She came down to breakfast with black shadows under her eyes and her face quite wan.

The Squire, busy with his own load of trouble, scarcely noticed her. Mrs. O'Shanaghgan took her place languidly at the head of the board. She poured out a cup of tea for her daughter and another for her husband.

"I must send to Dublin for some better tea," she said, looking at the Squire. "Can you let me have a pound after breakfast, Pat? I may as well order a small chest while I am about it."

The Squire looked at her with lack-luster eyes. Where had he got one pound for tea? But he said nothing.

Just then the gossoon Mike was seen passing the window with the post-bag hung over his shoulder. Mike was the postman in general for the O'Shanaghgan household for the large sum of twopence a week. He went daily to fetch the letters, and received his money proudly each Saturday night. Nora now jumped up from the table.

"The letters!" she gasped.

Mrs. O'Shanaghgan surveyed her daughter critically.

"Sit down again, Nora," she said. "What is the matter with you? You know I don't allow these manners at table."

"But it is the post, mammy," said the girl.

"Well, my dear, if you will be patient, Margaret will bring the post in."

Nora sat down again, trembling. Mrs. O'Shanaghgan gave her a cold stare, and helped herself languidly to a small snippet of leathery toast.

"Our cook gets worse and worse," she said as she broke it. "Dear, dear! I think I must make a change. I have heard of an excellent cook just about to leave some people of the name of Wilson in the town. They are English people, which accounts for their having a good servant."

At that moment the redoubtable Pegeen did thrust in her head, holding the post-bag at arm's length away from her.

"Here's the post, Miss Nora," she said; "maybe you'll fetch it, miss. I'm a bit dirty."

Nora could not restrain herself another moment. She rushed across the room, seized the bag, and laid it by her father's side. As a rule, the post-bag was quickly opened, and its small contents dispersed. These consisted of the local paper for the Squire, which was always put up with the letters, a circular or two, and, at long intervals, a letter for Mrs. O'Shanaghgan, and perhaps one from an absent friend for the Squire. No one was excited, as a rule, about the post at the Castle, and Nora's ill-suppressed anxiety was sufficiently marked now to make even her father look at her in some surprise. To the girl's relief, her mother unexpectedly came to the rescue.

"She thinks, perhaps, Terence will write," she said; "but I told him not to worry himself writing too often. Stamps cost money, and the boy will need every penny to keep up a decent appearance at my brother's."

"All the same, perhaps he will be an Irish boy enough to write a letter to his own sister," said the Squire. "So here goes; we'll look and see if there is anything inside here for you, my little Norrie."

The Squire unlocked the bag and emptied the contents on the table. They were very meager contents; nothing but the newspaper and one letter. The Squire took it up and looked at it.

"Here we are," he said; "it is for you, my dear."

"For me," said Mrs. O'Shanaghgan, holding out her hand. "Pass it across, Nora."

"No, it is not for you, my lady, as it happens. It is for Nora. Here, Norrie, take it."

Nora took it up. She was shivering now, and her hand could scarcely hold it. It was addressed to her, beyond doubt: "Miss O'Shanaghgan, Castle O'Shanaghgan," etc.

"Read it at once, Nora," said her mother. "I have not yet had any letter to speak of from Terry myself. If you read it aloud it will entertain us. It seems to be a thick letter."

"I don't think—I don't think it—it is from Terence," answered Nora.

"Nonsense, my dear."

"Open it, Norrie, and tell us," said the Squire. "It will be refreshing to hear a bit of outside news."

Nora now opened the envelope, and took a very thick sheet of paper out. The contents of the letter ran as follows:

"My Dear Nora—Your brother Terence came here a week ago, and has told us a great deal about you. We are enjoying having him extremely; but he has made us all anxious to know you also. I write now to ask if you will come and pay us a visit at once, while your brother is here. Ask your mother to spare you. You can return with Terence whenever you are tired of us and our ways. I have business at Holyhead next Tuesday, and could meet you there, if you could make it convenient to cross that day. I inclose a paper with the hours that the boats leave, and when they arrive at Holyhead. I could then take you up with me to London, and we could reach here that same evening. Ask my sister to spare you. You will be heartily welcome, my little Irish niece.—Your affectionate uncle,

"George Hartrick."

Nora could scarcely read the words aloud. When she had finished she let the sheet of paper flutter to the floor, and looked at her mother with glowing cheeks and sparkling eyes.

"I may go? I must go," she said.

"My dear Nora," said Mrs. O'Shanaghgan, "why that must?"

"Oh, mammy! oh, daddy! don't disappoint me," cried the girl. "Do—do let me go, please, please."

"Nora," said Mrs. O'Shanaghgan again, "I never saw you so unreasonable in your life; you are quite carried away. Your uncle, after long years, has condescended to send you an invitation, and you speak in this impulsive, unrestrained fashion. Of course, it would be extremely nice for you to go; but I doubt for a single moment if it can be afforded."

"Oh, daddy, daddy! please take my part!" cried Nora. "Please let me go, daddy—oh, daddy!" She rushed up to her father, flung her arms round his neck, and burst into tears.

Mrs. O'Shanaghgan rose from the table in cold displeasure. "Give me your uncle's letter," she said.

Nora did not glance at her; she was past speaking. So much hung on this; all the future of the O'Shanaghgans; the Castle, the old Castle, the home of her ancestors, the place in which she was born, the land she loved, the father she adored—all, all their future hung upon Nora's accepting the invitation which she had asked her uncle to give her. Oh! if they ever found out, what would her father and mother say? Would they ever speak to her again? But they must not find out, and she must go; yes, she must go.

"What is it, Nora? Do leave her alone for a moment, wife," said the Squire. "There is something behind all this. I never saw Light o' the Morning give way to pure selfishness before."

"It isn't—it isn't," sobbed Nora, her head buried on the Squire's shoulder.

"My darling, light of my eyes, colleen asthore, acushla machree!" said the Squire. He lavished fond epithets upon the girl, and finally took her into his arms, and clasped her tight to his breast.

Mrs. O'Shanaghgan, after staring at the two in speechless indignation for a moment, left the room. When she reached the door she turned round.

"I cannot stand Irish heroics," she said. "This is a disgraceful scene. Nora, I am thoroughly ashamed of you."

She carried her brother's letter away with her, however, and retired into the drawing room. There she read it carefully.

How nice it would be if Nora could go! And Nora was a beauty, too— an Irish beauty; the sort of girl who always goes down in England. She would want respectable dress; and then—with her taking ways and those roguish, dark-blue eyes of hers, with that bewitching smile which showed a gleam of the whitest and most pearly teeth in the world, with the light, lissome figure, and the blue-black hair—what could not Irish Nora achieve? Conquests innumerable; she might make a match worthy of her race and name; she might—oh, she might do anything. She was only a child, it is true; but all the same she was a budding woman.

Mrs. O'Shanaghgan sat and pondered.

"It seems a great pity to refuse," she said to herself. "And Nora does need discipline badly; the discipline of England and my brother's well-ordered home will work wonders with her. Poor child, her father will miss her. I really sometimes think the Squire is getting into his dotage. He makes a perfect fool of that girl; to see her there speaking in that selfish way, and he petting her, and calling her ridiculous names, with no meaning in them, and folding her in his arms as if she were a baby, and all for pure, downright selfishness, is enough to make any sensible person sick. Nora, too, who has always been spoken of as the unselfish member of the family, who would not spend a penny to save her life if she thought the Squire was going to suffer. Now she wants him to put his hand into his pocket for a considerable amount; for the child cannot go to my brother without suitable clothes—that is a foregone conclusion. But, dear me! all women are selfish when it comes to mere pleasure, and Nora is no better than the rest. For my part, I admire dear Terence's downright method of asking for so-and-so, and getting it. Nora is deceitful. I am much disappointed in her."

CHAPTER XI
THE DIAMOND CROSS

But although Mrs. O'Shanaghgan spoke of her daughter to herself as deceitful, she did not at all give up the idea of her accepting her uncle's invitation. George Hartrick had always had an immense influence over his sister Ellen. He and she had been great friends long ago, when the handsome, bright girl had been glad to take the advice of her elder brother. They had almost quarreled at that brief period of madness in Ellen Hartrick's life, when she had fallen in love with handsome Squire O'Shanaghgan; but that quarrel had long been made up. Mrs. O'Shanaghgan had married the owner of O'Shanaghgan Castle, and had rued her brief madness ever since. But her pride had prevented her complaining to her brother George. George still imagined that she kept her passionate love intact for the wild Irishman. Only one thing she had managed ever since their parting, many years ago, and that was, that her English brother should not come to see her in her Irish home. One excuse after the other she had offered, and at last she had told him frankly that the ways of the Irish were not his ways; and that, when he really wanted to see his sister, he must invite her to come to England to visit him.

Hartrick was hurt at Ellen's behavior, and as he himself had married about the same time, and his own young family were growing up around him, and the making of money and the toil of riches were claiming him more and more, he did not often think of the sister who was away in the wilds of Ireland. She had married one of the proud old Irish chiefs. She had a very good position in her way; and when her son and daughter required a little peep into the world, Hartrick resolved that they should have it. He had invited Terence over; and now Nora's letter, with its perplexity, its anguish, its bold request, and its final tenderness, had come upon him with a shock of surprise.

George Hartrick was a much stronger character than his sister. He was a very fine man, indeed, with splendid principles and downright ways; and there was something about this outspoken and queer letter which touched him in spite of himself. He was not easily touched; but he respected the writer of that letter. He felt that if he knew her he could get on with her.

He resolved to treat her confidence with the respect it seemed to him it deserved; and, without hesitation, he wrote her the sort of letter she had asked him to write. She should pay him a visit, and he would find out for himself the true state of things at Castle O'Shanaghgan. Whether he would help the Squire or not, whether there was any need to help him, he could not say, for Nora had not really revealed much of the truth in her passionate letter. She had hinted at it, but she had not spoken; she would wait for that moment of outpouring of her heart until she arrived at The Laurels.

Now, Mrs. O'Shanaghgan, standing alone in her big, empty drawing room, and looking out at the summer landscape, thought of how Nora might enter her brother's house. Fond as Mrs. O'Shanaghgan was of Terence—he was in truth a son after her own heart—she had a queer kind of pride about her with regard to Nora. Wild and untutored as Nora looked, her mother knew that few girls in England could hold a candle to her, if justice were done her. There was something about the expression in Nora's eyes which even Mrs. O'Shanaghgan could scarcely resist at times, and there were tones and inflections of entreaty in Nora's voice which had a strange power of melting the hearts of those who listened to her.

After about an hour Mrs. O'Shanaghgan went very slowly upstairs. Her bedroom was over the drawing room. It was just as large as the drawing room—a great bare apartment. The carpet which covered the floor was so threadbare that the boards showed through in places; the old, faded chintz curtains which hung at the windows were also in tatters; but they were perfectly clean, for Mrs. O'Shanaghgan did her best to retain that English cleanliness and order which she felt were so needed in the land of desolation, as she was pleased to call Ireland.

A huge four-post bedstead occupied a prominent place against one of the walls; there was an enormous mahogany wardrobe against another; but the whole center of the room was bare. The dressing-table, however, which stood right in the center of the huge bay, was full of pretty things—silver appointments of different kinds, brushes and combs heavily mounted in silver, glass bottles with silver stoppers, perfume bottles, pretty knick-knacks of all sorts. When Nora was a little child she used to stand fascinated, gazing at her mother's dressing-table. It was the one spot where any of the richness of the Englishwoman's early life could still be found. Mrs. O'Shanaghgan went up now and looked at her dressing-table, sweeping her eyes rapidly over its contents. The brushes and combs, the bottles of scent, the button-hooks, the shoe-horns, the thousand-and-one little nothings, polished and bright, stood upon the dressing-table; and besides these there was a large, silver-mounted jewel-case.

Mrs. O'Shanaghan was not at all afraid to leave this jewel-case out, exposed to view day after day, for no one all round the place would have touched so much as a pin which belonged to the Squire's lady. The people were poor, and would think nothing of stealing half a bag of potatoes, or helping themselves to a good sack of fruit out of the orchard; but to take the things from the lady's bedroom or anything at all out of the house they would have scorned. They had their own honesty, and they loved the Squire too much to attempt anything of the sort.

Mrs. O'Shanaghan now put a key into the lock of the jewel-case and opened it. When first she was married it was full of pretty things—long strings of pearls, a necklet of very valuable diamonds, a tiara of the same, rings innumerable, bracelets, head ornaments of different kinds, buckles for shoes, clasps for belts, pins, brooches. Mrs. O'Shanaghan, when Nora was a tiny child, used on every one of the little girl's birthdays to allow her to overhaul the jewel case; but of late years Nora had never looked inside it, and Mrs. O'Shanaghan had religiously kept it locked. She opened it now with a sigh. The upper tray was quite empty; the diamonds had long ago been disposed of. They had gone to pay for Terence's schooling, for Terence's clothes, for one thing and another that required money. They had gone, oh! so quickly; had melted away so certainly. That first visit of her son's to England had cost Mrs. O'Shanaghan her long string of pearls, which had come to her as an heirloom from her mother before her. They were very valuable pearls, and she had sold them for a tenth, a twentieth part of their value. The jeweler in Dublin, who was quite accustomed to receiving the poor lady's trinkets, had sent her a check for fifty pounds for the pearls, knowing well that he could sell them himself for at least three hundred pounds.

Mrs. O'Shanaghan now once more rifled the jewel case. There were some things still left—two or three rings and a diamond cross. She had never wanted to part with that cross. She had pictured over and over how it would shine on Nora's white neck; how lovely Nora would look when dressed for her first ball, having that white Irish cross, with its diamonds and its single emerald in the center, shining on her breast. But would it not be better to give Nora the chance of spending three or four months in England, the chance of educating herself, and let the cross go by? It was so valuable that the good lady quite thought that she ought to get seventy pounds for it. With seventy pounds she could fit Nora up for her English visit, and have a little over to keep in her own pocket. Only Nora must not go next Tuesday; that was quite impossible.

Mrs. O'Shanaghan quickly determined to make the sacrifice. She could still supply Nora with a little, very simple pearl necklet, to wear with her white dress during her visit; and the cross would have to go. There would be a few rings still left; after that the jewel case would be empty.

Mrs. O'Shanaghgan packed the precious cross into a little box, and took it out herself to register it, and to send it off to the jeweler who always bought the trinkets she sent him. She told him that she expected him to give her, without the smallest demur, seventy pounds for the cross, and hoped to have the money by the next day's post.

Having done this and dispatched her letter, she walked briskly back to the Castle. She saw Nora wandering about in the avenue. Nora, hatless and gloveless, was playing with the dogs. She seemed to have forgotten all about her keen disappointment of the morning. When she saw her mother coming up the avenue she ran to meet her.

"Why, mammy," she said, "how early you are out! Where have you been?"

"I dislike extremely that habit you have, Nora, of calling me mammy; mother is the word you should address your parent with. Please remember in future that I wish to be called mother."

"Oh, yes, mother!" answered Nora. The girl had the sweetest temper in the world, and no amount of reproof ever caused her to answer angrily. "But where have you been?" she said, her curiosity getting the better of her prudence.

"Again, Nora, I am sorry to say I must reprove you. I have been to the village on business of my own. It is scarcely your affair where I choose to walk in the morning."

"Oh, of course not, mam—I mean mother."

"But come with me down this walk. I have something to say to you."

Nora eagerly complied. There was something in the look of her mother's eyes which made her guess that the usual subject of conversation—her own want of deportment, her ignorance of etiquette—was not to be the theme. She felt her heart, which had sunk like lead within her, rise again to the surface. Her eyes sparkled and smiles played round her rosy lips.

"Yes, mother," she said; "yes."

"All impulse," said Mrs. O'Shanaghgan—she laid her hand on Nora's arm—"all impulse, all Irish enthusiasm."

"I cannot help it, you know," said Nora. "I was born that way. I am Irish, you know, mammy."

"You are also English, my dear," replied her mother. "Pray remember that fact when you see your cousins."

"My cousins! My English cousins! But am I to see them? Mother, mother, do you mean it?"

"I do mean it, Nora. I intend you to accept your uncle's invitation. No heroics, please," as the girl was about to fling her arms round her mother's neck; "keep those for your father, Nora; I do not wish for them. I intend you to go and behave properly; pray remember that when you give way to pure Irishism, as I may express your most peculiar manners, you disgrace me, your mother. I mean you to go in order to have you tamed a little. You are absolutely untamed now, unbroken in."

"I never want to be broken in," whispered Nora, tears of mingled excitement and pain at her mother's words brimming to her eyes. "Oh, mother!" she said, with a sudden wail, "will you never, never understand Nora?"

"I understand her quite well," said Mrs. O'Shanaghgan, her voice assuming an unwonted note of softness; "and because I do understand Nora so well," she added—and now she patted the girl's slender arm—"I want her to have this great advantage, for there is much that is good in you, Nora. But you are undisciplined, my dear; wild, unkempt. Little did I think in the old days that a daughter of mine should have to have such things said to her. Our more stately, more sober ways will be a revelation to you, Nora. To your brother Terence they will come as second nature; but you, my dear, will have to be warned beforehand. I warn you now that your Uncle George will not understand the wild excitement which you seem to consider the height of good breeding at O'Shanaghgan."

"Mother, mother," said Nora, "don't say anything against O'Shanaghgan."

"Am I doing so?" said the poor lady. She stood for a moment and looked around her. Nora stopped also and when she saw her mother's eyes travel to the rambling old house, to the neglected lawn, the avenue overgrown with weeds, it seemed to her that a stab of the cruelest pain was penetrating her heart.

"Mother sees all the ugliness; she is determined to," thought Nora; "but I see all the beauty. Oh! the dear, dear old place, it shan't go if Nora can save it." Then, with a great effort, she controlled herself.

"How am I to go?" she said. "Where is the money to come from?"

"You need not question me on that point," said Mrs. O'Shanaghgan. "I will provide the means."

"Oh, mother!" said Nora; "no, I would rather stay." But then she remembered all that this involved; she knew quite well that her mother had rifled the jewel-case; but as she had done so over and over again just for Terence's mere pleasure, might she not do so once more to save the old place?

"Very well," she said demurely; "I won't ask any questions."

"You had better not, for I have not the slightest idea of replying to them," answered Mrs. O'Shanaghgan. "I shall write to your uncle to-day. You cannot go next week, however."

"Oh! why not? He said Tuesday; he would meet me at Holyhead on Tuesday."

"I will try and provide a fit escort for you to England; But you cannot go next Tuesday; your wardrobe forbids it," answered Mrs. O'Shanaghgan.

"My wardrobe! Oh, mother, I really need not bother about clothes!"

"You may not bother about them, Nora; but I intend to," replied Mrs. O'Shanaghgan. "I must buy you some suitable dress."

"But how will you do it?"

"I have not been away from Castle O'Shanaghgan for a long time," said Mrs. O'Shanaghgan, "and it will be a nice change for me. I shall take you to Dublin, and get you what things are necessary. I will then see you off on board the steamer."

"But would not father be best?"

"Your father can come with us or not, just as he pleases; but I am the person who will see to your wardrobe for your English visit," replied her mother.

Nora, excited, bewildered, charmed, had little or nothing to oppose to this plan. After all, her mother was coming out in a new light. How indifferent she had been about Nora's dress in the past! For Terence were the fashionable coats and the immaculate neckties and the nice gloves and the patent-leather boots. For Nora! Now and then an old dress of her mother's was cut down to fit the girl; but as a rule she wore anything she could lay hands on, made anyhow. It is true she was never grotesque like Biddy Murphy; but up to the present dress had scarcely entered at all as a factor into her life.

The next few days passed in a whirl of bewildered excitement. Mrs. O'Shanaghgan received, as she expected, by return of post, seventy pounds from the Dublin jeweler for her lovely diamond cross. This man was rapidly making his fortune out of poor Mrs. O'Shanaghgan, and he knew that he had secured a splendid bargain for himself when he bought the cross.

Mrs. O'Shanaghgan, therefore, with a full purse, could give directions to her household during her brief absence, and altogether was much brightened and excited at the thought of Nora's visit. She had written herself to her brother, saying that she would be very glad to spare her daughter, and giving him one or two hints with regard to Nora's manners and bringing up.

"The Irish have quite different ideas, my dear brother," she wrote, "with regard to etiquette to those which were instilled into us; but you will bear patiently with my little wild Irish girl, for she has a very true heart, and is also, I think you will admit, nice-looking."

Mr. Hartrick, who read between the lines of his sister's letter, wrote to say that business would bring him to Holyhead on the following Tuesday week also, and, therefore, it would be quite convenient for him to meet Nora on that day.

The evening before she was to depart arrived at last. The Squire had spent a busy day. From the moment when Nora had told him that her mother had provided funds, and that she was to go to England, he had scarcely reverted to the matter. In truth, with that curious Irish phase in his character which is more or less the inheritance of every member of his country, he contrived to put away the disagreeable subject even from his thoughts. He was busy, very busy, attending to his farm and riding round his establishment. He was still hoping against hope that some money would come in his way long before the three months were up, when the mortgagee would foreclose on his property. He was not at all unhappy, and used to enter his house singing lustily or whistling loudly. Nora sometimes wondered if he also forgot how soon she was going to leave him. His first call when he entered the house had always been "Light o' the Morning, where are you? Come here, asthore; the old dad has returned," or some such expression. It came to the excited girl's heart with a pang how he would miss her when she was no longer there; how he would call for her in vain, and feel bewildered for a moment, and then remember that she was far away.

"But I shan't be long away," she thought; "and when I come back and save him and the old place, oh, how glad he will be! He will indeed then think me his Light o' the Morning, for I shall have saved him and the old home."

But the last evening came, and Nora considered whether she ought to recall the fact that she was going away, perhaps for a couple of months, to her father. He came in as usual, sat down heavily on the nearest settee, and stretched out his long legs.

"I wonder if I am getting old?" he said. "I declare I feel a bit tired. Come along here, Nora, and cheer me up. What news have you this evening, little woman?"

"Oh, father! don't you know?"

"Well, your eyes look bright enough. What is it, girleen?"

"I am going away to Dublin to-morrow."

"You? Bless you! so you are," said the Squire, with a hearty laugh. "Upon my soul I forgot all about it. Well, and you are going to have a good time, and you'll forget the old dad—eh?—you'll forget all about the old dad?"

"Father, father, you know better," said Nora—she flung her arms round his neck and laid her soft cheek against his—"as if I could ever forget you for a single moment," she said.

"I know it, a-colleen; I know it, heart's asthore. Of course you won't. I am right glad you are going; it will be a nice change for you. And what about the bits of duds—eh?—and the pretty trinkets? Why, you'll be going into grand society; you'll be holding your little head like a queen. Don't you forget, my pet, that you're Irish through and through, and that you come of a long line of brave ancestors. The women of your house never stooped to a shabby action, Nora; and never one of them sacrificed her honor for gold or anything else; and the men were brave, girleen, very brave, and had never fear in one of them. You remember that, and keep yourself upright and brave and proud, and come back to the old dad with as pure and loving a heart as you have now."

"Oh, father, of course, of course. But you will miss me? you will miss me?"

"Bedad! I expect I shall," said the Squire; "but I am not going to fret, so don't you imagine it."

"Have you," said Nora in a low whisper—"have you done anything about-about the mortgage?"

"Oh, you be aisy," said the Squire, giving her a playful poke; "and if you can't be aisy, be as aisy as you can," he continued, referring to the old well-known saying. "Things will come right enough. Why, the matter is weeks off yet. It was only yesterday I heard from an old friend, Larry M'Dermott, who has been in Australia, and has made a fine pile. He is back again, and I am thinking of seeing him and settling up matters with him. Don't you have an uneasy thought in your head, my child. I'll write to you when the thing is fixed up, as fixed it will be by all that's likely in a week or fortnight from now. But look here, Norrie, you'll want something to keep in your pocket when you are away. I had best give you a five-pound note."

"No, no," said Nora. "I wouldn't touch it; I don't want it."

"Why not? Is it too proud you are?"

"No; mother is helping me to this visit. I don't know how she has got money. I suppose in the old way."

"Poor soul!" said the Squire. "To tell you the truth, Norrie, I can't bear to look at that jewel-case of hers. I believe, upon my word, that it is nearly empty. She is very generous, is your mother. She's a very fine woman, and I am desperate proud of her. When M'Dermott helps me to tide over this pinch I'll have all those jewels back again by hook or by crook. Your mother shan't suffer in the long run, and I'll do a lot to the old place—the old house wants papering and painting. We'll dance a merry jig at O'Shanaghgan at your wedding, my little girl; and now don't keep me, for I have got to go out to meet Murphy. He said he would look around about this hour."

Nora left her father, and wandered out into the soft summer gloaming. She went down the avenue, and leaned for a time over the gate. The white gate was sadly in need of paint, but it was not hanging off its hinges as the gate was which led to the estate of Cronane. Nora put her feet on the last rung, leaned her arms on the top one, and swayed softly, as she thought of all that was about to happen, and the glorious adventures which would in all probability be hers during the next few weeks. As she thought, and forgot herself in dreams of the future, a low voice calling her name caused her to start. A man with shaggy hair and wild, bright eyes had come up to the other side of the gate.

"Why, then, Miss Nora, how are ye this evening?" he said. He pulled his forelock as he spoke.

Nora felt a sudden coldness come over all her rosy dreams; but she was too Irish and too like her ancestors to feel any fear, although she could not help remembering that she was nearly half a mile away from the house, and that there was not a soul anywhere within call.

"Good-evening, Andy," she said. "I must be going home now."

"No, you won't just yet," he answered. He came up and laid his dirty hand on her white sleeve.

"No, don't touch me," said Nora proudly. She sprang off the gate, and stood a foot or two away. "Don't come in," she continued; "stay where you are. If you have anything to say, say it there."

"Bedad! it's a fine young lady that it is," said the man. "It aint afeared, is it?"

"Afraid!" said Nora. "What do you take me for?"

"Sure, then, I take yez for what you are," said the man—"as fine and purty a slip of a girleen as ever dwelt in the old Castle; but be yez twice as purty, and be yez twice as fine, Andy Neil is not the man to forget his word, his sworn word, his oath taken to the powers above and the powers below, that if his bit of a roof is taken off his head, why, them as does it shall suffer. It's for you to know that, Miss Nora. I would have drowned yez in the deep pool and nobody would ever be the wiser, but I thought better of that; and I could here—yes, even now—I could choke yez round your pretty soft neck and nobody would be any the wiser, and I'd think no more of it than I'd think of crushing a fly. I won't do it; no I won't, Miss Nora; but there's *thim* as will have to suffer if Andy Neil is turned out of his hut. You spake for me, Miss Nora; you spake up for me, girleen. Why, the Squire, you're the light of his eyes; you spake up, and say, 'Lave poor Andy in his little hut; lave poor Andy with a roof over him. Don't mind the bit of a rint.' Why, then, Miss Nora, how can I pay the rint? Look at my arrum, dear." As the man spoke he thrust out his arm, pushing up his ragged shirt sleeve. The arm was almost like that of a skeleton's; the skin was starting over the bones.

"Oh, it is dreadful!" said Nora, all the pity in her heart welling up into her eyes. "I am truly, truly sorry for you, Andy, I would do anything in my power. It is just this: you know father?"

"Squire? Yes, I guess I know Squire," said the man.

"You know," continued Nora, "that when he takes what you might call the bit between his teeth nothing will move him. He is set against you, Andy. Oh, Andy! I don't believe he will listen."

"He had better," said the man, his voice dropping to a low growl; "he had better, and I say so plain. There's that in me would stick at nothing, and you had best know it, Miss Nora."

"Can you not go away, Andy?"

"I—and what for?"

"But can you?"

"I could, but I won't."

"I don't believe father will yield. I will send you some money from England if you will promise to go away."

"Aye; but I don't want it. I want to stay on. Where would my old bones lie when I died if I am not in my own counthry? I'm not going to leave my counthry for nobody. The cot where I was born shall see me die; and if the roof is took off, why, I'll put it back again. I'll defy him and his new-fangled ways and his English wife to the death. You'll see mischief if you don't put things right, Miss Nora. It all rests with yez, alannah."

"I am awfully sorry for you, Andy; but I don't believe you would seriously injure father, for you know what the consequences would be."

"Aye; but when a man like me is sore put to it he don't think of consequences. It's just the burning wish to avenge his wrongs; that's what he feels, and that's what I feel, Miss Nora, and so you had best take warning."

"Well, I am going away to-morrow," said the girl. "My father is in great trouble, and wants money very badly himself, and I am going to England."

"To be out of the way when the ruin comes. I know," said the man, with a loud laugh.

"No; you are utterly mistaken. Andy, don't you remember when I was a little girl how you used to let me ride on your shoulder, and once you asked me for a tiny bit of my hair, that time when it was all in curls, and I gave you just the end of one of my curls, and you said you would keep it to your dying day? Would you be cruel to Nora now, and just when her heart is heavy?"

"Your heart heavy? You, one of the quality—'taint likely," said the man.

"It is true; my heart is very heavy. I am so anxious about father; you won't make me more anxious—will you? You won't do anything—anything wrong—while I am away? Will you make me a promise that you will let me go with an easy mind?"

"You ask your father to give me three months' longer grace, and then we'll see."

"I will speak to him," said Nora very slowly. "I am sorry, because he is worried about other things, and he does not take it kindly when I interfere in what he considers his own province; but I'll do my best. I cannot stay another moment now, Andy. Good-by."

She waved her hand to him, and ran down the avenue, looking like a white wraith as she disappeared into the darkness.

CHAPTER XII
A FEATHER-BED HOUSE

Before she went to sleep that night Nora wrote a tiny note to her father:

"DEAREST DAD:

"For the sake of your Light o' the Morning, leave poor Andy Neil in his little cottage until I come back again from England. Do, dear dad; this is the last wish of Nora before she goes away.

"YOUR COLLEEN."

She thought and thought, and felt that she could not have expressed herself better. Fear would never influence the Squire; but he would do a good deal for Nora. She laid the letter just where she knew he would see it when he entered his ramshackle study on the following day; and the next morning, with her arms clasped round his neck and her kisses on his cheeks, she gave him one hearty hug, one fervent "God bless you, dad," and rushed after her mother.

The outside car was ready at the door. Mrs. O'Shanaghgan was already mounted. Nora sprang up, and they were rattling off into the world, "to seek my fortune," thought the girl, "or rather the fortune of him I love best."

The Squire, with his grizzled locks and his deep-set eyes, stood in the porch to watch Nora and her mother as they drove away.

"I'll be back in a twinkling, father; never you fret," called out his daughter, and then a turn in the road hid him from view.

"Why, Nora, what are you crying for?" said her mother, who turned round at that moment, and encountered the full gaze of the large dark-blue eyes swimming in tears.

"Oh, nothing. I'll be all right in a moment," was the answer, and then the sunshine broke all over the girl's charming face; and before they reached the railway station Nora was chatting to her mother as if she had not a care in the world.

Her first visit to Dublin and the excitement of getting really pretty dresses made the next two or three days pass like a flash. Mrs. O'Shanaghgan with money in her pocket was a very different woman from Mrs. O'Shanaghgan without a penny. She enjoyed making Nora presentable, and had excellent taste and a keen eye for a bargain. She fitted up her daughter with a modest but successful wardrobe, bought her a proper trunk to hold her belongings, and saw her on board the steamer for Holyhead.

The crossing was a rough one, but the Irish girl did not suffer from seasickness. She stood leaning over the taffrail chatting to the captain, who thought her one of the most charming passengers he ever had to cross in the *Munster*; and when they arrived at the opposite side, Mr. Hartrick was waiting for his niece. He often said since that he would never forget his first sight of Nora O'Shanaghgan. She was wearing a gray tweed traveling dress, with a little gray cap to match; the slender young figure, the rippling black hair, and the brilliant face flashed for an instant on the tired vision of the man of business; then there came the eager outstretching of two hands, and Nora had kissed him because she could not help herself.

"Oh, I am so glad to see you, Uncle George!" The words, the action, the whole look were totally different from what his daughters would have said or done under similar circumstances. He felt quite sure that his sister's description of Nora was right in the main; but he thought her charming. Drawing her hand through his arm, he took her to the railway station, where the train was already waiting to receive its passengers. Soon they were flying in *The Wild Irish Girl* to Euston. Nora was provided with innumerable illustrated papers. Mr. Hartrick took out a little basket which contained sandwiches, wine, and different cakes, and fed her with the best he could procure. He did not ask her many questions, not even about the Castle or her own life. He was determined to wait for all these things. He read something of her story in her clear blue eyes; but he would not press her for her confidence. He was anxious to know her a little better.

"She is Irish, though, and they all exaggerate things so dreadfully," was his thought. "But I'll be very good to the child. What a contrast she is to Terence! Not that Terence is scarcely Irish; but anyone can see that this child has more of her father than her mother in her composition."

They arrived at Euston; then there were fresh changes; a cab took them to Waterloo, where they once again entered the train.

"Tired, my dear niece?" said her uncle as he settled her for the final time in another first-class compartment.

"Not at all. I am too excited to be tired," was her eager answer. And then he smiled at her, arranged the window and blind to her liking, and they started once more on their way.

Mr. Hartrick lived in a large place near Weybridge, and Nora had her first glimpse of the lovely Surrey scenery. A carriage was waiting for the travelers when they reached their destination—a carriage drawn by a pair of spirited grays. Nora thought of Black Bess, and secretly compared the grays to the disadvantage of the latter. But she was determined to be as sweet and polite and English as her mother would desire. For the first time in her whole existence she was feeling a little shy. She would have been thoroughly at home on a dog cart, or on her favorite outside car, or on the back of Black Bess, who would have carried her swift as the wind; but in the landau, with her uncle seated by her side, she was altogether at a loss.

"I don't like riches," was her inward murmur. "I feel all in silken chains, and it is not a bit pleasant; but how dear mammy—oh, I must think of her as mother—how mother would enjoy it all!"

The horses were going slowly uphill, and now they paused at some handsome iron gates. These were opened by a neatly dressed woman, who courtesied to Mr. Hartrick, and glanced with curiosity at Nora. The carriage bowled rapidly down a long avenue, and drew up before a front door. A large mastiff rose slowly, wagged his tail, and sniffed at Nora's dress as she descended.

"Come in, my dear; come in," said her uncle. "We are too late for dinner, but I have ordered supper. You will want a good meal and then bed. Where are all the others? Where are you, Molly? Where are you, Linda? Your Irish cousin Nora has come."

A door to the left was quickly opened, and a graceful-looking lady, in a beautiful dress of black silk and quantities of coffee lace, stood on the threshold.

"Is this Nora?" she said. "Welcome, my dear little girl." She went up to Nora, laid one hand on her shoulder, and kissed her gravely on the forehead. There was a staid, sober sort of solemnity about this kiss which influenced Nora and made a lump come into her throat.

This gracious English lady was very charming, and she felt at once that she would love her.

"The child is tired, Grace," said her husband to Mrs. Hartrick. "Where are the girls? Why are they not present?"

"Molly has been very troublesome, and I was obliged to send her to her room," was her reply; "but here is Terence. Terence, your sister has come."

"Oh, Terry!" cried Nora.

The next moment Terence, in full evening dress, and looking extremely manly and handsome, appeared upon the scene. Nora forgot everything else when she saw the familiar face; she ran up to her brother, flung her arms round his neck, and kissed him over and over.

"Oh, it is a sight for sore eyes to see you!" she cried. "Oh, Terry, how glad, how glad I am that you are here!"

"Hush! hush! Nonsense, Nora. Try to remember this is an English house," whispered Terence; but he kissed her affectionately. He was glad to see her, and he looked at her dress with marked approval. "She will soon tame down, and she looks very pretty," was his thought.

Just then Linda was seen coming downstairs.

"Has Nora come?" called out her sweet, high-bred voice. "How do you do, Nora? I am so glad to see you. If you are half as nice as Terence, you will be a delightful addition to our party."

"Oh, but I am not the least bit like Terence," said Nora. She felt rather hurt; she did not know why.

Linda was a very fair girl. She could not have been more than fifteen years of age, and was not so tall as Nora; but she had almost the manners of a woman of the world, and Nora felt unaccountably shy of her.

"Now take your cousin up to her room. Supper will be ready in a quarter of an hour," said Mrs. Hartrick. "Come, George; I have something to say to you."

Mr. and Mrs. Hartrick disappeared into the drawing-room. Linda took Nora's hand. Nora glanced at Terence, who turned on his heel and went away.

"See you presently, sis," he called out in what he considered a very manly tone; and Nora felt her heart, as she expressed it, sink down into her boots as she followed Linda up the richly carpeted stairs. Her feet sank into the velvety pile, and she hated the sensation.

"It is all a sort of feather-bed house," she said to herself, "and I hate a feather-bed house. Oh, I can understand my dad better than ever to-night; but how mother would enjoy this!"

CHAPTER XIII
"THERE'S MOLLY"

As they were going upstairs Linda suddenly turned and looked full at her cousin.

"How very grave you are! And why have you that little frown between your brows? Are you vexed about anything?"

"Only I thought Terry would be more glad to see me," replied Nora.

"More glad!" cried Linda. "I saw you hugging him as I ran downstairs. He let you. I don't know how any one could show gladness more. But come along; this is your room. It is next to Molly's and mine. Isn't it pretty? Molly and I chose it for you this morning, and we arranged those flowers. You will have such a lovely view, and that little peep of the Thames is so charming. I hope you will like your room."

Nora entered one of the prettiest and most lovely bedrooms she had ever seen in her life. Never in her wildest dreams had she imagined anything so cozy. The perfectly chosen furniture, the elegant appointments of every sort and description, the view from the partly opened windows, the view of winding river and noble trees—all looked rich and cultivated and lovely; and the Irish girl, as she gazed around, found suddenly a great, fierce hatred rising up in her heart against what she called the mere prettiness. She turned and faced Linda, who was watching her with curiosity in her somewhat small blue eyes Linda was essentially English, very reserved and quiet, very self-possessed, quite a young lady of the world. She looked at Nora as if she meant to read her through.

"Well, don't you think the view perfect?" she said.

"Have you ever been in Ireland?" was Nora's answer.

"Never. Oh, dear me! have you anything as pretty as this in Ireland?"

"No," said Nora fiercely—"no." She left the window, turned back, and began to unpin her hat.

"You look as if you did not care for your room."

"It is a very, very pretty room," said Nora, "and the view is very, very pretty, but I am tired to-night. I did not know it; but I am. I should like to go to bed soon."

"So you shall, of course, after you have had supper. Oh, how awfully thoughtless of me not to know that you must be very tried and hungry! Molly and I are glad you have come."

"But where is Molly? I should like to see her."

Linda went up to Nora and spoke in a low whisper.

"She is in disgrace."

"In disgrace? Has she done anything naughty?"

"Yes, fearfully naughty. She is in hot water as usual."

"I am sorry," said Nora. She instantly began to feel a strong sensation of sympathy for Molly. She was sure, in advance, that she would like her.

"But is she in such dreadful disgrace that I may not see her?" she asked after a pause.

"Oh, I don't know. I don't suppose so."

Just then there was heard at the room door a gay laugh and a kind of scamper. A knock followed, but before Nora could answer the door was burst open, and a large, heavily made, untidy-looking girl, with a dark face and great big black eyes, bounded into the apartment.

"I have burst the bonds, and here I am," she said. "How do you do, Nora? I'm Molly. I am always and always in hot water. I like being in hot water. Now, tell-tale-tit, you can go downstairs and acquaint mother with the fact that I have burst the bonds, for kiss little Irish Nora I will."

"Oh, I am glad to see you," said Nora. Her depression vanished on the spot. She felt that, naughty as doubtless Molly was, she could get on with her.

"Come, let's take a squint at you," said the eldest Miss Hartrick; "come over here to the light."

Molly took Nora by both hands over to the window.

"Now then, let's have a category of your charms. Terence has been telling us that you are very pretty. You are. Come, Linda; come and look at her. Did you ever see such black hair? And it's as soft as silk."

Molly put up a rather large hand and patted Nora somewhat violently on the head.

"Oh, don't!" said Nora, starting back.

"My dear little cousin, I am a very rough specimen, and you must put up with me if you mean to get on at The Laurels. We are all stiff and staid here; we are English of the English. Everything is done by rule of thumb—breakfast to the minute, lunch to the minute, afternoon tea to the minute, dinner to the minute, even tennis to the minute. Oh! it's detestable; and I—I am expected to be good, and you know there's not a bit of goodness in me. I am all fidgets, and you can never be sure of me for two seconds at a time. I am a worry to mother and a worry to father; and as to Terence—oh, my dear creature, I am so truly thankful you are not like Terence! Here I drop a courtesy to his memory. What an awfully precise man he will make by and by! I did not know you turned out that kind of article in Ireland."

Nora's face, over which many emotions had been flitting, now looked grave.

"You know that Terence is my brother?" she said slowly.

Molly gazed at her; then she burst into a fit of hearty laughter.

"You and I will get on," she said. "I like you for sticking up for your brother. But now, my dear, I must go back. I am supposed to stay in my bedroom until to-morrow morning. Linda, if you tell—well, you'll have to answer to me when we are going to bed, that's all. By-by, Nora. I'll see you in the morning. Do get her some hot water, Linda. She's worth waiting on; she's a very nice sort of child, and very, very pretty. If that is the Irish sort of face, I for one shall adore it. Good-by, Nora, for the present."

Molly banged herself away—her mode of exit could scarcely be called by any other name. As soon as the door had closed behind her Linda laughed.

"I ought to tell, you know," she said in her precise voice; "it is very, very wrong of Molly to leave her bedroom when mother is punishing her."

"But what has she done wrong?" asked Nora.

"Oh, went against discipline. She is at school, you know, and she would write letters during lessons. It is really very wrong of her, and Miss Scott had to complain; so mother said she should stay in her room, instead of being downstairs to welcome you. She is a good soul enough; but we none of us can discipline her. She is very funny; you'll see a lot of her queer cranks while you are here."

"How old is she?" asked Nora.

"Between sixteen and seventeen; too old to be such a romp."

"Only a little older than I am," said Nora. "And how old are you, Linda?"

"Fifteen; they all tell me I look more."

"You do; you look eighteen. You are very old for your age."

"Oh, thank you for the compliment. Now, then, do brush your hair and wash your hands; there's the supper-gong. Mother will be annoyed if we are not down in a jiffy. Now, do be quick."

Nora washed her hands, brushed her hair, and ran downstairs with her cousin. As she ate during the somewhat stiff meal that followed she thought many times of Molly. She felt that, naughty as Molly doubtless was, she would make the English house tolerable. Terence sat near her at supper, by way of extending to her brotherly attentions; but all the time he was talking on subjects of local interest to his aunt and uncle.

Mr. Hartrick evidently thought Terence a very clever fellow, and listened to his remarks with a deference which Nora thought by no means good for him.

"He wants one of the dear old dad's downright snubs," was her inward comment. "I must have a talk with him to-morrow. If he progresses at this rate toward English refinement he will be unbearable at O'Shanaghgan when he returns; quite, quite unbearable. Oh, for a sniff of the sea! oh, for the wild, wild wind on my cheeks! and oh, for my dear, darling, bare bedroom! I shall be smothered in that heavily furnished room upstairs. Oh, it is all lovely, I know—very lovely; but I'm not made to enjoy it. I belong to the free, and I don't feel free here. The silken chains and the feather-bed life won't suit me; of that I am quite sure. Thank goodness, however, there's Molly; she is in a state of rebellion, too. I must not sympathize with her; but I am truly glad she is here."

CHAPTER XIV
BITS OF SLANG

Early the next morning Nora was awakened from a somewhat heavy sleep by someone pulling her violently by the arm.

"Wake up! wake up!" said a voice; and then Nora, who had been dreaming of her father, and also of Andy Neil, started up, crying as she did so, "Oh, don't, Andy! I know father will let you stay a little longer in the cot. Don't, don't, Andy!"

"Who, in the name of fortune, is Andy?" called the clear voice of Molly Hartrick. "Do wake up, Nora, and don't look so dazed. You really are a most exciting person to have staying in the house. Who is Andy, and what cot are you going to turn him out of? Is he a baby?"

Nora now began to laugh.

"I quite forgot that I was in England," she said. "Am I really in England? Are you—are you——Oh, now I remember everything. You are Molly Hartrick. What is the hour? Is it late? Have I missed breakfast?"

"Bless you, child! lie down and keep quiet; it's not more than six o'clock. I wanted to see some more of you all by myself. I am out of punishment now; it ended at midnight, and I am as free as anybody else; but as it is extremely likely I shall be back in punishment by the evening, I thought we would have a little chat while I was able to have it. Just make way for me in your bed; I'll nestle up close to you, and we'll be ever so jolly."

"Oh, do," said Nora, in a hearty tone.

Molly scrambled in, taking the lion's share of the bed, Nora lay on the edge.

"I am glad you are facing the light, for I can examine your features well," said Molly. "You certainly are very nice-looking. How prettily your eyebrows are arched, and what white teeth you have! And, although you have that wonderful black hair, you have a fair skin, and your cheeks have just enough color; not too much. I hate florid people; but you are just perfect."

"I wish you would not flatter me, Molly," said Nora; "nobody flatters me in Ireland."

"They don't? But I thought they were a perfect nation of flatterers. I am sure it is always said of them."

"Oh, if you mean the poor people," said Nora; "they make pretty speeches, but nobody thinks anything about that. Everybody makes pretty speeches to everybody else, except when we are having a violent scold by way of a change."

"How delicious!" said Molly. "And what sort of house have you? Like this?"

"No, not the least like this," answered Nora.

"With what emphasis you speak. Do you know that father told me you lived in a beautiful place, a castle hanging over the sea, and that your mountains and your sea and your old castle were things to be proud of?"

"Did he? Did your father really say that?" asked Nora. She sat up on her elbow; her eyes were shining; they assumed a look which Nora's eyes often wore when she was, as she expressed it, "seeing things out of her head." Far-off castles in the clouds would Nora look at then; rainbow-tinted were they, and their summits reached heaven. Molly gazed at her with deepening interest.

"Yes, Nora," she said; "he did say it. He told me so before Terence came; but I—do forgive me—I don't care for Terence."

"You must not talk against him to me," said Nora, "because he happens to be my brother; but I'll just whisper one thing back to you, Molly—if he was not my brother he would not suit me."

"How nice of you to say that! We shall get on splendidly. Of course, you must stick up for him, being your brother; he stuck up for you before you came. It is very nice and loyal of you, and I quite understand. But, dear me! I am not likely to see much of you while you are here."

"Why not? Are you not going to stay here?"

"Oh, my dear, yes; I'll stay. School has just begun over again, you know, and I am always in hot water. I cannot help it; it is a sort of way of mine. This is the kind of way I live. Breakfast every morning; then a lecture from mother or from father. Off I go in low spirits, with a great, sore heart inside me; then comes the hateful discipline of school; and every day I get into disgrace. I have a lot of lessons returned, and am low down in my class, instead of high up, and am treated from first to last as a naughty child. By the middle of the day I am a very naughty child indeed."

"But you are not a child at all, Molly; you are a woman. Why, you are older than I."

"Oh, what have years to do with it?" interrupted Molly. "I shall be a child all my days, I tell you. I shall never be really old. I like mischief and insubordination, and—and—let me whisper it to you, little Nora—vulgarity. Yes, I do love to be vulgar. I like shocking mother; I like shocking father. Since Terence came I have had rare fun shocking him. I have learned a lot of slang, and whenever I see Terence I shout it at him. He has got quite nervous lately, and avoids me. He likes Linda awfully, but he avoids me. But, to go on with my day. I am back from school to early dinner, generally in disgrace. I am not allowed to speak at dinner. Back again I go to school, and I am home, or supposed to be home, at half-past four; but not a bit of it, my dear; I don't get home till about six, because I am kept in to learn my lessons. It is disgraceful, of course; but it is a fact. Then back I come, and mother has a talk with me. However busy mother may be, and she is a very busy woman, Nora—you will soon find that out—she always has time to find out if I have done anything naughty; and, as fibs are not any of my accomplishments, I always tell her the truth; and then what do you think happens? An evening quite to myself in my bedroom; my dinner sent up to me there, and I eating it in solitary state. They are all accustomed to it. They open their eyes and almost glare at me when by a mere chance I do come down to dinner. They are quite uncomfortable, because, you see, I am waiting my opportunity to fire slang at one of them. I always do, and always will. I never could fit into the dull life of the English."

"You must be Irish, really," said Nora.

"You don't say so! But I am afraid I am not. I would give all the world to be, but am quite certain I am not. There, now, of course I'd be awfully scolded if it was found out that I had awakened you at this hour, and had confided my little history to you. I am over sixteen. I shall be seventeen in ten months' time. And that is my history, insubordination from first to last. I don't suppose anybody really likes me, unless it is poor Annie Jefferson at school."

"Who is Annie Jefferson, Molly?"

"A very shabby sort of girl, who is always in hot water too. I have taken to her, and she just adores me. There is no one else who loves me; and she, poor child, would not be admitted inside these walls; she is not aristocratic enough. Dear me, Nora! it is wrong of me to give you all this information so soon; and don't look anxious about me, little goose, for I have taken an enormous fancy to you."

"I will tell you one thing," said Nora after a pause, "if you will never tell again."

"Oh, a secret!" said Molly. "Tell it out, Nora. I love secrets. I'll never betray; I have no friends to betray them to. You may tell me with all the heart in the world."

"Well, it is this," said Nora; "we are not at all rich at home. We are poor, and have no luxuries and the dear old house is very bare; and, oh! but, Molly, there is no place like it—no place like it. It's worth all the world to me; and when I came here last night, and saw your great, rich, beautiful house, I—I quite hated it, and I almost hated Linda too; and even my uncle, who has been so kind, I could not get up one charitable thought for him, nor for your mother, who is such a beautiful, gracious lady; and even Terence—oh! Terry seemed quite English. Oh, I was miserable! But when I saw you, Molly, I said to myself, 'There is one person who will fit me'; and—oh, don't Molly! What is it?"

"Only, if you say another word I shall squeeze you to death in the hug I am giving you," said Molly. Her arms were flung tightly round Nora's neck. She kissed her passionately three or four times.

"We'll be friends. I'll stick up for you through thick and thin," said Molly. "And now I'm off; for if Linda caught me woe betide me."

"One word before you go, Molly," called out Nora.

"Yes," said Molly, standing at the door.

"Try to keep straight to-day, for my sake, for I shall want to say a great deal to you to-night."

"Oh, yes, so I will," answered Molly. "Now then, off I go."

The door was banged behind her. It awoke Mrs. Hartrick, who turned slowly on her pillow, and said to herself, "I am quite certain that wicked girl Molly has been disturbing our poor little traveler." But she fell asleep, and Nora lay thinking of Molly. How queer she was! And yet—and yet she was the only person in the English home who had yet managed to touch Nora's warm Irish heart.

The rest of the day passed somewhat soberly. Molly and Linda both started for school immediately after an early breakfast. Terence went to town with his uncle, and Nora and her aunt were left alone. She had earnestly hoped that she might have had one of her first important talks with Mr. Hartrick before he left that morning; but he evidently had no idea of giving her an opportunity. He spoke to her kindly, but seemed to regard her already as quite one of the family, and certainly was not disposed to alter his plans or put out his business arrangements on her account. She resolved, with a slightly impatient sigh, to abide her time, and followed her aunt into the morning-room, where the good lady produced some fancywork, and asked Nora if she would like to help her to arrange little squares for a large patchwork quilt which was to be raffled for at a bazar shortly to be held in the place.

Nora gravely took the little bits of colored silk, and, under her aunt's supervision, began to arrange them in patterns. She was not a neat worker, and the task was by no means to her taste.

"What time ought I to write in order to catch the post?" she said, breaking the stillness, and raising her lovely eyes to Mrs. Hartrick's face.

"The post goes out many times in the day, Nora; but if you want to catch the Irish mail, you must have your letter in the box in the hall by half-past three. There is plenty of time, my dear, and you will find notepaper and everything you require in the escritoire in the study. You can always go there if you wish to write your letters."

"Thank you," answered Nora.

"When you are tired of work, you can go out and walk about the grounds. I will take you for a drive this afternoon. I am sorry that you have arrived just when the girls have gone back to school; but you and Linda can have a good deal of fun in the evenings, you know."

"But why not Molly too?" asked Nora. She felt rather alarmed at mentioning her elder cousin's name.

Mrs. Hartrick did not speak at all for a moment; then she gave a sigh.

"I am sorry to have to tell you, Nora, that Molly is by no means a good girl. She is extremely rebellious and troublesome; and if this state of things goes on much longer her father and I will be obliged to send her to a very strict school as a boarder. We do not wish to do that, as my husband does not approve of boarding-schools for girls. At present she is spending a good deal of her time in punishment."

"I hope she won't be in punishment to-night," said Nora. "I like her so much."

"Do you, my dear? I hope she won't influence you to become insubordinate."

Nora felt restless, and some of the bits of colored silk fluttered to the floor.

"Be careful, my dear Nora," said her aunt in a somewhat sharp voice; "don't let those bits of silk get about on the carpet. I am most particular that everything in the house should be kept neat and in order. I will get you a little work-basket to keep your things in when next I go upstairs."

"Thank you, Aunt Grace," answered Nora.

"And now, as we are alone," continued the good lady, "you might tell me something of your life. Your uncle is very anxious that your mother should come and pay us a visit. He is very much attached to his sister, and it seems to me strange that they should not have met for so many years. You have a beautiful place at home, Nora—have you not?"

"Yes," said Nora; "the place is"—she paused, and her voice took an added emphasis—"beautiful."

"How emphatically you say it, dear! You have a pretty mode of speech, although very, very Irish."

"I am Irish, you see, Aunt Grace," answered Nora.

"Yes, dear, you need scarcely tell me that; your brogue betrays you."

"But mother was always particular that I should speak correctly," continued the girl. "Does my accent offend you, Aunt Grace?"

"No, dear; your uncle and I both think it quite charming. But tell me some more. Of course you are very busy just now with your studies, Nora. A girl of your age—how old did you say you were—sixteen?—a girl of your age has not a moment to lose in acquiring those things which are essential to the education of an accomplished woman of the present day."

"I am afraid I shall shock you very much indeed, Aunt Grace, when I tell you that my education is supposed to be finished."

"Finished!" said Mrs. Hartrick. She paused for a moment and stared full at Nora. "I was astonished," she continued, "when your uncle suggested that you should pay us a visit now. I said, as September had begun, you would be going back to school; but you accepted the invitation, or rather your mother did for you, without any allusion to your school. You must have got on very well, Nora, to be finished by now. How many languages do you know?"

"I can chatter in Irish after a fashion," said Nora; "and I am supposed, after a fashion also, to know my own tongue."

"Irish!" said Mrs. Hartrick in a tone of quivering scorn. "I don't mean anything of that sort. I allude to your acquaintance with French, German, and Italian."

"I do know a very little French," said Nora; "that is, I can read one or two books in French. Mother taught me what I know; but I do not know any

German or any Italian. I don't see that it matters," she continued, a flush coming into her cheeks. "I should never talk German or Italian in Ireland. I wouldn't be understood if I did."

"That has nothing to do with it, Nora; and your tone, my dear, without meaning it, of course, was just a shade pert just now. It is essential in the present day that all well-educated women should be able to speak at least in three languages."

"Then I am sorry, Aunt Grace, for I am afraid you will despise me. I shall never be well educated in that sense of the word."

Mrs. Hartrick was silent.

"I will speak to your uncle," she said after a pause. "While you are here you can have lessons. It would be possible to arrange that you went to school with Linda and Molly, and had French and German lessons while there."

"But I don't expect to be very long in England," said Nora, a note of alarm in her voice.

"Oh, my dear child, now that we have got you, we shall not allow you to go in a hurry. It is such a nice change for you, too; this is your first visit to England, is it not?"

"Yes, Aunt Grace."

"We won't let you go for some time, little Nora. Your brother is a dear fellow; your uncle and I admire him immensely, and he is quite well educated and so adaptable; and I am sure you would be the same, my dear, when you have had the many chances which will be offered to you here. You must look upon me as your real aunt, dear, and tell me anything that you wish. Don't be shy of me, my love; I can quite understand that a young girl, when she first leaves her mother, is rather shy."

"I never felt shy at home," answered Nora; "but then, you know, I was more with father than with mother."

"More with your father! Does he stay at home all day, then?"

"He is always about the place; he has nothing else to do."

"Of course he has large estates."

"They are not so very large, Aunt Grace."

"Well, dear, that is a relative term, of course; but from your uncle's description, and to judge from your mother's letters, it must be a very large place. By the way, how does she manage her servants? She must have a large staff at Castle O'Shanaghgan."

"I don't think we manage our servants particularly well," said Nora. "It is true they all stay with us; but then we don't keep many."

"How many, dear?"

"There's Pegeen—she is the parlor-maid—and there's the cook—we do change our cook sometimes, for mother is rather particular; then there is the woman who attends to the fowls, and the woman who does the washing, and—I think that is about all. Oh, there's the post-boy; perhaps you would consider him a servant, but I scarcely think he ought to be called one. We give him twopence a week for fetching the letters. He is a very good little boy. He stands on his head whenever he sees me; he is very fond of me, and that is the way he shows his affection. It would make you laugh, Aunt Grace, if you saw Michael standing on his head."

"It would make me shudder, you mean," said Mrs. Hartrick. "Really, Nora, your account of your mother's home is rather disparaging; two or three very rough servants, and no more. But I understood you lived in castle."

"Oh, a castle may mean anything; but it is not fair for you and Uncle George to think we are rich, for we are very poor. And," continued Nora, "for my part, I love to be poor." She stood up abruptly. In her excitement all her bits of silk tumbled to the floor. "May I go out and have a run, Aunt Grace?" she said. "I feel quite stiff. I am not accustomed to being indoors for so long at a time."

"You can go out, Nora, if you like," said her aunt in a displeased tone; "but, first, have the goodness to pick up all those bits you have dropped."

Nora, with flushed cheeks, stooped and picked up the bits of silk. She wrapped them in a piece of paper and put them on the table.

"You can stay out for an hour, my dear; but you are surely not going without a hat."

"I never wear a hat at home," said Nora.

"You must run upstairs and fetch your hat," said Mrs. Hartrick.

Poor Nora never felt more tried in the whole course of her life.

"I shall get as bad as Molly if this goes on," she thought to herself.

CHAPTER XV
TWO LETTERS

"DEAR MOTHER [wrote Nora O'Shanaghgan later on that same morning]: I arrived safely yesterday. Uncle George met me at Holyhead, and was very kind indeed. I had a comfortable journey up to town, and Uncle George saw that I wanted for nothing. When we got to London we drove across the town to another station, called Waterloo, and took a train on here. A carriage met us at the station with a pair of beautiful gray horses. They were not as handsome as Black Bess, but they were very beautiful; and we arrived here between eight and nine o'clock. This is just the sort of place you would like, mother; such thick carpets on the stairs, and such large, spacious, splendidly furnished rooms; and Aunt Grace has meals to the minute; and they have lots and lots of servants; and my bedroom—oh, mother! I think you would revel in my bedroom. It has such a terribly thick carpet on the floor—I mean it has a thick carpet on the floor; and there is a view from the window, the sort you have so often described to me— great big trees, and a lawn like velvet, and four or five tennis-courts, and a shrubbery with all the trees cut so exact and round and proper, and a peep of the River Thames just beyond. My cousins keep a boat on the river, and they often go out in the summer evenings. They are going to take me for a row on Saturday, when the girls have a holiday.

"I saw Terence almost immediately after I arrived. He looked just as you would like to see him, so handsome in his evening dress. He was a little stiff—at least, I mean he was very correct in his manner. We had supper when we arrived. I was awfully hungry, but I did not like to eat too much, for Terence seemed so correct—nice in his manner, I mean—and everything was just as you have described things when you were young. There are two girls, my cousins—Linda, a very pretty girl, fair, and so very neatly dressed; and Molly, who is not the least like the others. You would not like Molly; she is rather rough; but of course I must not complain of her. I have been sitting with Aunt Grace all the morning, until I could bear it no longer—I mean, until I got a little stiff in my legs, and then I had a run in the garden. Now I am writing this letter in Aunt Grace's morning-room, and if I look round I shall see her back.

"Good-by, dear mother. I will write again in a day or two.—Your affectionate daughter,

"NORA O'SHANAGHGAN."

"There," said Nora, under her breath, "that's done. Now for daddy."

She took out another sheet of paper, and began to scribble rapidly.

"Darling, darling, love of my heart! Daddy, daddy, oh! but it's I that miss you. I am writing to you here in this could, could country. Oh, daddy, if I could run to you now, wouldn't I? What are you doing without your Light o' the Morning? I am pent up, daddy, and I don't think I can stand it much longer. It's but a tiny visit I'll pay, and then I'll come back again to the mountains and the sea, and the old, old house, and the dear, darling dad. Keep up your heart, daddy; you'll soon have Light o' the Morning home. Oh! it's so proper, and I'm wrapped up in silk chains; they are surrounding me everywhere, and I can't quite bear it. Aunt Grace is sitting here; I am writing in her morning-room. Oh! if I could, wouldn't I scream, or shout, or do something awfully wicked; but I must not, for it is the English way. They have got the wild bird Nora into the English cage; and, darling dad asthore, it's her heart that will be broke if she stays here long. There's one comfort I have—or, bedad! I don't think I could bear it—and that's Molly. She's a bit of a romp and a bit of a scamp, and she has a daring spirit of her own, and she hates the conventionalities, and she would like to be Irish too. She can't, poor colleen; but she is nice and worth knowing, and she'll just keep my heart from being broke entirely.

"How are they all at home? Give them lashins and lavins of love from Nora. Tell them it's soon I'll be back with them. You go round and give a message to each and all; and don't forget Hannah Croneen, and little Mike, and Bridget Murphy, and Squire Murphy, and the rest—all and every one who remembers Nora O'Shanaghgan. Tell them it's her heart is imprisoned till she gets back to them; and she would rather have one bit of her own native soil than all the gold in the whole of England. I declare it's rough and wild I am getting, and my heart is bleeding. I have written a correct letter to mother, and given her the news; but I am telling you a bit of my true, true heart. Send for me if you miss me too much, and I'll fly back to you. Oh! it's chains wouldn't keep me, for go I must if this state of things continues much longer.—Your

"LIGHT O' THE MORNING."

The two letters were written, the last one relieving Nora's feelings not a little. She put them into separate envelopes and stamped them.

Mrs. Hartrick rose, went over to her desk, and saw Nora's letters.

"Oh, you have written to your parents," she said. "Quite right, my dear. But why put them into separate envelopes? They could go nicely in one. That, really, is willful waste, Nora, which we in England never permit."

"Oh, please, don't change them, Aunt Grace," said Nora, as Mrs. Hartrick took the two letters up and paused before opening one of the envelopes. "Please, please, let them go as they are. It's my own stamp," she continued, losing all sense of grammar in her excitement.

"Well, my dear, just as you please. There, don't excite yourself, Nora. I only suggested that, when one stamp would do, it was rather wasteful to spend two."

"Oh, daddy does like to get his own letters to his own self," said Nora.

"Your father, you mean. You don't, surely, call him by the vulgar word daddy?"

"Bedad! but I do," answered Nora.

Mrs. Hartrick turned and gave her niece a frozen glance. Presently she laid her hand on the girl's shoulder.

"I don't want to complain or to lecture you," she said; "but that expression must not pass your lips again while you are here."

"It shan't. I am ever so sorry," said the girl.

"I think you are, dear; and how flushed your cheeks are! You seem quite tired. Now, go upstairs and wash your hands; the luncheon-gong will ring in five minutes, and we must be punctual at meals."

Nora slowly left the room.

"Oh! but it's like lead my heart is," she said to herself.

The day passed very dismally for the wild Irish girl. After lunch she and her aunt had a long and proper drive. They drove through lovely country; but Nora was feeling even a little bit cross, and could not see the beauties of the perfectly tilled landscape, of the orderly fields, of the lovely hedgerows.

"It is too tidy," she said once in a choking sort of voice.

"Tidy!" answered Mrs. Hartrick. She looked at Nora, tittered a sigh, and did not speak of the beauties of the country again.

When they got back from their drive things were a little better, for Linda and Molly had returned from school; and, for a wonder, Molly was not in disgrace. She looked quite excited, and darting out of the house, took Nora's hand and pulled it inside her arm.

"Come and have a talk," she said. "I am hungering for a chat with you."

"Tea will be ready in fifteen minutes, Molly," called out Mrs. Hartrick, then entered the house accompanied by Linda.

Meanwhile Molly and Nora went round to the shrubbery at the back of the house.

"What is the matter with you?" said Molly. She turned and faced her companion.

Nora's eyes filled with sudden tears.

"It is only that I am keeping in so much," she said; "and—and, oh! I do wish you were not all quite so tidy. I am just mad for somebody to be wild and unkempt. I feel that I could take down my hair, or tear a rent in my dress—anything rather than the neatness. Oh! I hate your landscapes, and your trim hedges, and your trim house, and your—"

"Go on," said Molly; "let it out; let it out. I'll never repeat it. You must come in, in about a quarter of an hour, to a stiff meal. You will have to sit upright, let me tell you, and not lounge; and you will have to eat your bread and butter very nicely, and sip your tea, and not eat overmuch. Mother does not approve of it. Then when tea is over you will have to leave the room and go upstairs and get things out for dinner."

"My things out for dinner?" gasped Nora. "What do you mean?"

"Your evening-dress. Do you suppose you will be allowed to dine in your morning-dress?"

"Oh, to be sure," said Nora, brightening; "now I understand. Mother did get me a white frock, and she had it cut square in the neck, and the sleeves are a little short."

"You will look sweet in that," said Molly, gazing at her critically; "and I will bring you in a bunch of sweet-peas to put in your belt, and you can have a little bunch in your hair, too, if you like. You know you are awfully pretty. I am sure Linda is just mad with jealousy about it; I can see it, although she does not say anything. She is rather disparaging about you, is Linda; that is one of her dear little ways. She runs people down with faint praise. She was talking a lot about you as we were going to school this morning. She began: 'You know, I do think Nora is a pretty girl; but it is such a pity that—'"

"Oh, don't," said Nora, suddenly putting out her hand and closing Molly's lips.

"What in the world are you doing that for?" said Molly.

"Because I don't want to hear; she did not mean me to know that she said these things."

"What a curiosity you are!" said Molly. "So wild, so defiant, and yet—oh, of course, I like you awfully. Do you know that the vision of your face kept me good all day? Isn't that something to be proud of? I didn't answer one of my teachers back, and I did have a scolding, let me tell you. Oh, my music; you don't know what I suffer over it. I have not a single particle of taste. I have not the faintest ghost of an ear; but mother insists on my learning. I could draw; I could sketch; I can do anything with my pencil; but that does not suit mother. It must be music. I must play; I must play well at sight; I must play all sorts of difficult accompaniments for songs, because gentlemen like to have their songs accompanied for them; and I must be able to do this the very moment the music is put before me. And I must not play too loud; I must play just right, in perfect time; and I must be ready, when there is nothing else being done, to play long pieces, those smart kind of things people do play in the present day; and I must never play a wrong note. Oh, dear! oh, dear! and I simply cannot do these things. I don't know wrong notes from right. I really don't."

"Oh, Molly!" cried Nora.

"There you are; I can see that you are musical."

"I think I am, very. I mean I think I should always know a wrong note from a right one; but I have not had many opportunities of learning."

"Oh, good gracious me! what next?" exclaimed Molly.

"I don't understand what you mean," said Nora.

"My dear, I am relieving my feelings, just as you relieved yours a short time ago. Oh, dear! my music. I know I played atrociously; but that dreadful Mrs. Elford was so cross; she did thump so herself on the piano, and told me that my fingers were like sticks. And what could I do? I longed to let out some of my expressions at her. You must know that I am feared on account of my expressions—my slang, I call them. They do shock people so, and it is simply irresistible to see them shudder, and close their eyes, and draw themselves together, and then majestically walk out of the room. The headmistress is summoned then, and I—I am doomed. I get my pieces to do out of school; and when I come home mother lectures me, and sends me to my bedroom. But I am free to-night. I have been good all day; and it is on account of you, Nora; just because you are a little Irish witch; and I sympathize with you to the bottom of my soul."

"Molly! Molly!" here called out Linda's voice; "mother says it's time for you and Nora to come in to wash your hands for tea."

"Oh, go to Jericho!" called out Molly.

Linda turned immediately and went into the house.

"She is a tell-tale-tit," said Molly. "She will be sure to repeat that to mother; and do you think I shall be allowed any cake? There is a very nice kind of rice-cake which cook makes, and I am particularly fond of it. You'll see I am not to have any, just because I said 'Go to Jericho!' I am sure I wish Linda would go."

"But those kind of things are rather vulgar, aren't they?" said Nora. "Father wouldn't like them. We say all kinds of funny things at home, but not things like that. I wish you would not."

"You wish I would not what?"

"Use words like 'Go to Jericho!' Father would not like to hear you."

"You are a very audacious kind of girl, let me tell you, Nora," said Molly. She colored, and looked annoyed for a moment, then burst into a laugh. "But I like you all the better for not being afraid of me," she continued. "Come, let's go into the house; we can relieve our feelings somehow to-night; we'll have a lark somehow; you mark my words. In the meantime mum's the word."

CHAPTER XVI
A CHEEKY IRISH GIRL

At tea the girls were very stiff. Molly and Nora were put as far as possible asunder. They did not have tea in the drawing room, but in the dining room, and Mrs. Hartrick presided. There was jam on the table, and two or three kinds of cake, and, of course, plenty of bread and butter.

As Molly had predicted, however, the news of her expression "Go to Jericho!" had already reached Mrs. Hartrick's ears, and the fiat had gone forth that she was only to eat bread and butter. It was handed to her, in a marked way, by her mother, and Linda's light-blue eyes flashed with pleasure. Nora felt at that moment that she almost hated Linda. She herself ate resignedly, and without much appetite. Her spirits were down to zero. It seemed far less likely than it did before she left O'Shanaghgan that she could help her father out of his scrape. It was almost impossible to break through these chains of propriety, of neatness, of order. Would anybody in this trim household care in the very least whether the old Irishman broke his heart or not? whether he and the Irish girl had to go forth from the home of their ancestors? whether the wild, beautiful, rack-rent sort of place was kept in the family or not?

"They none of them care," thought Nora. "I don't believe Uncle George will do anything; but all the same I have got to ask him. He was nice about my letter, I will own that; but will he really, really help?"

"A penny for your thoughts, Nora, my dear," said Mrs. Hartrick at this moment.

Nora glanced up with a guilty flush.

"Oh, I was only thinking," she began.

"Yes, dear, what about?"

"About father." Nora colored as she spoke, and Linda fixed her eyes on her face.

"Very pretty indeed of you, my dear, to think so much of your father," said Mrs. Hartrick; "but I cannot help giving you a hint. It is not considered good manners for a girl to be absent-minded while she is in public. You are more or less in public now; I am here, and your cousins, and it is our bounden duty each to try and make the others pleasant, to add to the enjoyment of the meal by a little graceful conversation. Absent-mindedness is very dull for others, my dear Nora; so in future try not to look quite so abstracted."

Nora colored again. Molly, at the other end of the table, bit her lip furiously, and stretched out her hand to help herself to another thick piece of bread and butter. In doing so she upset a small milk-jug; a stream of milk flowed down the tablecloth, and Mrs. Hartrick rose in indignation.

"This is the fourth evening running you have spilt something on the tablecloth, Molly. Go to your room immediately."

Molly rose, dropped a mocking courtesy to her mother, and left the room.

"Linda dear, run after your sister, and tell her that, for her impertinence to me, she is to remain in her room until dinner-time."

"Oh! please forgive her this time; she didn't mean it really," burst from Nora's lips.

"Nora!" said Mrs. Hartrick.

"Oh! I am sorry for her; please forgive her."

"Nora!" repeated her aunt again.

"It is because you do not understand her that she goes on like that; she is such a fine girl, twice—twice as fine as Linda. Oh, I do wish you would forgive her!"

"Thank you," said Linda in a mocking voice. She had got as far as the door, and had overheard Nora's words. She now glanced at her mother, as much as to say, "I told you so," and left the room.

Nora had jumped to her feet. She had forgotten prudence; she had forgotten politeness; her eyes were bright with suppressed fire, and her glib Irish tongue was eager to enter into the fray.

"I must speak out," she said. "Molly is more like me than anybody else in this house, and I must take her part. She would be a very, very good girl if she were understood."

"What are your ideas with regard to understanding Molly?" said Mrs. Hartrick in that very calm and icy voice which irritated poor Nora almost past endurance. She was speechless for a moment, struggling with fresh emotion.

"Oh! I wish——" she began.

"And I wish, my dear Nora, that you would remember the politeness due to your hostess. I also wish that you would consider how very silly you are when you speak as you are now doing. I do not know what your Irish habits are; but if it is considered in Ireland rather a virtue than otherwise to spill a milk jug, and allow the contents to deface the tablecloth, I am sorry for you, that is all."

"You cannot understand. I—I am sorry I came," said Nora.

She burst into sudden tears, and ran out of the room. In a few moments Linda came back.

"Molly is storming," she said; "she is in an awful rage."

"Sit down, Linda, and don't tell tales of your sister," answered Mrs. Hartrick in an annoyed voice.

"Dear me, mother!" said Linda; "and where is Nora?"

"Nora is a very impertinent little girl. She is wild, however, and unbroken. We must all have patience with her. Poor child! it is terrible to think that she is your father's niece. What a contrast to dear Terence! He is a very nice, polite boy. I am sorry for Nora. Of course, as to Molly, she is quite different. She has always had the advantage of my bringing-up; whereas poor Nora—well, I must say I am surprised at my sister-in-law. I did not think your father's sister would have been so remiss."

"There is one thing I ought to say," said Linda.

"What is that, dear? Linda, do sit up straight, and don't poke your head."

Linda drew herself up, and looked prettily toward her mother.

"What do you wish to say?"

"It is this. I think Nora will be a very bad companion for Molly. Molly will be worse than ever that Nora is in the house."

"Well, my dear Linda, it is your duty to be a good deal with your cousin. You are too fond of poking holes in others; you are a little hard upon your sister Molly. I do not wish to excuse Molly; but it is not your place as her younger sister to, as it were, rejoice in her many faults."

"Oh, I don't, mother," said Linda, coloring.

"Linda dear, I am afraid you do. You must try and break yourself of that very unchristian habit. But, on the whole, my dear, I am pleased with you. You are careful to do what I wish; you learn your lessons correctly; I have good reports of you from your schoolmistresses; and if you are careful, my dear, you will correct those little habits which mar the perfect whole."

"Thank you, dear mother," said Linda. "I will try to do what you wish."

"What I particularly want you to do just now is to be gentle and patient with your cousin; you must remember that she has never had your advantages. Be with her a good deal; talk to her as nicely as you can; hint to her what I wish. Of course, if she becomes quite incorrigible, it will be impossible for me to have her long with you and Molly; but the child is much to be pitied; she is a very pretty creature, and with a little care could be made most presentable. I by no means give her up."

"Dear mother, how sweetly Christian-like and forgiving you are!" said Linda.

"Oh, hush, my dear; hush! I only do my duty; I hope I shall never fail in that."

Mrs. Hartrick rose from the tea-table, and Linda soon afterward followed her. Mr. Hartrick was seen coming down the avenue. He generally walked from the station. He came in now.

"What a hot day it is!" he said. "Pour me out a cup of tea, Linda. I am very thirsty."

He flung himself into an easy chair, and Linda waited on him.

"Well," he said, "where are the others? Where is the little Irish witch, and where is Molly?"

"I am sorry to say that Molly is in disgrace, as usual," said Mrs. Hartrick.

"Oh, dear, dear!" said Mr. Hartrick; "we ought to send her to school, poor child! I am sorry for her."

"And I intended to give her quite a pleasant evening," said Mrs. Hartrick, "in honor of her cousin's arrival. She was in disgrace yesterday when Nora arrived; and I had thought of giving the girls a delightful evening. I had it all planned, and was going to ask the Challoners over; but really Molly is so incorrigible. She was very pert to me, although she did bring a better report from school; she used some of her objectionable language to Linda, and was more awkward even than usual."

"Look at the tablecloth, father," said Linda.

"I think, Linda, you had better run out of the room," said Mr. Hartrick. He spoke in an annoyed voice.

"Certainly, father, I will go; but don't you want another cup of tea first?"

"Your mother shall pour it out for me. Go, my dear—go."

"Only, mother, is it necessary that we should not ask the Challoners because Molly is naughty? The rest of us would like to have them."

"I will let you know presently, Linda," said her mother; and Linda was obliged, to her disgust, to leave the room.

"Now, then, my dear," said Mr. Hartrick, "I don't at all like to call you over the coals; but I think it is a pity to speak against Molly so much as you do in her sister's presence. Linda is getting eaten up with conceit; she will be an intolerable woman by and by, so self-opinionated, and so pleased with herself. After all, poor Molly may have the best of it in the future; she is a fine child, notwithstanding her naughtiness."

"I thought it likely you would take her part, George; and I am sorry," answered Mrs. Hartrick in a melancholy tone; "but I am grieved to tell you that there is something else to follow. That little Irish girl is quite as cheeky, even more cheeky than Molly. I fear I must ask you to say a word to her; I shall require her to be respectful to me while she is here. She spoke very rudely to me just now, simply because I found it my duty to correct Molly."

"Oh, that won't do at all," said Mr. Hartrick. "I must speak to Nora."

"I wish you would do so."

"I will. By the way, Grace, what a pretty creature she is!"

"She is a beautiful little wildflower," said Mrs. Hartrick. "I have taken a great fancy to her, notwithstanding her rudeness. She has never had the smallest care; she has simply been allowed to grow up wild."

"Well, Nature has taken care of her," said Mr. Hartrick.

"Yes, dear, of course; but you yourself know the advantage of bringing up a girl nicely."

"And no one is more capable of doing that than you are," said Mr. Hartrick, giving his wife an admiring glance.

"Thank you, dear, for the compliment; but I should be glad if you would speak to Nora. Now that she is here, I have no doubt that we shall soon discipline her; and I should like her to pay quite a long visit—that is, of course, if she becomes conformable to my ways."

"She will be sure to do that, Grace," replied the husband. "I am glad you mean to be good to her, and to take her in hand, poor little lass!"

"I thought she might have some good masters and get some valuable lessons while she is here," said Mrs. Hartrick. "Would you believe it, George?—that little girl of sixteen calmly informed me that her education was finished. At the same time, she said she knew no language but her own, and just a smattering of that dead tongue, Irish. She cannot play; in short, she has no accomplishments whatever, and yet her education is finished. I must say I do not understand your sister. I should have thought that she was a little more like you."

"There never was a more particular girl than Ellen used to be," said Mr. Hartrick; "but I must have a long talk with Nora. I'll see her this evening. I know she has a good deal she wants to talk to me about."

"A good deal she wants to talk to you about, George?"

"Oh, yes, my dear; but I will explain presently. She is a proud little witch, and must not be coerced; we must remember that her spirit has never been broken. But I'll talk to her, I'll talk to her; leave the matter in my hands, Grace."

"Certainly, dear; she is your niece, remember."

CHAPTER XVII
TWO DESCRIPTIONS

Some of Nora's words must have sunk into Mrs. Hartrick's heart, for, rather to Molly's own astonishment, she was allowed to dress nicely for dinner, and to come down. Her somewhat heavy, dark face did not look to the best advantage. She wore a dress which did not suit her; her hair was awkwardly arranged; there was a scowl on her brow. She felt so sore and cross, after what she considered her brave efforts to be good during the morning, that she would almost rather have stayed up in her room. But Nora would not hear of that. Nora had rushed into Molly's room, and had begged her, for her sake, to come downstairs. Nora was looking quite charming in that pretty white frock which Mrs. O'Shanaghgan had purchased for her in Dublin. Her softly rounded figure, her dazzlingly fair complexion, were seen now for the first time to the best advantage. Her thick black hair was coiled up becomingly on her graceful little head, and, with a bunch of sweet peas at her belt, there could scarcely have been seen a prettier maiden. When she appeared in the drawing room, even Terence was forced to admit that he had seldom seen a more lovely girl than his sister. He went up to her and began to take notice of her.

"I am sorry I was obliged to be out all day. I am studying the different museums very exhaustively," said Terence in that measured tone of his which drove poor Nora nearly wild. She replied to him somewhat pertly, and he retired once more into his shell.

"Pretty as my sister is," he soliloquized, "she really is such an ignorant girl that few fellows would care to speak to her. It is a sad pity."

Terence, the last hope of the house of O'Shanaghgan, was heard to sigh profoundly. His aunt, Mrs. Hartrick, and his cousin Linda would, doubtless, sympathize with him.

"Dinner was announced, and the meal went off very well. Molly was absolutely silent; Nora, taking her cue from her, hardly spoke; and Linda, Terence, and Mrs. Hartrick had it all their own way. But just as dessert was placed on the table, Mr. Hartrick looked at Nora and motioned to her to change seats and to come to one close to him.

"Come now," he said, "we should like to hear your account of Castle O'Shanaghgan. Terence has told us all about it; but we should like to hear your version."

"And a most lovely place it must be," said Mrs. Hartrick from the other end of the table. "Your description, Terence, makes me quite long to see it; and if it were not that I am honestly very much afraid of the Irish peasantry, I should be glad to go there during the summer. But those terrible creatures, with their shillalahs, and their natural aptitude for firing on you from behind a hedge, are quite too fearful to contemplate. I could not run the risk of assassination from any of them. They seem to have a natural hatred for the English and—why, what is the matter, Nora?"

"Only it's not true," said Nora, her eyes flashing. "They are not a bit like that; they are the most warmhearted people in the whole world. Terence, have you been telling lies about your country? If you have, I am downright ashamed of you."

"But I have not. I don't know what you mean," answered Terence.

"Oh, come, come, Nora!" said her uncle, patting her arm gently; but Nora's eyes blazed with fire.

"It's not a bit true," she continued. "How can Aunt Grace think of that? The poor things have been driven to desperation, because—because their hearts have been trampled on."

"For instance," said Terence in a mocking voice, which fell like ice upon poor Nora's hot, indignant nature—"for instance, Andy Neil—he's a nice specimen, is he not?"

"Oh," said Nora, "he—he is the exception. Don't talk of him, please."

"That's just it," said Terence, laughing. "Nora wants to give us all the sweets, and to conceal all the bitters. Now, I am honest, whatever I am."

"Oh, are you?" said Nora, in indignation. "I should like to know," she continued, "what kind of place you have represented Castle O'Shanaghgan to be."

"I don't know why I should be obliged to answer to you for what I say, Nora," cried her brother.

"You describe it now, Nora. We will hear your description," said her uncle.

Nora sat quite still for a moment; then she raised her very dark-blue eyes.

"Do you really want me to tell you about O'Shanaghgan?" she said slowly.

"Certainly, my dear."

"Certainly, Nora. I am sure you can describe things very well," said her aunt, in an encouraging voice, from the other end of the table.

"Then I will tell you," said Nora. She paused for a moment, then, to the astonishment and disgust of Mrs. Hartrick, rose to her feet.

"I cannot talk about it sitting down," she said. "There's the sea, you know—the wild, wild Atlantic. In the winter the breakers are—oh! I have sometimes seen them forty feet high."

"Come, come, Nora!" said Terence,

"It is true, Terry; the times when you don't like to go out."

Terence retired into his shell.

"I have seen the waves like that; but, oh! in the summer they can be so sweet and conoodling."

"What in the world is that?" said Mrs. Hartrick.

"Oh, it is one of our Irish words; there's no other way to express it. And then there are the cliffs, and the great caves, and the yellow, yellow sands, and the shells, and the seaweeds, and the fish, and the boating, and—and—"

"Go on, Nora; you describe the sea just like any other sea."

"Oh, but it is like no other sea," said Nora. "And then there are the mountains, their feet washed by the waves."

"Quite poetical," said Mrs. Hartrick.

"It is; it is all poetry," said Nora. "You are not laughing at me, are you, Aunt Grace? I wish you could see those mountains and that sea, and then the home—O'Shanaghgan itself."

"Yes, Nora; tell us," said her uncle, who did not laugh, and was much interested in the girl's description.

"The home," cried Nora; "the great big, darling, empty house."

"Empty! What a very peculiar description!" said Mrs. Hartrick.

"Oh, it is so nice," said Nora. "You don't knock over furniture when you walk about; and the dining-room table is so big that, even if you did spill a jug of milk, father would not be angry."

Mrs. Hartrick uttered a sigh.

"Oh, we are wild over there," continued Nora; "we have no conventionalities. We share and share alike; we don't mind whether we are rich or poor. We are poor—oh! frightfully poor; and we keep very few servants; and—and the place is bare; because it can be nothing but bare; but there's no place like O'Shanaghgan."

"But what do you mean by bare?" said Mrs. Hartrick.

"Bare?" said Nora. "I mean bare; very few carpets and very little furniture, and—and——But, oh! it's the hearts that are warm, and that is the only thing that matters."

"It must be a right-down jolly place; and, by Jehoshaphat! I wish I was there," interrupted Molly.

"Molly!" said her mother.

"Oh, leave her alone for the present," said Mr. Hartrick. "But do you mean," he continued, looking at Nora in a distressed way, "that—that my sister lives in a house of that sort?"

"Mother?" said Nora. "Of course; she is father's wife, and my mother; she is the lady of O'Shanaghgan. It is a very proud position. We don't want grand furniture nor carpets to make it a proud position. She is father's wife, and he is O'Shanaghgan of Castle O'Shanaghgan. He is a sort of king, and he is descended from kings."

"Well, Terence, I must say this does not at all coincide with your description," said his uncle, turning and looking his nephew full in the face.

"I didn't wish to make things too bad, sir. Of course, we are not very rich over there; but still, Nora does exaggerate."

"Look here, Nora," said her uncle, suddenly turning and pulling her down to sit beside him, "you and I must have a little chat. We will just go and have it right away. You shall tell me your version of the story quite by ourselves." He then rose and drew her out of the room.

"Where shall we go?" he said when they stood for a moment in the conservatory, into which the big dining room opened.

"Do you really mean it?" said Nora.

"Mean what, dear?"

"To talk to me about—about my letter? Do you mean it?"

"Certainly I do, and there is no time like the present. Come—where shall we go?"

"Where we can be alone; where none of the prim English can interrupt."

"Nora, you must not be so prejudiced. We are not so bad as all that."

"Oh, I know it. I wish you were bad; it's because you are so awfully good that I hate—I mean, that I cannot get on with any of you."

"Poor child! you are a little wild creature. Come into my study; we shall be quite safe from interruption there."

CHAPTER XVIII
A COMPACT

Mr. Hartrick, still holding Nora's hand, took her down a corridor, and the next moment they found themselves in a large room, with oak bookcases and lined with oak throughout; but it was a stately sort of apartment, and it oppressed the girl as much as the rest of the house had done.

"I had thought," she murmured inwardly, "that his study would be a little bare. I cannot think how he can stand such closeness, so much furniture." She sighed as the thought came to her.

"More and more sighs, my little Irish girl," said Mr. Hartrick. "Why, what is the matter with you?"

"I cannot breathe; but I'll soon get accustomed to it," said Nora.

"Cannot breathe? Are you subject to asthma, my dear?"

"Oh, no, no; but there is so much furniture, and I am accustomed to so little."

"All right, Nora; but now you must pull yourself together, and try to be broad-minded enough to take us English folk as we are. We are not wild; we are civilized. Our houses are not bare; but I presume you must consider them comfortable."

"Oh, yes," said Nora; "yes."

"Do you dislike comfortable houses?"

"Hate them!" said Nora.

"My dear, dear child!"

"You would if you were me—wouldn't you, Uncle George?"

"I suppose if I were you I should feel as you do, Nora. I must honestly say I am very thankful I am not you."

Nora did not reply at all to that.

"Ah, at home now," she said, "the moon is getting up, and it is making a path of silver on the waves, and it is touching the head of Slieve Nagorna.

The dear old Slieve generally keeps his snow nightcap on, and I dare say he has it by now. In very hot weather, sometimes, it melts and disappears; but probably he has got his first coat of snow by now, just on his very top, you know. Then, when the moon shines on it and then on the water—why, don't you think, Uncle George, you would rather look at Slieve Nagorna, with the snow on him and the moon touching his forehead, and the path of silver on the water, than—than be just comfortable?"

"I don't see why I should not have both," said Mr. Hartrick after a pause; "the silver path on the water and the grand look of Slieve Nagorna (I can quite fancy what he is like from your description, Nora), and also have a house nicely furnished, and good things to eat, and——. But I see we are at daggers drawn, my dear niece. Now, please tell me what your letter means."

"Do you really want me to tell you now?"

"Yes."

"Do you know why I have really come here?"

"You said something in your letter; but you did not explain yourself very clearly."

"I came here," said Nora, "for a short visit. I want to go back again soon. Time is flying. Already a month of the three months is over. In two months' time the blow will fall unless—unless you, Uncle George, avert it."

"The blow, dear? What blow?"

"They are going," said Nora—she held out both her hands—"the place, the sea, the mountains, the home of our ancestors, they are going unless— unless you help us, Uncle George."

"My dear Nora, you are very melodramatic; you must try and talk plain English. Do you mean to say that Castle O'Shanaghgan—"

"Yes, that's it," said Nora; "it is mortgaged. I don't quite know what mortgaged means, but it is something very bad; and unless father can get a great deal of money—I don't know how much, but a good deal—before two months are up, the man to whom Castle O'Shanaghgan is mortgaged will take possession of it. He is a horrid Englishman; but he will go there, and he will turn father out, and mother out, and me—oh, Terence doesn't matter. Terence never was an Irishman—never, never; but he will turn us out. We will go away. Oh, it does not greatly matter for me, because I am young; and it does not greatly matter for mother, because she is an English woman. Oh, yes, Uncle George, she is just like you—she likes comfort; she likes richly furnished rooms; but she is my mother, and of course I love her; she will stand it, for she will think perhaps we will come here to this country. But it is father I am thinking of, the old lion, the old king, the dear, grand old father. He won't understand, he'll be so puzzled. No other place will suit him; he won't say a word; it's not the way of the O'Shanaghgans to grumble. He won't utter a word; he will go away, and he will—die. His heart will be broken; he will die."

"Nora, my dear child!"

"It is true," said Nora. Her face was ghastly white; her words came out in broken sobs. "I see him, Uncle George; every night I see him, with his bowed head, and his broken heart, and his steps getting slower and slower. He'll be so puzzled, for he is such a true Irishman, Uncle George. You don't know what we are—happy one day, miserable the next. He thinks somehow, somehow, that the money will be paid. But, oh, Uncle George!—I suppose I have got a little bit of the English in me after all—I know it will not be paid, that no one will lend it to him, not any of his old friends and cronies; and he will have to go, and it will break his heart, unless, unless you help him. I thought of you; I guessed you must be rich. I see now that you are very rich. Oh, how rich!—rich enough for carriages, and thick carpets, and easy-chairs, and tables, and grand dresses, and—and all those sort of things; and you will help—won't you? Please, do! please, do! You'll be so glad some day that you helped the old king, and saved him from dying of a broken heart. Please, help him, Uncle George."

"My dear little girl!" said Mr. Hartrick. He was really affected by Nora's speech; it was wild; it was unconventional; there was a great deal of false sentiment about it; but the child herself was true, and her eyes were beautiful, and she looked graceful, and young, and full of passion, almost primeval passion, as she stood there before him. Then she believed in him. If she did not believe in anyone else in the house, she believed in him. She thought that if she asked him he would help.

"Now, tell me," he said after a pause, "does your mother know what you have come here for?"

"Mother? Certainly not; I told you in my letter that you must not breathe a word of it to mother; and father does not know. No one knows but I—Nora, I myself."

"This has been completely your own idea?"

"Completely."

"You are a brave girl."

"Oh, I don't know about being brave. I had to do something. If you belonged to Patrick O'Shanaghgan you would do something for him too. Have you ever seen him, Uncle George?"

"Yes, at the time of my sister's wedding, but not since."

"And then?"

"He was as handsome a fellow as I ever laid eyes on, and Irish through and through."

"Of course. What else would he be?"

"I have not seen him since. My sister, poor Ellen, she was a beautiful girl when she was young, Nora."

"She is stately, like a queen," said Nora. "We all admire her very, very much."

"And love her, my dear?"

"Oh yes, of course I love mother."

"But not as well as your father?"

"You could not, Uncle George, if you knew father."

"Well, I shall not ask any more. You really do want me to help?"

"If you can; if it will not cost you too much money."

"And you mean that your father is absolutely, downright poor?"

"Oh, I suppose so. I don't think that matters a bit. We wouldn't like to be rich, neither father nor I; but we do want to keep O'Shanaghgan."

"Even without carpets and chairs and tables?" said Mr. Hartrick.

"We don't care about carpets and chairs and tables," said Nora. "We want to keep O'Shanaghgan, the place where father was born and I was born."

"Well, look here, Nora. I can make you no promises just now; but I respect you, my dear, and I will certainly do something—what I cannot possibly tell you, for I must look into this matter for myself. But I will do this: I will go to O'Shanaghgan this week and see my sister, and find out from the Squire what really is wrong."

"You will?" said Nora. She thought quickly. Her father would hate it; but, after all, it was the only chance. Even she had sufficient common sense to know that Mr. Hartrick could not help unless he went to the old place.

"Oh, you will do it when you see it," she said, with sudden rapture. "And you'll take me home with you?"

"Well, I think not, Nora. Now that you are here you must stay. I am fond of you, my little girl, although I know very little about you; but I do think that you have very mistaken ideas. I want you to love your English cousins for your mother's sake, and to love their home for your mother's sake also; and I should like you to have a few lessons, and to take some hints from your Aunt Grace, for you are wild, and need training. If I go to O'Shanaghgan for you, will you stay at The Laurels for me?"

"I will do anything, anything for you, if you save father," said Nora. She fell on her knees before her uncle could prevent her, took his hand, and kissed it.

"Then it is a compact," said Mr. Hartrick; "but remember I only promise to go. I cannot make any promises to help your father until I have seen him."

CHAPTER XIX
SHE WILL SOON TAME DOWN

"I am going to Ireland to-morrow, Grace," said Mr. Hartrick to his wife that evening.

"To Ireland!" she cried. "What for?"

"I want to see my sister Ellen. I feel that I have neglected her too long. I shall run over to O'Shanaghgan, and stay there for two or three nights."

"Why are you doing this, George?" said Mrs. Hartrick very slowly.

Mr. Hartrick was silent for a moment; then he said gravely:

"I have heard bad news from that child."

"From Nora?"

"Yes, from Nora."

"But Terence has never given us bad news."

"Terence is not a patch upon Nora, my dear Grace."

"There I cannot agree with you. I infinitely prefer Terence to Nora," was Mrs. Hartrick's calm reply.

"But I thought you admired the child."

"Oh, I admire what the child may become," was the cautious answer. "I cannot admire a perfectly wild girl, who has no idea of self-discipline or self-restraint. And remember one thing, George: whatever she says to you, you must take, to use a vulgarism, with a grain of salt. An Irish girl cannot help exaggerating. She has doubtless exaggerated the condition of things."

"I only pray God she has," was Mr. Hartrick's reply.

"If things are even half as bad as she represents them, it is high time that I should pay my sister a visit."

"Why? What does she say?"

"She has given me a picture of the state of affairs at that house which wrings my heart, Grace. To think that my beautiful sister Ellen should be subjected to such discomforts, to such miseries, is intolerable. I intend to go to O'Shanaghan to-morrow, and will see how matters are for myself."

Mrs. Hartrick was again silent for a moment or two; then she said gravely:

"Doubtless you are right to do this; but I hope, while you are away, you will do nothing rash."

"What do you mean?"

"I mean that, from the little I have seen of Nora, she is a very impetuous creature, and has tried perhaps to wring a promise from you."

"I will tell you quite simply what she has said, Grace, and then you will understand. She says her father has mortgaged the Castle evidently up to the hilt. The mortgagees will foreclose in a couple of months, unless money can be found to buy them off. Now, it has just occurred to me that I might buy Castle O'Shanaghan for ourselves as a sort of summer residence, put it in order, and allow Patrick O'Shanaghan to live there, and my sister. By and by the place can go to Terence, as we have no son of our own. I have plenty of money. What do you think of this suggestion, Grace?"

"It might not be a bad one," said Mrs. Hartrick; "but I could not possibly go to a place of that sort unless it were put into proper repair."

"It is, I believe, in reality a fine old place, and the grounds are beautiful," said Mr. Hartrick. "A few thousand pounds would put it into order, and we could furnish it from Dublin. You could have a great many guests there, and—"

"But what about the O'Shanaghans themselves?"

"Well, perhaps they would go somewhere else for the couple of months we should need to occupy the house during the summer. Anyhow, I feel that I must do something for Ellen's sake; but I will let you know more after I have been there."

Mrs. Hartrick asked a few more questions. After a time she said:

"Is Nora to remain here?"

"Yes. I was going to speak to you about that. It is a sad pity that so pretty a girl should grow up wild. We had better keep her with us for the next two or three years. She will soon tame down and learn our English habits; then, with her undeniable Irish charm and great beauty, she will be able to do something with her life."

"I shall be quite pleased to have her," said Mrs. Hartrick in a cordial tone. "I like training young girls, and Nora is the sort who would do me credit if she really were willing to take pains."

"I am sure she will be; she is an honest little soul."

"Oh, I see you are bewitched by her."

"No, not bewitched; but I admire honesty and candor, and the child has got both."

"Well, well!" said Mrs. Hartrick, "if it is arranged that Nora is to stay here, I will go and see Miss Flowers at Linda's and Molly's school to-morrow, and ask if Nora can be admitted as a pupil. There is no use in losing time, and she may as well start her lessons next week. By all means, George, go and do your best for the poor things. Of course your sister ought not to be allowed to be in money difficulties."

"I should think not," said Mr. Hartrick.

The next day Mr. Hartrick bade Nora and his own family good-by, and started on his expedition to Ireland. Nora was quivering with impatience. When she had seen the last of him she turned back into the house, and was there met by her brother Terence.

"Come here, Nora. I want to speak to you," he said.

She followed him into the nearest room. He closed the door behind them.

"May I ask what you have been saying to Uncle George?"

"You may ask, of course, Terry; but I don't mean to tell you," answered Nora.

"It is because of you he is going to Ireland?"

"It is because of something I have said."

"How do you think our mother will like it? You know how proud she is; how all these years she has determined to put a good face on things, and not to allow her relations in England to know the truth. I have followed her cue, and have been careful to make the very best of things at Castle O'Shanaghgan."

"Oh, it is easy to tell lies," said Nora, with scorn.

"Nora, you talk in a very silly way, and I often have no patience with you," answered her brother. "If I have regard to my mother's feelings, why should you despise me? You are supposed to consider our father's feelings."

"That is very different; the whole thing is different," said Nora. She flushed, bit her lip, and then turned away.

"You must hear me," said Terence, looking at her with some impatience; "you must, you shall. You are quite intolerable with your conceit and your silly, silly Irish ways."

"Well, go on. What have you to say to me?"

"That I think you were guilty of dishonor in talking as you did at dinner last night. You spoke of the place and the poverty in a way which quite put me to the blush. I hope in future, while you are here, you will cease to run the O'Shanaghgans down. It is not worthy of you, Nora, and I am ashamed of you."

"Run them down—I?" said poor Nora in astonishment.

"Yes, you."

She was silent for a moment; she was making a great effort to recover her equanimity. Was Terence right? Had she done wrong to speak before her aunt and cousins as she had done? Of course her uncle was different; it was absolutely necessary that he at least should know the truth. A distressful sense of dismay at her own impetuosity came over her. Terence watched her narrowly. He was fond of Nora in his heart of hearts, and also proud of her; and now that he saw she was really sorry he went up to her, put his arm round her neck, and kissed her.

"Never mind, little girl," he said, "you are young. Try to be guided by me in future, and do not give yourself away. We Irish wear our hearts on our sleeves, and that sort of thing does not go down in England."

"Oh, how I hate this cold England!" said the Irish girl, with passion.

"There you are again, all your feelings expressed too broadly. You will never endure life if you go on as you have begun, Nora."

"Terence," said Nora, looking up at him, "when are you going home?"

"When am I going home? Thank you, I am very comfortable here."

"Don't you think that just at present, when father is in trouble, his only son, the heir of O'Shanaghgan, ought to be with him?"

"Poor old O'Shanaghgan," said the lad, with impatience; "you think that it comprises the whole of the world. I tell you what it is, Nora, I am made differently, and I infinitely prefer England. My uncle has been kind enough to offer me a small post in his business. Did I not tell you?"

"No, no; I never knew what my uncle's business was."

"He is a merchant prince, Nora; an enormously rich man. He owns warehouses upon warehouses. He has offered me a post in one—a very good post, and a certain income."

"And you mean to accept?" said Nora, her eyes flashing fire.

"Well, I am writing to mother on the subject. I think it would be well to do so."

"You, an O'Shanaghgan, will descend to trade?" replied the girl.

"Oh, folly! folly! Nora, your ideas are really too antiquated."

Nora did not speak at all for a moment; then she walked toward the door.

"I cannot understand you," she said. "I am awfully sorry. I was born different; I was made different. I cannot understand why you should bring dishonor to the old place."

"By earning a little money to keep us all from beggary," retorted the lad in a bitter tone; but Nora did not hear him; she had left the room. Her eyes were smarting with unshed tears. She went out into the shrubbery in search of Molly.

"But for Molly I should break my heart," she thought.

CHAPTER XX
STEPHANOTIE

Mrs. Hartrick made all necessary arrangements, and on the following Monday Nora accompanied her cousin to school. Molly was much delighted.

"Now I shall be able to work," she said, "and I won't be guilty of slang when you are by. Don't whisper it to Linda. She would be in the seventh heaven of bliss, and I detest pleasing her; but I would do anything in the world for you, Nora creena."

Nora gave her cousin's arm an affectionate squeeze.

"I have never been to school," said Nora; "you must instruct me what I am to do."

"Oh, dear, dear!" said Molly, "you won't need instruction; you are as sharp and smart as any girl could be. You'll be a little puzzled at first about the different classes, and I'll give you hints about how to take notes and all that sort of thing. But you will quickly get into the way of it, and then you'll learn like a house on fire."

"I wish you two wouldn't whisper together so much," said Linda in an annoyed voice. "I am going over my French parsing to myself, and you do interrupt me so."

"Then walk a little farther away from us," said Molly rudely.

She turned once more to her cousin.

"I will introduce you to the very nicest girls in my form," she said. "I do hope you'll be put into my form, for then in the evenings you and I can do our work together. I expect you know about as much as I do."

"But that's just it—I don't," said Nora. "I have not learned a bit in the school way. I had a governess for a time, but she did not know a great deal. Of course mother taught me too; but I have not had advantages. I should not be surprised if I were put into the lowest form."

They now arrived at the school, and a few minutes later Nora found herself in a huge classroom in which about sixty other girls were assembled.

Miss Flowers presently sent a pupil-teacher to ask Miss O'Shanaghgan to have an interview with her in her private room.

Miss Flowers was about fifty years of age. She had white hair, calm, large, well-opened blue eyes, a steadfast mouth, and a gracious and at the same time dignified manner. She was not exactly beautiful; but she had the sort of face which most girls respected and which many loved. Nora looked earnestly at her, and in her wild, impulsive Irish fashion, gave her heart on the spot.

"What is your name, my dear?" said the head-mistress kindly.

Nora told it.

"You are Irish, Mrs. Hartrick tells me."

"Yes, Miss Flowers, I have lived all my life in Ireland."

"I must find out what sort of instruction you have had. Have you ever been at school before?"

"Never."

"How old are you?"

"Sixteen, Miss Flowers."

"What things have you been taught?"

"English subjects of different sorts," replied Nora. "A little music—oh, I love music, I do love music!—and a little French; and I can speak Irish," she added, raising her beautiful, dark-blue eyes, and fixing them on the face of the head-mistress. That winsome face touched Miss Flowers' heart.

"I will do what I can for you," she said. "For the present you had better study alone. At the end of a week or so I shall be able to determine what form to put you in. Now, go back to the schoolroom and ask Miss Goring to come to me."

Miss Goring was the English mistress. Miss Flowers saw her alone for a minute or two.

"Do what you can for the Irish girl," she said. "She is a very pretty creature; she is evidently ignorant; but I think she has plenty of talent."

Miss Goring went back, and during the rest of the morning devoted herself to Nora. Nora had varied and strange acquirements at her finger's ends. She was up in all sorts of folk lore; she could clothe her speech in picturesque and striking language. She could repeat poetry from Sir Walter Scott, from Shakspere, from the old Irish bards themselves; but her grammar was defective, although her reading aloud was very pretty and sweet.

Her knowledge of history was vague, and might be best described by the expression, up and down. She knew all about the Waldenses; she had a vivid picture in her mind's eye of St. Bartholomew's Eve. The French Revolution appalled and, at the same time, attracted her. The death of Charles I. drew tears from her eyes; but she knew nothing whatever of the chronological arrangements of history; and the youngest girl in the school could have put her to shame with regard to the Magna Charta. It was just the same with every branch of knowledge which Nora had even a smattering of.

At last the great test of all came—could she play or could she not? She had spoken often of her passionate love for music. Miss Goring took her into the drawing room, away from the other girls.

"I am not supposed to be musical," she said, "but I think I know music when I hear it. If you have talent, you shall have plenty of advantages here. Now, sit down and play something for me."

"What! At that piano?" said Nora, her eyes sparkling. Miss Goring had opened a magnificent Broadwood grand.

"Yes," she said. "It is rather daring of me to bring you here; but I want you to have fair play."

"I never played on a really good piano in my life," said Nora. "May I venture?"

"Yes. I do not believe you will injure it."

"May I play as loud as I like, and as soft as I like?"

"Certainly. You may play exactly as you please; only play with all your heart. You will be taught scientific music doubtless; but I want to know what you can do without education, at present."

Nora sat down. At first she felt a little shy, and all her surroundings were so strange, the piano was so big; she touched it with her small, taper fingers, and it seemed to her that the deep, soft notes were going to overpower her. Then she looked at Miss Goring and felt uncomfortable; but she touched the notes again, and she began to forget the room, and Miss Goring, and the grand piano; and the soul of music stood in her eyes and touched the tips of her fingers. The music was quite unclassical, quite unconventional; but it was music—a wild kind of wailing chant—the notes of the Banshee itself. Nora played on, and the tears filled her eyes and streamed down her cheeks.

"Oh, it hurts so!" she said at last, and she looked full up at Miss Goring. Behold, the cold, gray eyes of the English teacher were also full of tears.

"You terrify me," she said. "Where did you hear anything like that?"

"That is the wail of the Banshee. Shall I play any more?"

"Nothing more so eerie."

"Then may I sing for you?"

"Can you sing?"

"I was never taught; but I think I can sing." Nora struck a few chords again. She sang the pathetic words, "She is Far from the Land," and Miss Goring felt the tears filling her eyes once more.

"Upon my word!" she said, as she led her pupil back to the schoolroom, "you can play and you can sing; you have music in you. It would be worth while to give you good lessons."

Nora's musical education was now taken up with vigor. Miss Goring spoke to Miss Flowers about it, and Miss Flowers communicated with Mrs. Hartrick; and Mrs. Hartrick was extremely pleased to find that she had a musical genius in her midst, and determined to give that same musical genius every chance. Accordingly, the very best master in the school arranged to give Nora lessons, and a mistress of striking ability took her also in hand. Nora's wild music, the music that came from her heart, and the song that bubbled from her lips, were absolutely silenced. She must not sing at will; she must on no account play at will. The dullest of exercises were given to her for the purpose of molding her fingers, and the dullest of voice exercises were also given to her for the purpose of molding her voice. She struggled against the discipline, and hated it. She was essentially a child of nature, and this first putting on of the chains of education was the reverse of pleasant.

"Oh, Molly," she said, "what is the good of singing those hateful, screaming exercises, and those scales? They are too detestable, and those little twists and turns. My fingers absolutely feel quite nervous. What is the use? What is the use?"

Molly also sighed and said, "What is the use?" But then the musical mistress and the great master looked at Nora all over when she made similar remarks, and would not even vouchsafe to answer.

"Father would never be soothed with that sort of music," she said. "I think he would be very glad we had not a good piano. Oh, Molly, what does it all mean?"

"I don't know," said Molly. "It's like all other education, nothing but grind, grind; but I suppose something will come of it in the long run."

"What are you talking about, girls?" said Mrs. Hartrick, who just then appeared upon the scene. "Nora, I am pleased; to get very good reports of your music."

"Oh!" said Nora, "I am glad you have come, Aunt Grace; and I shall be able to speak to you. Must I learn what takes all the music out of me?"

"Silly child. There is only one road to a sound musical education, and that is the road of toil. At present you play by ear, and sing by ear. You have talent; but it must be cultivated. Just believe that your elders know what they are about."

Nora did not say anything. Mrs. Hartrick, after looking at her gravely for a moment, continued her gentle walk round the shrubbery. Molly uttered a sigh.

"There's no good, Nora," she said. "You'll have to go through with it. I suppose it is the only way; but it's hard to believe it."

"Well, at any rate, I enjoy other things in my school life," said Nora. "Miss Goring is so nice, and I quite love Miss Flowers; and, after all, I am in your form, Molly, and we do like doing our lessons together."

"To be sure we do; life is quite a different thing for me since you have come here," was Molly's retort.

"And you have been very good indeed about your naughty words, you know," said Nora, nestling up to her cousin.

"Have I? Well, it's owing to you. You see, now, I have someone to help me—someone to understand me."

"Ah!" said Nora; "but I won't be here very long."

"Not here very long! Why, you must. What is the use of beginning school and then stopping it?"

"School or no school, my place is by father's side. It is a long, long time since we heard from Uncle George. As soon as ever he comes back I go."

"Father has been a whole month in Ireland now," said Molly. "I cannot imagine what he is doing. I think mother fidgets rather. She has very long letters from him, and——"

"And, do you know," said Nora, "that father has not written to me once—no, not once since Uncle George went over? I am absolutely in the dark."

"I wonder you stand it," said Molly. "You are so impetuous. I cannot imagine why you don't fly back."

"I could not," said Nora.

"Could not? What is there to hinder you?"

"I have given my word."

"Your word? To whom?"

"To your father. He went to Ireland to please me."

"Oh, did he? That's exciting," said Molly. "Father went to Ireland to please a little chit like you. Now, what does this mean?"

"It means exactly what I have said. He went because I begged him to; because I explained things to him, and he said he would go. But he made a condition, and I am bound to stick to my part of it."

"And that was— —How your eyes shine, Nora!"

"That was, that I am to stay patiently here, and get as English as ever I can. Oh! I must stick to my part of the bargain."

"Well, I cannot say you look very happy," said Molly, "although you are such a favorite at the school. If I was not very fond of you myself I should be jealous. If I had a friend whom I really worshiped, before you appeared on the scene, it was Stephanotie Miller, the American girl."

"Oh, isn't she charming?" said Nora. "She makes me laugh. I am sure she has Irish blood in her."

"Not a bit of it; she's a Yankee of the Yankees."

"Well, she has been sent to school to get tame, just as I have been," said Nora; "but I don't want you to lose her friendship. After all, I care very little for anyone in the school but you, Molly; only Stephanotie makes me laugh."

"We'll have her to tea tomorrow. I'll run in now and ask mother. I shan't mind a bit if you are not going quite to take her from me. After all, she can be friends with both of us. I'll run into the house this moment, and ask mother if we may have Stephanotie to tea."

Molly rushed into the house. Her mother was seated in the morning room, busily writing.

"Well, my dear, well?" she said. "I hear you—you need not bang the door. What is it, Molly?"

"Oh, mother! do look up and listen."

Mrs. Hartrick raised her head slowly.

"Yes, dear?" she said.

"I have behaved a great deal better lately—have I not, mother?"

"You certainly have, Molly; and I am pleased with you. If you would restrain some of your impetuosity, I should be glad to tell you how pleased I am."

"It is all owing to Nora."

"To Nora, my dear! Nora is as wild as you are."

"All the same, it is owing to Nora; and she is not as wild as I am. I mean that I have been downright vulgar; but if you think there is one trace of that in little Nora, it is because you do not know her a bit."

"What is your special request, Molly? I am very busy just now, and cannot discuss your cousin's character. You have improved, and I am pleased with you."

"Then, if you are pleased with me, mother, will you do me a favor?"

"What is that?"

"Stephanotie Miller has never been at our house."

"Stephanotie Miller. What an outlandish name! Who is she?"

"She is a dear, jolly, sweet, handsome American girl. She came to school last term, and she is in the same form with Nora and me; and we both adore her, yes we do. Whatever she does, and whatever she says, we think simply perfection; and we want to ask her here. She is staying with a rather tiresome aunt, in a little house in the village, and she has come over to be Englishized. May she have tea with us tomorrow?"

"I will inquire about her from Miss Flowers; and if she seems to be a nice girl I shall have no objection."

"But we want her to come tomorrow," said Molly. "It is Saturday, you know, and a whole holiday. We thought she might come to lunch, or, if you objected to that, immediately after lunch."

"And what about Linda? Does Linda like her?"

"Holy Moses, no!" said Molly.

"Molly!"

"Oh, mother! do forgive me, and don't say she mustn't come because I said 'Holy Moses.' It's all Linda; she excites the vulgar in me always. But may Stephie come, mother? You are always having Linda's friends here."

"I will not be reproved by you, Molly."

"But, please, dear mother, let her come. Nora and I want her so badly."

"Well, dear, I will try and see Miss Flowers tomorrow morning."

"Won't you judge of her for yourself, mother? There never was a better judge than you are."

This judicious flattery had its effect on Mrs. Hartrick, She sat quite still for a moment, pondering. After all, to be a pupil at Mrs. Flowers' school was in itself a certificate of respectability, and Molly had been very good lately—that is, for her; and if she and Nora wanted a special friend to spend the afternoon with them, it would be possible for Mrs. Hartrick quickly to decide whether the invitation was to be repeated.

"Very well," she said, looking at her daughter, "for this once you may have her; and as you have wisely expressed it, Molly, I can judge for myself."

"Oh, thank you, thank you, mother!"

Molly rushed out of the room. She was flying headlong down the passage, when she came plump up against Linda.

"Now, what is up?" said that young person. "Really, Molly!"

"Oh, hurrah! I have won my way for once," said Molly. "Stephanotie is coming tomorrow to spend the whole afternoon."

"Stephanotie—that horrid Yankee?" said Linda.

"Horrid Yankee yourself!" was Molly's vulgar retort.

"But she cannot come. I have asked Mabel and Rose Armitage, and you know they cannot stand Stephanotie."

"Well, you, and your Mabel and Rose, can keep away from Stephanotie—that's all," said Molly. "Anyhow, she is coming. Don't keep me. I must tell Nora."

Linda made way for her sister to fly past her, as she afterward expressed it, like a whirlwind. She stood still for a moment in deep consideration. Stephanotie was a daring, bright, go-ahead young person, and had she ever taken, in the very least, to Linda, Linda would have worshiped her. Stephanotie was extremely rich, and the bouquets she brought to school, and the bon-bons she kept in her pocket, and the pretty trinkets she wore, and the dresses she exhibited had fascinated Linda more than once. For, rich as the Hartricks were, Mrs. Hartrick had far too good taste to allow her daughters more pocket-money, or more trinkets, or more bon-bons than their companions. Linda, in her heart of hearts, had greatly rebelled against her mother's rule in this particular, and had envied Stephanotie what she called her free life. But Stephanotie had never taken to Linda, and she had taken to Molly, and still more had she taken to Nora; and, in consequence, Linda pretended to hate her, and whenever she had an opportunity used to run her down.

Linda and her friends, Rose and Mabel Armitage, with several other girls, formed quite a clique in the school against Stephanotie and what she termed her "set"; and now to think that this very objectionable American girl was to spend the next day at The Laurels because Molly, forsooth! wished it, was quite intolerable.

Linda thought for a moment, then went into the room where her mother was busy writing. Mrs. Hartrick had just finished her letter. She looked up when Linda approached.

"Well, darling?" she said. Mrs. Hartrick was very fond of Linda, and petted her a great deal more than Molly.

"Oh, mother! I am vexed," said Linda. "Is it quite settled?"

"Is what settled, my dear?"

"Is it quite settled that Stephanotie is to come to-morrow?"

"By the way, I was going to ask you about her, Linda. What sort of girl is she?"

"I do not wish to say anything against my schoolfellows, mother; but if you could only see her—"

Mrs. Hartrick raised her eyebrows in alarm.

"Molly has taken so violently to her," she answered, "and so has Nora; and I thought that just for once—"

"So you have given leave, mother?"

"Yes; I have."

"And my friends are coming—those two charming girls, the Armitages."

"Yes, dear; I greatly admire both the Armitage girls. I am glad they are coming; but why should not Miss Miller come also?"

"Only, she is not in their 'set,' mother—that is all. I wish—I do wish you would ask her to postpone her visit. If she must come, let her come another Saturday."

"I will think about it," said Mrs. Hartrick. "I have certainly promised and——But I will think about it."

Linda saw that she could not press her mother any further. She went away in great disquietude.

"What is to be done?" she thought. "If only mother would speak to Molly at once; but Molly is so impetuous; and once Stephanotie is asked, there will be no getting out of it. She is just the sort of girl to tell that unpleasant story about me, too. If mother knew that, why, I should at last be in her black books. Well, whatever happens, Stephanotie must not be asked to spend the afternoon here to-morrow. I must somehow contrive to put some obstacle in the way."

CHAPTER XXI
THE ROSE-COLORED DRESS

Meanwhile Molly rushed off to Nora. "Linda means mischief, and I must put my foot down immediately," she said.

"Why, Molly, what is up?"

"Put on your hat, darling, and come with me as fast as ever you can."

"Where to?"

"Mother has given in about Stephanotie. Linda will put her finger in the pie if she possibly can. I mean Stephanotie to get her invitation within the next five minutes. Now, then, come along, Nora. Do be quick."

Mrs. Hartrick never allowed the girls to go out except very neatly dressed; but on this occasion they were seen tearing down the road with their garden hats on and minus their gloves. Had anyone from The Laurels observed them, good-by to Molly's liberty for many a long day. No one did, however. Linda during the critical moment was closeted with her mother. When she reappeared the girls were halfway to the village. They reached it in good time, and arrived at the house of Miss Truefitt, Stephanotie's aunt.

Miss Truefitt was an old-fashioned and precise little lady. She had gone through a great deal of trouble since the arrival of her niece, and often, as she expressed it, did not know whether she stood on her head or her heels; but she was fond of Stephanotie, who, notwithstanding her wild ways, was very affectionate and very taking. And now, when she saw Molly and Nora appearing, she herself entered the hall and opened the door for them.

"Well, my dears," she said, "Stephie is in her bedroom; she has a headache, and wanted to lie down for a little."

"Oh, just let me run up to her. I won't keep her a minute," said Molly.

"Come in here with me," said Miss Truefitt to Nora. She opened the door of her neat little parlor. Nora entered. The room was full of gay pictures and gay books, and scattered here and there were very large boxes of bon-bons.

"How she can eat them all is what puzzles me," said Miss Truefitt; "she seems to live on them. The quantity she demolishes would wreck the health of any English girl. Ah, here comes Molly."

But Molly did not come downstairs alone; the American girl was with her. Stephanotie rushed into the room.

"I am going to The Laurels to-morrow, auntie. I am going quite early; this dear old Molly has asked me. You guess I'll have a good time. There will be a box of bon-bons for Nora, sweet little Irish Nora; and a box for dear little Molly, a true native of England, and a fine specimen to boot. Oh, we shall have a nice time; and I am so glad I am asked!"

"It is very kind of Mrs. Hartrick to send you an invitation, Stephie," said her aunt.

"Oh, bother that, Aunt Violet! You know perfectly well she would not ask me if Molly and Nora had not got it out of her."

"Well, we did try our best and most conoodling ways," said Nora in a soft voice.

"Ah, didn't you, you little Irish witch; and I guess you won, too. Well, I'm going; we'll have a jolly lark with Linda. If for no other reason, I should be glad to go to upset her apple cart."

"Dear me, Stephie! you are very coarse and vulgar," said Miss Truefitt.

"Not a bit of it, auntie. Have a bon-bon, do." Stephanotie rushed across the room, opened a big box of bon-bons, and presented one, as if it were a pistol, full in Miss Truefitt's face.

"Oh, no, thank you, my dear!" said that lady, backing; "the indigestion I have already got owing to the way you have forced your bon-bons upon me has almost wrecked my health. I have lost all appetite. Dear me, Stephie! I wish you would not be so dreadfully American."

"The process of Englishizing me is a slow one," said Stephanotie. She turned, walked up to the glass, and surveyed herself. She was dressed in rich brown velveteen, made to fit her lissome figure. Her hair was of an almost fiery red, and surrounded her face like a halo; her eyes were very bright china-blue, and she had a dazzlingly fair complexion. There were people who thought Stephanotie pretty; there were others who did not admire her at all. She had a go-ahead, very independent manner, and was the sort of girl who would be idolized by the weaker members of the school. Molly, however, was by no means a weak member of the school, nor, for that matter, was Nora, and they both took great pleasure out of Stephanotie.

"My bark is worse than my bite," said that young person. "I am something like you, Molly. I am a bit of a scorcher; but there, when I am trained in properly I'll be one of the best of good creatures."

"Well, you are booked for to-morrow now," said Molly; "and Jehoshaphat! if you don't come in time—"

"Oh, Molly!" whispered Nora.

"There, I won't say it again."

Poor Miss Truefitt looked much shocked. Molly and Nora bade her good-by, and nodded to Stephanotie, who stood upon the doorstep and watched them down the street; then she returned to her aunt.

"I did think," said Miss Truefitt slowly, "that the girls belonging to your school were ladylike; but to come here without gloves, and that eldest girl, Miss Hartrick, to use such a shocking expression."

"Oh, bless you, Aunt Vi! it's nothing to the expressions she uses at school. She's a perfect horror of a girl, and I like her for that very reason. It is that horrid little Linda would please you; and I must say I am sorry for your taste."

Stephanotie went upstairs to arrange her wardrobe for the next day.

She had long wished to visit Molly's home. The Laurels was one of

the prettiest places in the neighborhood, and Molly and Linda were

considered as among the smartest girls at the school. Stephanotie wished

to be hand-and-glove with Molly, not because she was supposed to be

rich, or respectable, or anything else, but simply because her nature

fitted to that of the wild, enthusiastic American girl. But, all the

same, now that she had got the entrée, as she expressed it, of the

Hartricks' home, she intended to make a sensation.

"When I do the thing I may as well do it properly," she said to

herself. "I will make them open their eyes. I have watched Mrs. Hartrick

in church; and, oh dear me! have not I longed to give her a poke in the

back. And as to Linda, she thinks a great deal of her dress. She

does not know what mine will be when I take out my very best and most

fascinating gown."

Accordingly Stephanotie rifled her trunk, and from its depths she produced a robe which would, as she said, make the members of The Laurels sit up. It was made of rose-colored silk, and trimmed with quantities of cream lace. The skirt had many little flounces on it, and each was edged with lace. The bodice was cut rather low in the neck, and the sleeves did not come down anything like as far as the wrists. The rose-colored silk with its cream lace trimmings was altogether the sort of dress which might be worn in the evening; but daring Stephanotie intended to appear in it in the morning. She would encircle her waist with a cream-colored sash, very broad, and with much lace upon it; and would wear many-colored beads round her neck, and many bracelets on her arms.

"The whole will have a stylish effect, and will at any rate distinguish me from everyone else," was her inward comment. She shook out the dress, and then rang the bell. One of the servants appeared.

"I want to have this robe ironed and made as presentable as possible," said Stephanotie; "see you have it all done and put in my wardrobe ready for wear tonight. I guess it will fetch 'em," she added, and then she rushed like a whirlwind into the presence of Miss Truefitt.

"Auntie," she said, "would you like to see me done up in style?"

"I don't know, I am sure, my dear," said Miss Truefitt, looking at her with nervous eyes.

"Oh, dear, Aunt Vi! if you were to see mother now you wouldn't know her; she is wonderfully addicted to the pleasures of the toilet. There is nothing so fascinating as the pleasures of the toilet when once you yield to its charms. She rigged me up pretty smart before I left New York, and I am going to wear my rose-colored silk with the cream lace to-morrow."

"But you are not going to an evening party, my dear."

"No; but I shall stay all the evening, and I know I'll look killing. The dress suits me down to the ground. It is one of my fads always to be in something red; it seems to harmonize with my hair."

Miss Truefitt uttered a deep sigh.

"What are you sighing for, Aunt Vi?"

"Nothing, dear; only please don't offer me a bon-bon. The mere sight of those boxes gives me a feeling of nausea."

"But you have not tried the crystallized figs," cried Stephanotie; "they are wonderfully good; and if you feel nausea a peppermint-drop will set you right. I have a kind of peppermint chocolate in this box which is extremely stimulating to the digestive organs."

"No, no, Stephie. I beg—I really do beg that you will take all the obnoxious boxes out of the room."

"Very well, auntie; but you'll come up to-morrow to see me in my dress?"

The next day was Saturday, a holiday of course. Stephanotie had put her hair into Hinde's curlers the night before, and, in consequence, it was a perfect mass of frizzle and fluff the next morning. Miss Truefitt, who wore her own neat gray locks plainly banded round her head, gave a shudder when she first caught sight of Stephanotie.

"I was thinking, dear, during the night," she said, "of your pink silk dress, and I should very much prefer you to wear the gray cashmere trimmed with the neat velvet at the cuffs and collar. It would tone down your—"

"Oh, don't say it," said Stephanotie; "my hair is a perfect glory this morning. Come yourself and look at it—here; stand just here; the sun is shining full on me. Everyone will have to look twice at me with a head like this."

"Indeed, that is true," said Miss Truefitt; "and perhaps three times; and not approve of you then."

"Oh, come, auntie, you don't know how bewitching I look when I am got up in all my finery."

"She is hopelessly vulgar," thought poor Miss Truefitt to herself; "and I always supposed Agnes would have such a nice, proper girl, such as she was herself in the old days; but that last photograph of Agnes shows a decided falling off. How truly glad I am that I was never induced to marry an American! I would rather have my neat, precise little house and a small income than go about like a figure of fun. That poor child will never be made English; it is a hopeless task. The sooner she goes back to America the better."

Meanwhile Stephanotie wandered about the house, thinking over and over of the happy moment when she would appear at The Laurels. She thought it best to put on her rose-colored dress in time for early dinner. It fitted her well, but was scarcely the best accompaniment to her fiery-red hair.

"Oh, lor', miss!" said Maria, the servant, when she first caught sight of Stephanotie.

"You may well say, 'Oh, lor'!' Maria," replied Stephanotie, "although it is not a very pretty expression. But have a bon-bon; I don't mean to be cross."

She whirled across the room, snatched hold of one of her boxes of bon-bons, and presented it to Maria. Maria was not averse to a chocolate peppermint, and popped one into her mouth. The next instant Miss Truefitt appeared. "Now, Stephanotie," she said, "do you think for a single moment—Oh, my dear child, you really are too awful! You don't mean to say you are going to The Laurels like that?"

"Have a bon-bon?" was Stephanotie's response.

"You are downright rude. I will not allow you to offer me bon-bons again."

"But a fresh box of them has just arrived. I got them by the eleven o'clock post to-day," was Stephanotie's reckless answer; "and, oh, such beauties! And I had a letter from mother to say that I might order as many as ever I liked from Fuller's. I mean to write to them to ask them to send me ten shillings' worth. I'll ask for the newest varieties. There surely must be bon-bons which would not give you indigestion, Aunt Vi."

"I must ask you to take off that dress, Stephanotie. I forbid you to go to The Laurels in such unsuitable attire."

"Oh, lor'! and it's lovely!" said Maria, *sotto voce*, as she was leaving the room.

"What an unpleasant smell of peppermint!" said Miss Truefitt, sniffing at that moment. "You know, Stephanotie, how I have begged of you not to eat those unpleasant sweets in the dining room."

"I didn't," said Stephanotie; "it was only Maria."

Maria backed out of the room with another violent "Oh, lor'!" and ran down to the kitchen.

"I'll have to give notice," she said. "It's Miss Stephanotie; she's the most dazzlingly brilliant young lady I ever set eyes on; but mistress will never forgive me for eating that peppermint in her presence."

"Rinse the mouth out, and take no notice," was the cook's somewhat heartless rejoinder. "How do you say she was dressed, Maria?"

"Pink, the color of a rose, and that ravishing with lace. I never see'd such a dress," said Maria. "She's the most beautiful young lady and the queerest I ever set eyes on."

Stephanotie and her aunt were having a battle upstairs, and in the end the elder lady won. Stephanotie was obliged to take off the unsuitable dress and put on the gray cashmere. As subsequent events proved, it was lucky for her that she did do so.

CHAPTER XXII
LETTERS

By the post on the following morning there came two letters for Nora. She hailed them with a cry of delight.

"At last!" she said.

Mrs. Hartrick was not in the room; she had a headache, and did not get up to breakfast. Terence had already started for town. He had secured the post he desired in his uncle's office, and thought himself a very great man of business. Linda did not count for anything.

Nora flung herself into an easy-chair, and opened the first of her letters. It was from her mother. She was soon lost in its contents.

"MY DEAR NORA [wrote Mrs. O'Shanaghgan]: Be prepared for very great, startling, and at the same time gratifying, news. Your dear Uncle George, who has been spending the last three weeks with us, has made an arrangement which lifts us, my dear daughter, out of all pecuniary embarrassments. I will tell you as briefly as possible what has taken place. He had a consultation with your father, and induced him, at my suggestion, to unburden his mind to him. You know the Squire's ways. He pooh-poohed the subject and fought shy of it; but at last I myself brought him to task, and the whole terrible and disgraceful state of things was revealed. My dear Nora, my dear little girl, we were, it appears, on the brink of bankruptcy. In a couple of months O'Shanaghgan would no longer have been ours.

I cannot say that I should ever have regretted leaving this ramshackle and much-dilapidated place, but of course I should have shrunk from the disgrace, the exposure, the feeling that I was the cynosure of all eyes. That, indeed, would have cut me to the quick. Had your father consented to sell O'Shanaghgan and live in England, it would have been a moment of great rejoicing for me; but the place to be sold up over his head was quite a different matter. This, my dear Nora, seems to have been the position of affairs when your dear uncle, like a good providence or a guardian angel, appeared on the scene. Your uncle, my dearest Nora, is a very rich man. My dear brother has been careful with regard to money matters all his life, and is now in possession of a very large supply of this world's goods. Your dear uncle was good enough to come to the rescue, and has bought O'Shanaghgan from the man to whom your father owed the mortgage. O'Shanaghgan now belongs to your Uncle George."

"Never!" cried Nora, springing to her feet.

"What is the matter, Nora?" said Linda.

"Don't talk to me for the present, or I'll say something you won't like to hear," replied Nora.

"Really, I must say you are copying Molly in your manner."

"Don't speak to me," said Nora. Her face was crimson; she had never felt such a wild, surging sense of passion in the whole of her existence. Linda's calm gray eyes were upon her, however. She managed to suppress any more emotion, saw that her cousin was burning with curiosity, and continued the letter.

"Although, my dearest Nora, Castle O'Shanaghgan now belongs to your Uncle George, don't suppose for a single moment that he is going to be unkind to us. Far from it. To all appearance the place is still ours; but with, oh! such a difference. Your father is still, in the eyes of the tenants and of the country round, the owner of Castle O'Shanaghgan; but, after consulting with me, your Uncle George felt that he must not have the reins. His Irish nature, my dear—But I need not discuss that. You know as well as I do how reckless and improvident he is."

"Oh, mother!" gasped Nora. She clenched her little white teeth, and had great difficulty in proceeding with her letter. Linda's curiosity, however, acted as a restorative, and she went on with her mother's lengthy epistle.

"All things are now changed, and I may as well say that a glorious era has begun. Castle O'Shanaghgan is now your uncle's property, and it will soon be a place to be proud of. He is having it refurnished from attic to cellar; carpets, curtains, mirrors, furniture of all sorts have already begun to arrive from one of the most fashionable shops in Dublin. Gardeners have been got to put the gardens to rights, the weeds have been removed from the avenue, the grass has been cut, the lawns have been mown; the whole place looks already as if it had undergone a resurrection. My bedroom, dear Nora, is now a place suitable for your mother to sleep in; the bare boards are covered with a thick Brussels carpet. The Axminster stair carpets arrived yesterday. In the dining room is one of the most magnificent Turkey carpets I have ever seen; and your uncle has insisted on having the edge of the floor laid with parquetry. Will you believe me, Nora?—your father has objected to the sound of the hammering which the workmen make in putting in the different pieces of wood. You can scarcely believe it possible; but I state a fact. The stables are being filled with suitable horses; and with regard to that I am glad to say your father does take some interest. A victoria has arrived for me, and a pony-trap for you, dear; for it seems your Uncle George has taken a great fancy to you, my little Nora. Well, dear, all this resurrection, this wonderful restoration of Castle O'Shanaghgan has occurred during your absence. You will come back to a sort of fairyland; but it is one of your uncle's stipulations that you do not come back at present; and, of course, for such a fairy godfather, such a magician, no promise is too great to give. So I have told him, dear Nora, that you will live with your kind and noble Aunt Grace, and with your charming cousin Linda, and your cousin Molly— about whom I do not hear so much—as long as he wishes you to do so. You will receive the best of educations, and come back at Christmas to a suitable home. You must have patience until then. It is your uncle's proposal that at Christmas-time you and your cousins also come to O'Shanaghgan, and that we shall have a right good old-fashioned Christmas in this place, which at last is beautiful and worthy of your ancient house. You must submit patiently, therefore, dear Nora, to remaining in England. You will probably spend the greater portion of your time there for the next few years, until you are really accomplished. But the holidays you, with your dear cousins and your uncle and aunt, will always spend at O'Shanaghgan. You must understand, dear, that the house really belongs to your uncle; the place is his, and we are simply his tenants, from whom he nobly asks no rent. How proud I am of my dear brother, and how I rejoice in this glorious change!— Your affectionate mother,

"ELLEN O'SHANAGHGAN.".

The letter dropped from Nora's fingers.

"And was it I who effected all this?" she said to herself. "And I thought I was doing good."

The other letter lay unopened on her lap. She took it up with trembling hands, and broke the seal. It was a short letter compared to her mother's, but it was in the handwriting she loved best on earth.

"LIGHT O' THE MORNING [it began]: Why, then, my darling, it's done—it is all over. The place is mine no longer; it belongs to the English. To think I, O'Shanaghgan of Castle O'Shanaghgan, should live to write the words. Your mother put it to me, and I could not refuse her; but, oh, Nora asthore, heart of my life, I can scarcely bear to live here now. What with the carpets and the curtains, and the fuss and the misery, and the whole place being turned into a sort of furniture-shop, it is past bearing. I keep out most of my time in the woods, and I won't deny to you, my dearest child, that I have shed some bitter tears over the change in O'Shanaghgan; for the place isn't what it was, and it's heart-breaking to behold it. But your mother is pleased, and that's one comfort. I always did all I could for her; and when she smiles at me and looks like the sun—she is a remarkably handsome woman, Nora—I try to take a bit of comfort. But I stumble over the carpets and the mats, and your mother is always saying, 'Patrick, take care where you are going, and don't let the dogs come in to spoil the new carpets.' And the English servants that we have now taken are past bearing; and it's just as if I were in chains, and I would almost as lief the place had been sold right away from me as see it in its changed condition. I can add no more now, my child, except to say that, as I am under great and bitter obligations to your Uncle George,

I must agree to his request that you stay in England for the present; but Christmas is coming, and then I'll clasp you in my arms, and I'll have a grain of comfort again.—Your sorrowful old father,

PATRICK O'SHANAGHGAN."

Nora's cheeks flushed brighter than ever as she read these two letters. The first had cut her to the heart; the second had caused that desire for weeping which unless it is yielded to amounts to torture.

Oh! if Linda would not stay in the room. Oh! if she might crouch away where she, too, could shed tears over the changed Castle O'Shanaghgan. For what did she and her father want with a furniture-shop? Must she, for all the rest of her days, live in a sort of feather-bed house? Must the bareness, the space, the sense of expansion, be hers no more? She was half a savage, and her silken fetters were tortures to her.

"It will kill him," she murmured. She said the words aloud.

"What will kill him? What is wrong? Do, please, tell me," said Linda.

Nora looked at her with flashing eyes.

"How bright your cheeks are, Nora, and how your eyes shine! But you look very, very angry. What can be the matter?"

"Matter? There is plenty the matter. I cannot tell you now," said Nora.

"Then I'll go up and ask mother; perhaps she will tell me. It has something to do with that old place of yours, I have not the slightest doubt. Mother has got a very long letter from Ireland; she will tell me perhaps."

"Yes, go; and don't come back again," said Nora, almost rudely.

"She gets worse and worse," thought Linda as she slowly mounted the stairs. "Nora is anything but a pleasure in the house. At first when she came she was not quite so bad; she had a pretty face, and her manners had not been coarsened from contamination with Molly. Now she is much changed. Yes, I'll go to mother and talk to her. What an awful afternoon we are likely to have with that American girl here and Nora changing for the worse hour by hour."

Linda knocked at her mother's door. Mrs. Hartrick was not well, and was sitting up in bed reading her letters.

"My head is better, Linda," she said. "I shall get up presently. What is it, darling?"

"It is only the usual thing," said Linda, with a deep sigh. "I am always being rubbed the wrong way, and I don't like it."

"So it seems, my pet. But how nicely you have done your hair this morning! How very neat and ladylike you are becoming, Linda! You are a great comfort to me, dear."

"Thank you, mother; I try to please you," said Linda. She seated herself on her mother's bed, suppressed a sigh, then said eagerly:

"Nora is awfully put out. Is there bad news from that wild place, Castle O'Shanaghgan?"

"Bad news?" cried Mrs. Hartrick. "Has the child had letters?"

"Yes, two; she had been reading them instead of eating her breakfast, and the sighs and the groans, and the flashing eyes and the clenched teeth, and the jumping to her feet and the flopping herself down again have been past bearing. She won't let out anything except that she is downright miserable, and that it is a burning shame."

"What can she mean, mother? Is the old place sold? I always expected they were terribly poor."

"The best, most splendid news," said Mrs. Hartrick. "My dear Linda, you must be mistaken. Your father says that he has given your aunt and uncle leave to tell Nora everything. I thought the child would be in the seventh heaven of bliss; in fact, I was almost dreading her arrival on the scene, she is so impetuous."

"Well, mother, she is not in any seventh heaven of bliss," replied Linda; "so perhaps they have not told her. But what is it, mother dear? Do tell me."

"It is this, darling—your father has bought Castle O'Shanaghgan."

"Oh! and given it to the O'Shanaghgans. Why did he do that?"

"He has bought it, but he has not given it to the O'Shanaghgans. Some day, if Terence turns out worthy, the old place will doubtless be his, as we have no son of our own; but at present it is your father's property; he has bought it."

"Then no wonder poor Nora is sad," said Linda. "I can understand her; she is fond of the old place."

"But why should she be sad? They are not going; they are to stay there, practically owners of all they possess; for, although the property is really your father's, he will only exercise sufficient control to prevent that poor, wild, eccentric uncle of yours from throwing good money after bad. To all intents and purposes the O'Shanaghgans still hold possession; only now, my dear Linda, they will have a beautiful house, magnificently furnished. The grounds are carefully attended to, good gardeners provided, English servants sent for, and the whole place made suitable for your father's sister."

"But does Nora know of this?"

"I suppose so. I know your father said she was to be told."

"She is very miserable about something. I cannot understand her," said Linda. "I tell you what, I'll just go down and tell her. Perhaps those two letters were nothing but grumbles; and the O'Shanaghgans did not know then the happiness that was in store for them."

"You can tell her if you like, dear."

"I will, I will," said Linda. She jumped off her mother's bed and ran downstairs.

Nora was standing in the conservatory. She was gazing straight before her, not at the great, tall, flowering cactus nor the orchids, nor the mass of geraniums and pelargoniums of every shade and hue—she was seeing a picture of a wild, wild lonely place, of a bare old house, of a seashore that was like no other seashore in the world. She was looking at this picture with all the heart of which she was capable shining in her eyes; and she knew that she was looking at it in imagination only, and that she would never see the real picture again, for the wild old place was wild no longer, and in Nora's opinion the glory had departed. She turned when Linda's somewhat mincing voice fell upon her ears.

"How you startled me!" she said. "What is it?"

"Oh, good news," said Linda. "I am not quite so bad as you think me, Nora, and I am delighted. Mother has told me everything. Castle O'Shanaghgan is yours to live in as long as ever you care to do so. Of course it belongs to us; but that does not matter, and it is furnished from attic to cellar most splendidly, and there are English servants, and there are—"

"Everything abominable and odious and horrible!" burst from Nora's lips. "Oh, don't keep me; don't keep me! I am smothered at the thought—O'Shanaghgan is ruined—ruined!"

She ran away from her cousin out into the air. At headlong speed did she go, until at last she found herself in the most remote and least cultivated part of the plantation.

Oh, to be alone! Now she could cry, and cry she did right bitterly.

CHAPTER XXIII
THE BOX OF BON-BONS

It occurred to Stephanotie that, as she could not wear the rose-colored dress, as she must go perforce to the Hartricks' in her dove-colored cashmere, with its very neat velvet collar and cuffs, she would at least make her entrance a little striking.

"Why not take a box of bon-bons to Mrs. Hartrick?" she said to herself. "There's that great big new box which I have not opened yet It contains dozens of every kind of sweetmeat. I'll present it to her; she'll be pleased with the attention."

The box was a very large one; on its lid was painted a picture of two or three cupids hovering in the air, some of them touching the shoulders of a pretty girl who was supposed to be opening a box of chocolates. There was a good deal of color and embossed writing also on the cover, and altogether it was as showy and, in Stephanotie's opinion, as handsome a thing as anybody could desire.

She walked through the village, holding the box, tied with great bunches of red ribbon, in her hand. She scorned to put a brown-paper cover over it; she would take it in all its naked glory into the midst of the Hartrick household.

On her way she met the other two girls who were also going to spend an afternoon at The Laurels. Rose and Mabel Armitage were the daughters of a neighbouring squire. They were nice girls, but conventional.

There was nothing original about either of them; but they were very much respected in the school, not only on account of their father's position—he represented the county in the House—but also because they were good, industrious, and so-called clever. The Armitages took prizes at every examination. Their French was considered very nearly Parisian in accent; their drawings were all in absolutely perfect proportions. It is true the trees in Rose's landscapes looked a little stiff; but how carefully she laid on her water-colors; how honestly she endeavored to copy her master's smallest requirements! Then Mabel played with great correctness, never for a single moment allowing a wrong note to appear; and they both sang, very prettily, simple little ballads; and they were dressed with exquisite neatness and propriety in very quiet colors—dark blues, very dark reds, pretty, neat blouses, suitable skirts. Their hair was shiny, and sat in little tight tendrils and pretty curls round their heads. They were as like as two peas—each girl had a prim little mouth with rosy lips; each girl possessed an immaculate set of white teeth; each girl had a little, straight nose and pretty, clear gray-blue eyes; their foreheads were low, their eyebrows penciled and delicately marked. They had neat little figures; they were neat in every way, neat in soul too; admirable little people, but commonplace. And, just because they were commonplace, they did not like fiery-red-haired Stephanotie; they thought Molly the essence of vulgarity; they secretly admired beautiful Nora, but thought her manners and style of conversation deplorable; and they adored Linda as a kindred spirit.

Seeing them walking on in advance, like a little pair of doves, Stephanotie quickened her steps until she came up to them.

"Hallo!" she said; "you guess where I'm off to?"

"I am sure I cannot say," answered Rose, turning gently round.

Mabel was always Rose's echo.

"I cannot say," she repeated.

"Well, I can guess where you're going. You're going to have a right down good time at The Laurels—guess I'm right?"

"We are going to spend an afternoon at The Laurels," said Rose.

"An afternoon at The Laurels," echoed Mabel.

"And so am I—that's the best of the fun," said Stephanotie; "and I mean to give her something to remember me by."

"Whom do you mean?" said Rose.

"Why, my good, respected hostess, Mrs. Hartrick."

"What do you mean to give her?" asked Rose.

"This. How do you like it? It's full of bon-bons."

Rose, notwithstanding her virtuous and commonplace mind, had a secret leaning toward bon-bons. She did not dare to confess it even to Mabel; for Mabel also had a secret leaning, and did not dare to confess it to Rose. It was not *comme il faut* in their family for the girls of the house to indulge in bon-bons; but still, they would have liked some of those delicious sweets, and had often envied Stephanotie when she was showing them to her companions.

Of course, not for worlds would they have been friendly with the terrible American girl; but they did envy her her boxes of sweets.

"How gay!" said Rose, looking at the startling cover, with its cupids and its greedy-looking maiden.

"How jolly," said the American girl—"how luscious when you're eating them! Would you like to see them inside?"

"Oh, I think not," said Rose.

"Better not," said Mabel.

"But why better not?" continued Stephanotie. "It's natural that girls like us should like sweetmeats, bon-bons, or anything of that sort. Here, there's a nice little bit of shelter under this tree, and there's no one looking. I'll untie the ribbons; just hold the box, Rose."

Rose held it. Stephanotie hastily pulled off the red ribbons and lifted the cover. Oh, how delicious the inside did look!—rows upon rows of every imaginable sweet—cream-colored sweets, rose-colored, green, white; plums, apples, pears, figs, chocolates; every sort that the heart of girl could desire lay before them in rows on rows.

"They are, every one of them, for Mrs. Hartrick," said Stephanotie, "and you mustn't touch them. But I have got two boxes in my pocket; they make it bulge out; I should be glad to get rid of them. We'll tie this up, but you'll each have one of my boxes."

In a jiffy the big box was tied up again with its huge crimson bows, and each of the Armitage girls possessed one of the American girl's boxes of bon-bons.

"Aren't they pretty? Do have some; you don't know how long you may be kept waiting for your tea," said Stephanotie as she danced beside her companions up the avenue.

In this fashion, therefore, did the three enter the house, for both of the Armitages had yielded to temptation, and each girl was just finishing a large bon-bon when they appeared on the scene.

Mrs. Hartrick was standing in the great square central hall, waiting for her guests.

Stephanotie ran up to her.

"It's very good of you indeed to ask me," she said; "and please accept this—won't you? It's from an American girl, a trophy to remember her by."

"Indeed?" said Mrs. Hartrick, flushing very brightly. She stepped back a little; the huge box of bon-bons was forced into her hands.

"Jehoshaphat!" exclaimed Molly.

"Molly!" said her mother.

Linda uttered a little sigh. Rose and Mabel immediately became as discreet and commonplace and proper as they could be; but Stephanotie knew that the boxes of bon-bons were reposing in each of their pockets and her spirits rose higher than ever.

"Where is Irish Nora?" she said. "It's she that is fond of a good sweet such as they make for us in the States. But have the box—won't you, Mrs. Hartrick? I have brought it to you as a token of my regard."

"Indeed? Thank you very much, Miss Miller," said Mrs. Hartrick in a chilly voice. She laid the box on a side-table.

CHAPTER XXIV
THE TELEGRAM,

The girls went out into the grounds. The afternoon happened to be a perfect one; the air was balmy, with a touch of the Indian summer about it. The last roses were blooming on their respective bushes; the geraniums were making a good show in the carefully laid out beds. There were clumps of asters and dahlias to be seen in every direction; some late poppies and some sweet-peas and mignonette made the borders still look very attractive, and the chrysanthemums were beginning to appear.

"In a week's time they will be splendid," said Linda, piloting her two friends through the largest of the greenhouses.

"Do come away," said Molly; "when Linda speaks in that prim voice she's intolerable. Come, Nora; come, Stephie—we'll just have a run by ourselves."

Nora was still looking rather pale. The shock of the morning had caused the color to fade from her cheeks; she could not get the utterly changed O'Shanaghgan out of her head. She longed to write to her father, and yet she did not dare.

Stephanotie looked at her with the curious, keen glance which an American girl possesses.

"What is it? Do say," she said, linking her hand inside Nora's. "Is it anything that a bon-bon will soothe, or is it past that?"

"It is quite past that; but don't ask me now, Stephie. I cannot tell you, really."

"Don't bother her," said Molly; "she has partly confided in me, but not wholly. We'll have a good time by ourselves. What game do you think we had best play, Stephie?"

"I'm not one for games at all," answered Stephanotie. "Girls of my age don't play games. They are thinking seriously of the business of life—the flirtations and the jolly time they are going to have before they settle down to their staid married life. You English are so very childish."

"And we Irish are childish too," said Nora. "It's lovely to be childish," she added. "I hate to put away childish things."

"Oh, dear! so that is the Irish and English way," said Stephanotie. "But there, don't let us talk nationalities; let's be cozy and cheerful. I can tell you I did feel annoyed at coming here such a dowd; it was not my fault. I meant to make an impression; I did, really and truly. It was very good of you, Molly, to ask me; and I know that proud lady, your mother, didn't want to have me a bit. I am nothing but Stephanotie Miller, and she doesn't know the style we live in at home. If she did, maybe she would open her eyes a little; but she doesn't, and that's flat; and I am vulgar, or supposed to be, just because I am frank and open, and I have no concealment about me. I call a spade a spade."

"Oh, hurrah! so do I," said Molly, the irrepressible.

"Well, my dear, I don't use your words; they wouldn't suit me at all," said the American girl. "I never call out Jehoshaphat the way you do, whoever Jehoshaphat *is*; but I have my little eccentricities, and they run to pretty and gay dresses—dresses with bright colors and quantities of lace on them—and bon-bons at all hours, in season and out of season. It's easy to content me, and I don't see why my little innocent wishes should not be gratified."

"But you are very nicely dressed now," said Nora, looking with approval at the gray cashmere.

"Me nicely dressed!" screamed Stephanotie. "Do you call this dress nice? Why, I do declare it's a perfect shame that I should be made such a spectacle. It don't suit my hair. When I am ordering a dress I choose shades of red; they tone me down. I am fiery to-day—am I not, Molly?"

"Well, you certainly are," said Molly. "But what—what did you do to it?"

"To my locks, do you mean?"

"Yes. They do stick out so funnily. I know mother was shocked; she likes our heads to be perfectly smooth.'

"Like the Armitages', for instance," said Stephanotie.

"Well, yes; something like theirs. They are pretty girls, are they not?"

"Yes," said Stephanotie; "but don't they give you the quivers? Don't you feel as if you were rubbed the wrong way the moment you speak to them?"

"I don't take to them," said Molly; "but I think they're pretty."

"They're just like what O'Shanaghgan is now," thought Nora, who did not speak. "They are all prim and proper; there's not a single wildness allowed to come out anywhere."

"But they're for all the world like anybody else," said Stephanotie. "Don't they love sweeties just! If you' had seen them—the greedy way they took the bon-bons out of the little boxes I gave them. Oh, they're just like anybody else, only they are playing parts; they are little actors; they're always acting. I'd like to catch them when they were not. I'd like to have them for one wild week, with you, Molly, and you, Nora. I tell you there would be a fine change in them both."

"There's a telegraph-boy coming down the avenue," cried Molly suddenly. "I'll run and see what is the matter?"

Nora did not know why her heart beat. Telegrams arrived every day at The Laurels. Nevertheless she felt sure that this was no ordinary message; she stood now and stared at that boy as though her eyes would start from their sockets.

"What is the matter?" said Stephanotie.

"Nothing—nothing."

"You're vexed about something. Why should you be so distant with me?"

"I am not, Stephie. I am a little anxious; it is difficult always to be just the same," said Nora.

"Oh, don't I know it, my darling; and if you had as much to do with Aunt Vi Truefitt as I have, you would realize how often *my* spirits turn topsy-turvy. I often hope that I'll be Englishized quickly, so that I may get back to my dear parents. But there, Molly is coming back."

"The telegram was for mother," she said. "Do let us play."

Nora looked at Molly. Her face was red; it was usually pale. Nora wondered what had brought that high color into her cheeks. Molly seemed excited, and did not want to meet her cousin's eyes.

"Come, let us have a race," she said. "I don't want to put away childish things. I want to have a good game while I am in the humor. Let us see who will get first to the top of that hill. I like running uphill. I'm off; catch me who may!"

Molly started. Her figure was stout, and she ran in a somewhat awkward way. Nora flew after her. She soon reached her side.

"There, stop running," she said. "What is up?"

"What is up?" echoed Molly.

"Yes; what was in that telegram?"

"The telegram was for mother."

"But you know what was in it. I know you do."

"Nothing—nothing, Nora. Come, our race isn't over yet. I'm off again; you cannot catch me this time."

Molly ran, panting as she did so.

"I cannot tell her; I won't," she said to herself. "I wish her eyes were not so sharp. She is sure to find out; but I have begged and prayed of mother not to tell her, at least until after Stephanotie and the others have gone. Then, I suppose, she must know."

Molly reached the top of the hill. She was so blown that she had to fling herself on the grass. Nora again reached her side.

"Tell me, Molly," she said; "there is something the matter?"

"There is a telegram for mother, and I cannot tell you anything whatever about it," said Molly in a cross voice. "There, I'm off once more. I promised Linda that I would help her to look after the Armitage girls. Prim and proper as they are, they are sometimes a little bit too much for my dainty sister Linda. You take care of Stephie; she's right good fun. Let me go, Nora; let me go."

Molly pulled her hand almost roughly out of her cousin's grip, and the next moment was rushing downhill as fast as she could in the direction of the summer-house. There she knew she would find Linda and her two friends.

CHAPTER XXV
THE BLOW

Notwithstanding all the efforts of at least five merry girls, there was a cloud over the remainder of that afternoon. Nora's face was anxious; her gay laugh was wanting; her eyes wore an abstracted, far-away look. The depression which the letters of the morning had caused was now increased tenfold. If she joined in the games it was without spirit; when she spoke there was no animation in her words. Gone was the Irish wit, the pleasant Irish humor; the sparkle in the eyes was missing; the gay laughter never rose upon the breeze. At tea things were just as bad. Even at supper matters had not mended.

Molly now persistently avoided her cousin. Stephanotie and she were having a wild time. Molly, to cover Nora's gloom, was going on in a more extravagant way than usual. She constantly asked Jehoshaphat to come to her aid; she talked of Holy Moses more than once; in short, she exceeded herself in her wildness. Linda was so shocked that she took the Armitage girls to a distant corner, and there discoursed with them in low whispers. Now and then she cast a horrified glance round at where her sister and the Yankee, as she termed Stephanotie, were going on together. To her relief, toward the end of the evening, Mrs. Hartrick came into the room. But even her presence could not suppress Molly now. She was beside herself; the look of Nora sitting gloomily apart from the rest, pretending to be interested in one of Sir Walter Scott's novels, was too much for her. She knew that a bad time was coming for Nora, and her misery made her reckless. Mrs. Hartrick, hearing some of her naughtiest words, said in an icy tone that Miss Truefitt had sent a maid for Stephanotie; and a few moments afterward the little party broke up.

As soon as the strange girls had departed, Mrs. Hartrick turned immediately to Molly.

"I am shocked at your conduct," she said. "In order to give you pleasure I allowed Miss Miller to come here; but I should have been a wiser and happier woman if I had taken dear Linda's advice. She is not the sort of girl

I wish either you or Nora ever to associate with again. Now, go straight to your room, and don't leave it until I send for you."

Molly stalked off with a defiant tread and eyes flashing fire; she would not even glance at Nora. Linda began to talk in her prim voice. Before she could utter a single word Nora had sprung forward, caught both her aunt's hands, and looked her in the face.

"Now," she said, "I must know. What did that telegram say?"

"What telegram, Nora? My dear child, you forget yourself."

"I do not forget myself, Aunt Grace. If I am not to go quite off my head, I must know the truth."

"Sit down, Nora."

"I cannot sit; please put me out of suspense. Please tell me the worst at once."

"I am sorry for you, dear; I really am."

"Oh, please, please speak! Is anything—anything wrong with father?"

"I hope nothing serious."

"Ah! I knew it," said Nora; "there is something wrong."

"He has had an accident."

"An accident? An accident? Oh, what? Oh! it's Andy; it must be Andy. Oh, Aunt Grace, I shall go mad; I shall go mad!"

Mrs. Hartrick did not speak. Then she looked at Linda. She motioned to Linda to leave the room. Linda, however, had no idea of stirring. She was too much interested; she looked at Nora as if she thought her really mad.

"Tell me—tell me; is father killed?"

"No, no, my poor child; no, no. Do calm yourself, Nora. I will let you see the telegram; then you will know all that I know."

"Oh, please, please!"

Mrs. Hartrick took it out of her pocket. Nora clutched it very hard, but her trembling fingers could scarcely take the little flimsy pink sheet out of its envelope. At last she had managed it. She spread it before her; then she found that her dazed eyes could not see the words. What was the misery of the morning to the agony of this moment?

"Read it for me," she said in a piteous voice. "I—I cannot see."

"Sit down, my dear; you will faint if you don't."

"Oh! everything is going round. Is he—is he dead?"

"No, dear; nothing very wrong."

"Read—read!" said Nora.

Mrs. Hartrick did read. The following words fell upon the Irish girl's ears:

"O'Shanaghgan was shot at from behind a hedge this, morning. Seriously injured. Break it to Nora."

"I must go to him," said Nora, jumping up. "When is the next train? Why didn't you tell me before? I must go—I must go at once."

Now that the worst of the news was broken, she had recovered her courage and some calmness.

"I must go to him," she repeated.

"I have telegraphed. I have been mindful of you. I knew the moment you heard this news you would wish to be off to Ireland, so I have telegraphed to know if there is danger. If there is danger you shall go, my dear child; indeed, I myself will take you."

"Oh! I must go in any case," repeated Nora. "Danger or no danger, he is hurt, and he will want me. I must go; you cannot keep me here."

Just then there came a loud ring at the hall-door.

"Doubtless that is the telegram," said Mrs. Hartrick. "Run, Linda, and bring it."

Linda raced into the hall. In a few moments she came back with a telegram.

"The messenger is waiting, mother," she said.

Mrs. Hartrick tore it open, read the contents, uttered a sigh of relief, and then handed the paper on to Nora to read.

"There," she said; "you can read for yourself."

Nora read:

"Better. Doctor anticipates no danger. Tell Nora I do not wish her to come. Writing.

"HARTRICK."

"There, my dear, this is a great relief," said Mrs. Hartrick.

"Oh! I am going all the same," said Nora.

"No; that I cannot possibly allow."

"But he wants me, even if he is not in danger. It was bad enough to be away from him when he was well; but now that he is ill——You don't understand, Aunt Grace—there is no one can do anything for father as I can. I am his Light o' the Morning."

"His what?" said Mrs. Hartrick.

"Oh, that is what he calls me; but I have no time to explain now. I must go; I don't care."

"You are an ungrateful girl, Nora. If you had lived through the misery I have lived through the last few hours this telegram would fill you with thankfulness. It is your duty to stay here. You are under a promise to your kind uncle. He has rescued your father and mother from a most terrible position, and your promise to him saying that you would stay quietly here you cannot in all honor break. If your father were in danger it would be a different matter. As it is, it is your duty to stay quietly here, and show by your patience how truly you love him."

Nora sat silent. Mrs. Hartrick's words were absolute. The good lady felt that she was strictly following the path of duty.

"I can understand the shock you have had," she continued, looking at the girl, who now sat with her head slightly drooping, her hands clasped tightly together, her attitude one of absolute despair.

"Linda," she said, turning to her daughter, "fetch Nora a glass of wine. I noticed, my dear, that you ate scarcely any supper."

Nora did not speak.

Linda returned with a glass of claret.

"Now drink this off, Nora," said her aunt; "I insist."

Nora was about to refuse, but she suddenly changed her mind.

"I shall go whether she gives me leave or not," was her inward thought. "I shall want strength." She drank off the wine, and returned the empty glass to her cousin.

"There now, that is better," said Mrs. Hartrick; "and as you are unaccustomed to wine you will doubtless sleep soundly after it. Go up to your bedroom, dear. I will telegraph the first thing in the morning to O'Shanaghgan, and if there is the slightest cause for alarm will promise to take you there immediately. Be content with my promise; be patient, be brave, I beg of you, Nora. But, believe me, your uncle knows best when he says you are not to go."

"Thank you, Aunt Grace," said Nora in a low voice. She did not glance at Linda. She turned and left the room.

CHAPTER XXVI
TEN POUNDS

Molly was standing by the open window of her room when Nora came in. She entered quite quietly. Every vestige of color had left her face; her eyes, dark and intensely blue, were shining; some of her jet-black hair had got loosened and fell about her neck and shoulders. Molly sprang toward her.

"Oh, Nora!" she said.

"Hush!" said Nora. "I have heard; father is hurt—very badly hurt, and I am going to him."

"Are you indeed? Is mother going to take you?" said Molly.

"No; she has refused. A telegram has come from my uncle; he says I am not to go—as if a thousand telegrams would keep me. Molly, I am going."

"But you cannot go alone."

"I am going."

"When?" said Molly.

"Now—this very minute."

"What nonsense! There are no trains."

"I shall leave the house and stay at the station. I shall take the very next train to town. I am going."

"But, Nora, have you money?"

"Money?" said Nora. "I never thought of that."

"Mother won't give you money if she does not wish you to go."

"I'll go to my room and see." Nora rushed away. She came back in a few moments with her purse; she flung the contents on Molly's bed. Molly took up the silver coins as they rattled out of Nora's purse. Alack and alas! all she possessed was eight shillings and a few coppers.

"You cannot go with that," said Molly; "and I have nothing to lend you, or I would; indeed, I would give you all I possess, but mother only gives me sixpence a week. Nothing would induce her to give me an allowance. I have sixpence a week just as if I were a baby, and you can quite understand I don't save out of that. What is to be done?"

Nora looked nonplused. For the first time the vigorous intention, the fierce resolve which was bearing her onward, was checked, and checked by so mighty a reason that she could not quite see her way out of the present difficulty. To ask her Aunt Grace for money would be worse than useless. Nora was a sufficient reader of character to be quite certain that Mrs. Hartrick when she said a thing meant it. She would be kind to Nora up to a certain point. Were her father in what they called danger she herself would be the first to help Nora to go to him.

"How little they know how badly he wants me!" thought the girl; "how all this time he is pining for me—he who never knew illness in his life— pining, pining for me! Nothing shall keep me from him. I would steal to go to him; there is nothing I would not do."

"Nora, how queer you look!" said Molly.

"I am thinking," said Nora. "I wonder how I am to get that money? Oh, I have it. I'll ask Stephanotie to lend it to me. Do you think she would?"

"I don't know. I think it very likely. She is generous, and she has heaps of money."

"Then I'll go to her," said Nora.

"Stay, Nora; if you really want to run away——"

"Run away?" said Nora. "If you like to call it so, you may; but I'm going. My own father is ill; my uncle and aunt don't hold the same position to me that my father holds. I will go to him—I will."

"Then I tell you what it is," said Molly, "you must do this thing carefully or you'll be locked up in your bedroom. Mother would think nothing of locking the door of your bedroom and keeping you there. You don't know mother when once her back is up. She can be immensely kind up to a certain point, and then—oh! I know it—immensely cruel."

"What is to be done?" said Nora. "I hate doing a thing in this kind of way—in the dark, as it were."

"You must listen to me," said Molly; "you must be very careful. I have had some little scampers in my time, and I know how to manage matters. There is only one way for you to go."

"What is that?"

"You and I must go off and see Stephanotie; but we cannot do so until everyone is in bed."

"How can we go then?"

"We can easily climb down from this window. You see this pear-tree; it almost touches the window. I have climbed down by it more than once; we can get in again the same way."

"Oh, yes. If we must sneak out of the house like thieves," said Nora, "it's as good as any other way."

"I tell you it's the only way," said Molly. "We must be off on our way to London before mother gets up tomorrow morning. You don't know anything whatever about trains."

"But I can look them out," said Nora.

"Well, go back to your room. Mother will not be going to bed for quite an hour. We cannot help it; we can do nothing until she is safe in bed. Go away at once, Nora; for if she finds you here talking to me she will suspect something. I cannot tell you what mother is when once her suspicions are aroused; and she has had good cause to suspect me before now."

"But do you really mean to say you'll come with me?"

"I certainly mean to say I won't let you go alone. Now then, go away; just pack a few things, and slip back to me when I knock on the wall. I know when mother has gone to bed; it is necessary that she should be asleep, and that Linda should be asleep also; that is all we require. Leave the rest to me."

"And you are certain Stephanotie can lend us the money?"

"We can but ask her. If she refuses we must only come back again and make the best of things."

"I will never come back," said Nora. "I will go to the first pawnbroker's and pawn everything of value I possess; but go to my father I will."

"I admire your courage," said Molly. "Now then, go back to your room and wait for my signal."

Nora returned to her room. She began to open and shut her drawers. She did not care about being quiet. It seemed to her that no one could keep her from her father against her will. She did not recognize the all-potent fact that she had no money herself for the journey. Still, the money must be obtained. Of course Stephanotie had it, and of course Stephanotie would lend it; it would only be a loan for a few days. When once Nora got to Ireland she would return the money immediately.

She opened her drawers and filled a little black bag which she had brought with her from home. She put in the trifles she might need on her journey; the rest of her things could stay; she could not be bothered with them one way or the other. Then she sat quite still on the edge of her bed. How earnestly she wished that her aunt would retire for the night, that Linda would be quiet! Linda's room adjoined Nora's—it opened into Nora's—and Linda, when occasions roused her suspicions, could be intensely watchful. She did not seem to be going to bed; she kept moving about in her room. Poor Nora could scarcely restrain herself from calling out, "Oh, do be quick, Linda! What are you staying up for?" but she refrained from saying the fatal words. Presently she heard the creak of Linda's bed as she got into it. This was followed by silence.

Nora breathed a sigh of relief, but still the dangers were not past. Her little black bag lay quite ready on the chair, and she herself sat on the edge of her bed. Mrs. Hartrick's steps were heard coming up the stairs, and the next moment the door of Nora's room was opened and the good lady looked in.

"Not in bed, Nora," she said; "but this is very wrong."

"Oh, I could not sleep," said Nora.

Mrs. Hartrick went up to her.

"Now, my dear child," she said, "I cannot rest until I see you safe in bed. Come, I must undress you myself. What a wan little face! My dear girl, you must trust in God. Your uncle's telegram assures us that there is no danger; and if there is the smallest occasion I will take you myself to your father tomorrow."

"Oh! if you would only promise to take me," said poor Nora, suddenly rising to her feet, twining her arms round her aunt's neck, and looking full into her face. "Oh! don't say you will take me to my father if there is danger; say you'll take me in any case. It would break my heart to stay away. I cannot—cannot stay away from him."

"Now, you are talking in an unreasonable way, Nora—in a way I cannot for a moment listen to. Your uncle wishes you to stay where you are. He would not wish that if there was the least occasion for you to go to Ireland."

"Then you will not take me tomorrow?"

"Not unless your father is worse. Come, I must help you to get your things off."

Nora felt herself powerless in Mrs. Hartrick's hands. The good lady quickly began to divest her of her clothes, soon her night-dress was popped on, and she was lying down in bed.

"What is that black bag doing here?" said Mrs. Hartrick, glancing at the bag as she spoke.

"I was packing my things together to go to father."

"Well, dear, we must only trust there will be no necessity. Now, goodnight. Sleep well, my little girl. Believe me, I am not so unsympathetic as I look."

Nora made no reply. She covered her face with the bedclothes; a sob came from her throat. Mrs. Hartrick hesitated for a moment whether she would say anything further; but then, hoping that the tired-out girl would sleep, she went gently from the room. In the passage she thought for a moment.

"Why did Nora pack that little bag?" she said to herself. "Can it be possible—but no, the child would not do it. Besides, she has no money."

Mrs. Hartrick entered her own room at the other end of the corridor and shut the door. Then stillness reigned over the house—stillness absolute and complete.

No light had been burning under Molly's door when Mrs. Hartrick had passed. Molly, indeed, wiser than Nora, had got into bed and lay there, dressed, it is true, but absolutely in the dark. Nora also lay in her bed; every nerve was beating frantically; her body seemed to be all one great pulse. At last, in desperation, she sprang out of bed—there came the welcome signal from Molly's room. Nora struck a light and began to dress feverishly. In ten minutes she was once more in her clothes. She now put on the dark-gray traveling dress she had worn when coming to The Laurels. Her hat and jacket were quickly put on, and, carrying the little black bag, she entered Molly's room.

"What hour is it?" said Nora. "It must be long past midnight."

"Oh, no; nothing of the kind. It is not more than eleven o'clock."

"Oh! I thought it was one or two. Do you know that your mother came to see me and insisted on my getting into bed?"

"You were a great goose, Nora. You should have lain down as I did, in your clothes; that would have saved a little time. But come, mother has been quite quiet for half an hour and more; she must be sound asleep. We had better go."

"Yes, we had better go," said Nora. "I packed a few things in this bag; it is quite light, and I can carry it. My money is in it, too—eight shillings and fivepence. I do trust Stephanotie will be able to lend us the rest."

Molly had not been idle while Nora was in her room. She had taken care to oil the hasp of the window; and now, with extreme caution, she lifted it up, taking care that it did not make the slightest sound as she did so. The next moment both girls were seated on the window-ledge. Molly sprang on to the pear-tree, which creaked and crackled under her weight; but Mrs. Hartrick was already in the land of dreams. Molly dropped on to the ground beneath, and then it was Nora's turn.

"Shall I shut the window before I get on to the pear-tree?" whispered Nora.

"No, no; leave it open. Come just as you are."

Nora reached out her arms, grasped the pear tree, and slipped down to the ground.

"Now then, we must be off," said Molly. "I hope Pilot won't bark." She was alluding to the big watchdog. "But there, I'll speak to him; he is very fond of me."

The girls stole across the grass. The dew lay heavy on it; their footsteps made no sound. Presently they reached the front of the house, and Pilot, with a deep bay, flew to meet them.

"Pilot! Pilot! quiet; good dog!" said Molly. She went on her knees, flung her arms round the dog, and began to whisper in his ear.

"He understands," she said, looking up at Nora. The great creature seemed to do so; he wagged his feathery tail from side to side and accompanied the girls as far as the gate.

"Now, go home, go home," said Molly. She then took Nora's hand, and they ran down the road in the direction of the village.

"If it were not that you are so miserable I should enjoy this awfully," said Molly.

"But how do you mean to wake Stephie?" asked Nora at last.

"Well, luckily for us, her aunt, Miss Truefitt, is rather deaf. Miss Truefitt has a bedroom at the back of the house, and Stephanotie sleeps in front. I shall fling gravel at the window. There is not a soul, as you see, in the streets. It's well that it is such a quiet place; it will serve our purpose all the better."

They now found themselves outside Miss Truefitt's house. Molly took up a handful of gravel and flung it in a great shower at Stephanotie's window. Both girls then waited eagerly for a response. At first there was none; once again Molly threw the gravel.

"I do hope she will wake soon," she said, turning to Nora; "that gravel makes a great noise, and some of the neighbors may pop out their heads to see what is the matter. There! I saw a flicker of light in the room. She is thinking it is thieves; she won't for a single moment imagine that we are here. I do hope Miss Truefitt won't awaken; it will be all up with us if she does."

"No, no, it won't," said Nora; "there's not a person in this place I could not get to help me in a cause like this. The one who is absolutely invulnerable, who cannot be moved, because she imagines herself to be right, is your mother."

"There's Stephie at the window now," said Molly. A little figure in a night-dress was seen peeping out.

"It's us, Stephie. Let us in; it's most awfully important," whispered Molly's voice in deep sepulchral tones from below.

"But say, what's the matter?" called Stephanotie, opening her window and popping out her curly head.

"I can't talk to you in the street. Slip down and open the hall-door and let us in," said Molly. "It's most vital."

"It's life or death," whispered Nora. There was something in Nora's tremulous tones which touched Stephanotie, and at the same time stimulated her curiosity to such an extent that she flew into her clothes, dashing about perfectly reckless of the fact that she was making a loud noise; but, luckily for her, Miss Truefitt was deaf and the servants slept in a remote part of the old house. Soon Stephanotie was tumbling downstairs, the chain was taken off the door, and the two girls were admitted.

"Where shall I take you?" said Stephanotie. "It's all as dark as pitch. You know Aunt Vi won't hear of gas in the house. But stay, we can go into the dining room. I suppose you can tell me by the light of a solitary glim." As she spoke she pointed to the candle which she was holding high above her head.

"Yes, yes, or with no light at all," said Nora.

Stephanotie now opened the door of the dining room, and the three girls entered. Stephanotie placed the candle on the table and turned and faced them.

"Well," she said, "what's up? What do you want me to do?"

"I want you to lend me all the money you have," said Nora.

"All the money I have—good gracious!"

"Oh, Jehoshaphat! be quick about it," said Molly. "We cannot stand here talking; we want to catch the very next train to town."

"But why should I lend you all the money I have?"

"Oh, I'll tell her, Nora; don't you speak," said Molly. "Nora's father has been awfully hurt; he was shot at from behind a hedge by some scoundrel in Ireland. A telegram came to-day about him to mother, and mother won't take Nora to Ireland unless her father is in danger, and Nora is determined to go."

"I guess I'd about do the same," said Stephanotie, nodding her head. "If poppa was shot at from behind a hedge, I guess there's nothing would keep me away from him. But is it for that you want the money?"

"Yes," said Nora, plunging her hands into the depths of her black bag; "there's only eight shillings and five-pence here, and I can't get to Ireland with that."

"Haul out the spoil," said Molly; "make no bones about it. I'm going with Nora, because the child isn't fit to travel alone."

"You coming with me?" said Nora. "I didn't know that."

"I don't mean to leave you, my dear, until I see you safe in the midst of your family; besides, I have a bit of curiosity with regard to that wonderful old place of yours."

"Oh, it's lost, the place is quite lost," said Nora, remembering for the first time since the blow had fallen the feather-bed condition of Castle O'Shanaghgan.

"Well, lost or found, I'd like to have a peep at it," said Molly; "so fork out the spoil, Stephie, and be quick."

"I will, of course," said Stephanotie. "But how much do you want?"

"All you possess, my dear; you cannot give us more than all you possess."

"And when am I likely to have it back?"

"Oh, as if that mattered," said Molly; "the thing is to get Nora home. You won't be any the worse for this, if that is what you mean."

"Oh, I am not really thinking of that; but my school fees have to be paid, and the money only came from America two days ago for the purpose. You know Aunt Vi is very poor."

"Poor or rich, don't keep us waiting now," said Molly. "Look at Nora. Do you think for a single moment that your school bills matter when her heart is breaking?"

"And you shall have the money back, Stephie, every farthing, if I die to get it for you," said Nora with sudden passion.

"I don't doubt you, darling," said the generous-hearted American girl. "Well, I'll go up to my room and see what I can do." She left the room, ran upstairs, and quickly returned with a fat purse. It contained gold and notes; and very soon Molly found, to her infinite delight, that it would be by no means necessary for her and Nora to take all Stephie's wealth.

"Ten pounds will be sufficient," said Molly. "I have not the slightest idea what the fares to Ireland are, but I have no doubt we shall do nicely with this sum. May we have these two five-pounds notes, Stephie?"

"You may and welcome," said Stephanotie. "I have nearly thirty pounds here; but it's on account of the school bills. As a rule, poppa is not quite so generous. He says it is better for young girls like me not to have too much money. I guess I'd eat too many bon-bons if I had a lot of money at my disposal. But had you not better take it in gold? It is much easier to change."

"To be sure," said Molly. "Holy Moses! it's you that have got the sense, Stephie."

"Thank you for the compliment," replied Stephanotie. "Well, then, here you are—ten sovereigns. Good luck to you both. What do you mean to do?"

"Go to the station and find out about the trains, and start the very first moment possible," said Molly.

"I do wish I was going with you. It would be no end of a lark."

"Why don't you come?" asked Molly.

"I wish I might; but there, I suppose I had better not. I must look perfectly innocent to-morrow, or I may get into an awful scrape for this. You must both go now, or Aunt Vi when she turns in her sleep may wake. She turns in her sleep about three times during the night; and whenever she turns she wakes, so she tells me. I guess it's about time for her first turn now, so the sooner you are off the better."

"Oh, thank you, Stephie! I shall never, never forget your kindness," said Nora. She flung her arms impulsively round Stephanotie's neck, and the next moment the girls left the house.

CHAPTER XXVII
ADVENTURES—AND HOME AGAIN

The girls now went straight to the railway station; the hour was a quarter to twelve. They entered and asked at once if there was a train up to town. Yes; the last train would be due in ten minutes. Molly now took the management of affairs; she purchased a third-class ticket for herself and another for Nora.

"If we go third-class we shall not be specially remarked," she said. "People always notice girls who travel first-class."

The tickets being bought, the girls stood side by side on the platform. Molly had put on her shabbiest hat and oldest jacket; her gloves had some holes in them; her umbrella was rolled up in such a thick, ungainly fashion that it looked like a gamp. Nora, however, exquisitely neat and trim, stood by her companion's side, betraying as she did so traces of her good birth and breeding.

"You must untidy yourself a bit when we get into the train," said Molly. "I'll manage it."

"Oh, never mind about my looks; the thing is to get off," said Nora. "I'm not a scrap afraid," she added; "if Aunt Grace came to me now she could not induce me to turn back; nothing but force would make me. I have got the money, and to Ireland I will go."

"I admire you for your determination," said Molly. "I never knew that an Irish girl could have so much spunk in her."

"And why not? Aren't we about the finest race on God's earth?"

"Oh, come, come," said Molly; "you mustn't overdo it. Even you sometimes carry things a trifle too far."

Just then the train came in. There was the usual bustle of passengers alighting and others getting in; the next moment the girls had taken their seats in a crowded compartment and were off to town. They arrived in London between twelve and one o'clock, and found themselves landed at Waterloo. Now, Waterloo is not the nicest station in the world for two very young girls to arrive at midnight, particularly when they have not the faintest idea where to go.

"Let us go straight to the waiting room and ask the woman there what we had best do," said Molly, who still immensely enjoyed taking the lead.

Nora followed her companion quite willingly. Her worst fears about her father were held in abeyance, now that she was really on her way to him. The girls entered the waiting room. A tired-looking woman was busy putting out the gas, and reducing the room to darkness for the night. She turned round as the girls came in.

"I'm shutting up, ladies," she said.

"Oh, but please advise us," said Molly.

"How so, miss? What am I to do?"

"You'll be paid well," said Molly, "so you need not look so angry. Can you take us home to your place until the morning?"

"What does this mean?" said the woman.

"Oh, I'll explain," said Molly. "We're two runaways. I don't mind telling you that we are, because it's a fact. It is important that we should leave home. We don't want to be traced. Will you give us lodging?—any sort. We don't mind how small the room is. We want to be at Euston at an early hour in the morning; we are going to Holyhead."

"Dear, dear!" said the woman; "and does this really mean money?"

"It means five shillings," said Molly.

"Ten" was on Nora's lips; but Molly silenced her with a look.

"There's no use in overpaying her; she won't be half as civil," whispered Molly to Nora.

"It's five shillings you'll get," she repeated in a firm voice. "Here, I have got the change; you can look in my purse."

"Molly opened her purse as she spoke. The woman, a Mrs. Terry by name, did look in. She saw the shine of gold and several half-crowns.

"Well, to be sure!" she said. "But you'll promise not to get me into a scrape?"

"We won't even ask you your name. You can let us out of the house in time for us to catch the first train from Euston. We shall be off and away before we are discovered."

"And we'll remember you all our lives if you'll help us," said Nora. Then she added, tears filling her pretty eyes, "It's my father, please, kind woman; he has been shot at and is very ill."

"And who wants to keep you from your father, you poor thing?" said the woman. "Oh, if it's that, and there's no lovers in the question, I don't mind helping you both. It don't do for young girls to be wandering about the streets alone at night. You come with me, honeys. I can't take you for nothing, but I'll give you supper and breakfast, and the best bed I can, for five shillings."

Accordingly, in Mrs. Terry's company, the two girls left Waterloo Station. She walked down a somewhat narrow side-street, crossed another, and they presently found themselves in a little, old-fashioned square. The square was very old indeed, belonging to quite a dead-and-gone period of the world. The woman stopped at a house which once had been large and stately; doubtless in days gone by it had sheltered goodly personages and had listened to the laughter of the rich and well-to-do; but in its old age the house was let out in tenements, and Mrs. Terry owned a couple of rooms at the very top.

She took the girls up the dirty stairs, opened the door of a not uncomfortable sitting room, and ushered them in.

"There now, honeys," she said; "the best I can do for you both is the sofa for one and my bed for the other."

"No, no," said Nora, "we would not dream of taking your bed; and, for that matter, I could not sleep," she added. "If you will let me have a couple of chairs I shall lie down on them and wait as best I can until the morning. Oh, I have often done it at home and thought it great fun."

"Well, you must each have a bit of supper first; it don't do for young girls to go to bed hungry, more particularly when they have a journey before them. I'll get you some bread and cheese and a glass of milk each—unless, indeed, you would prefer beer?"

"Oh, no, we would much rather have milk," said Molly.

The woman bustled about, and soon came in with a jug of milk, a couple of glasses, some bread, and some indifferent butter.

"You can have the cheese if you really want it," she said.

"No; this will do beautifully," answered Nora.

"Well then, my dears, I'll leave you now for the night. The lamp will burn all night. It will be lonely for young girls to be in the dark; and I'll promise to call you at five o'clock. There's a train leaves Euston between six and seven that you had better catch, unless you want them as is hindering you from flight to stop you. I am interested in this poor young lady who wants to see her father."

"Oh, thank you; you are a perfect darling!" said Nora. "I'll come and see you some day when I am happy again, and tell you all about it."

"Bless your kind heart, honey! I'm glad to be able to do something for those who are in trouble. Now then, lie down and have a bit of sleep. I'll wake you sure and certain, and you shan't stir, the two of you, until you have had a hot cup of tea each."

Mrs. Terry was as good as her word. She called the girls in good time, and gave them quite a comfortable breakfast before they started. The tea was hot; the bread was good—what else did they want?

Nora awoke from a very short and broken slumber.

"Soon I shall be back again," she thought. "No matter how changed and ruined the place is, I shall be with him once more. Oh, my darling, my heart's darling, I shall kiss you again! Oh! I am happy at the thought."

Mrs. Terry herself accompanied them to Euston. It was too early to get a cab; she asked them if they were good walkers. They said they were. She took them by the shortest routes; and, somewhat tired, but still full of a strange exultation, they found themselves at the great station. Mrs. Terry saw them into their train, and with many loudly uttered blessings started them on their journey. She would not touch anything more than the five shillings, and tears were in her eyes as she looked her last at them.

"God bless them, and particularly that little Irish girl. Haven't she just got the cunningest, sweetest way in all the world?" thought the good woman. "I do hope her father will be better when she gets to him. Don't she love him just!"

Yes, it had been the most daring scheme, the wildest sort of adventure, for two girls to undertake, and yet it was crowned with success. They were too far on their journey for Mrs. Hartrick, however much she might wish it, to rescue them. She might be as angry as she pleased; but nothing now could get them back. She accordingly did the very best thing she could do— telegraphed to Mr. Hartrick to say that they had absolutely run away, but begged of him to meet them in Dublin. This the good man did. He met them both on the pier, received them quietly, without much demonstration; but then, looking into Nora's anxious face, his own softened.

"You have come, Nora, and against my will," he said. "Are you sorry?"

"Not a bit, Uncle George," she answered. "I would have come against the wills of a thousand uncles if father were ill."

"Then I have nothing to say," he answered, with a smile, "at least to you; but, Molly, I shall have something to talk to you about presently."

"It was very good of you to meet us, father. Was mother terribly angry?"

"What could you expect her to be? You have behaved very badly."

"I don't think so. I did the only possible thing to save Nora's heart from breaking."

"It seems to me," said Mr. Hartrick slowly, "that you all think of nothing but the heart of Nora. I am almost sorry now that I ever asked her to come to us in England."

"Oh, it's home again; it's home again!" cried the Irish girl as she paced up and down the platform. "Molly, do listen to the brogue. Isn't it just delicious? Come along, and let's talk to this poor old Irish beggar."

"Oh, but he doesn't look at all pleasant," said Molly, backing a little.

"Bless the crayther, but he is pleasant," said Nora. "I must go and have a chat with him." She caught hold of Molly's hand, and dragged her to the edge of the pavement, where an old man, with almost blind eyes, was seated in front of a large basket of rosy apples.

"And how are you this morning, father?" said Nora.

"Oh, then, it's the top of the morning to yez, honey," was the instant reply. "And how is yourself?"

"Very well indeed," said Nora.

"Then it's I that am delighted to see yez, though see yez I can't. Oh, then, I hope that it's a long life and plenty you'll have before you, my sweet, dear, illigant young lady—a good bed to lie on, and plenty to eat and drink. If you has them, what else could ail yez? Good-by to yez; good-by to yez."

Nora slipped a couple of pence into his hand.

"The blessings of the Vargin and all the Saints be on your head, miss. Oh! it's I that am glad to see yez. God's blessing on yez a thousand times."

Nora took the old man's hand and wrung it. He raised the white little hand to his lips and kissed it.

"There now," he said, "I have kissed yez; and these lips shan't see wather again for many a long day—that they shan't. I wouldn't wash off the taste of your hand, honey, for a bag of yellow gold."

"What an extraordinary man!" said Molly. "Have you known him all your life?"

"Known him all my life!" said Nora. "Never laid eyes on him before; that's the way we always talk to one another. Oh, I can tell you we love each other here in Ireland."

"It seems so," answered Molly, in some astonishment. "Dear me! if you address a total stranger so, how will you speak to those you really love?"

"You wait and see," answered Nora, her dark-blue eyes shining, and a mist of tears dimming their brightness; "you wait and see. Ah, it's past words we are sometimes; but you wait and you'll soon see."

Mr. O'Shanaghgan was pronounced better, although Mr. Hartrick had to admit that he was weak and fretful; and, now that Nora had come, it was extremely likely that her presence would do her father a sight of good.

"I knew it, Uncle George," she answered as they seated themselves in the railway carriage preparatory to going back to O'Shanaghgan—"I knew it, and that was why I came. You, uncle, are very wise," she added; "and yours is a beautiful, neat, orderly country; and you are very kind, and very clever; and you have been awfully good to the Irish girl—awfully good; and she is very ignorant; and you know a great deal; but one thing she does know best, and that is, the love and the longing in the heart of her own dear father. Oh, hurrah! I'm home again; I'm home again! Erin go bragh! Erin go bragh!"

CHAPTER XXVIII
THE WILD IRISH

The somewhat slow Irish train jogged along its way; it never put itself out, did that special train, starting when it pleased, and arriving when it chose at its destination. Its guard, Jerry by name, was of a like mind with itself; there was no hurry about Jerry; he took the world "aisy," as he expressed it.

"What's the good of fretting?" he used to say. "What can't be cured must be endured. I hurry no man's cattle; and my train, she goes when she likes, and I aint going to hurry her, not I."

On one occasion Jerry was known to remark to a somewhat belated traveler:

"Why, then, miss, is it hurrying ye are to meet the train? Why, then, you can take your time."

"Oh, Jerry!" said this anxious person, fixing her eyes on his face in great excitement, "I forgot a most important parcel at a shop half a mile away."

"Run and fetch it, then, honey," replied Jerry, "and I'll keep her a bit longer."

This the lady accordingly did. When she returned, the heads of all the other angry passengers were out of the windows expostulating with Jerry as to the cause of the delay.

"Hurry up, miss," he said then. He popped her into a compartment, and she, as he called the train, moved slowly out of the station.

At times, too, without the smallest provocation, Jerry would stop this special train because a little "pigeen" had got off one of the trucks and was running along the line. He and the porter shouted and raced after the animal, caught it, and brought it back to the train. On another occasion he calmly informed a rather important passenger, "Ye had best get out here, for she's bust." "She" happened to be the engine.

Into this train now got English Molly and Irish Nora. Mr. Hartrick pronounced it quite the vilest service he had ever traveled by. He began to grumble the moment he got into the train.

"It crawls," he said; "and it absolutely has the cheek to call itself an express."

But Nora, with her head out of the window, was shouting to Jerry, who came toward her full of blessings, anxious to shake her purty white hand, and telling her that he was as glad as a shower of gould to have her back again in the old country.

At last, however, the slow, very slow journey came to an end; and just after sunset the party found themselves at the little wayside station. Here a sight met Nora's eyes which displeased her exceedingly. Instead of the old outside car which her father used to drive, with the shabby old retainer, whose livery had long ago seen its best days, there arrived a smart groom, in the newest of livery, with a cockade in his hat. He touched his hat respectfully to Mr. Hartrick, and gave a quick glance round at Nora and Molly.

"Is the brougham outside, Dennis?" was Mr. Hartrick's response.

"Yes, sir; it has been waiting for half an hour; the train is a bit late, as usual, sir."

"You need not tell me that this train is ever in time," said Mr. Hartrick. "Well, girls, come along; I told Dennis to meet us, and here we are."

Molly thought nothing at all of the neat brougham, with its pair of spirited grays; she was accustomed to driving in the better-class of carriage all her life; but Nora turned first pale and then crimson. She got into the carriage, and sat back in a corner; tears were brimming to her eyes.

"This is the first. How am I to bear all the rest?" she said to herself.

Mr. Hartrick, who had hoped that Nora would be pleased with the brougham, with Dennis himself, with the whole very stylish get-up, was mortified at her silence, and, taking her hand, tried to draw her out.

"Well, little girl," he said, "I hope you will like the improvements I have made in the Castle. I have done it all at your instigation, remember."

"At my instigation?" cried Nora. "Oh, no, Uncle George, that you have not."

He looked at her in some amazement, then closed his lips, and said nothing more. Molly longed to get her father alone, in order to explain Nora's peculiar conduct.

"It is difficult for an Englishman to understand her," thought Molly. "I do, and I think her altogether charming; but father, who has gone to this enormous expense and trouble, will be put out if she does not show a little gratitude. I will tell her that she must; I will take the very first opportunity."

And now they were turning in at the well-known gates. These gates were painted white, whereas they had been almost reduced to their native wood. The avenue was quite tidy, no weeds anywhere; but Nora almost refused to look out. One by one the familiar trees seemed to pass by her as she was bowled rapidly along in the new brougham, as if they were so many ghosts saying good-by. But then there was the roar—the real, real, grand roar—of the Atlantic in her ears. No amount of tidiness, nothing could ever alter that sound.

"Oh, hurrah for the sea!" she said. She flung down the window and popped out her head.

Mr. Hartrick nodded to Molly. "She will see a great deal more to delight her than just the old ocean," he said.

Molly was silent. They arrived at the house; the butler was standing on the steps, a nice, stylish-looking Englishman, in neat livery. He came down, opened the carriage door, let down the steps, and offered his arm to Nora to alight; but she pushed past him, bounded up the steps, and the next moment found herself in her mother's arms.

"How do you do, my dear Nora?" said Mrs. O'Shanaghgan. "I am glad to see you, dear, but also surprised. You acted in your usual headstrong fashion."

"Oh, another time, mother. Mummy, how are you? I am glad to see you again; but don't scold me now; just wait. I'll bear it all patiently another time. How is the dad, mummy?—how is the dad?"

"Your father is doing nicely, Nora; there was not the slightest occasion for you to hurry off and give such trouble and annoyance."

"I don't suppose I have given annoyance to father," said Nora. "Where is he—in his old room?"

"No; we moved him upstairs to the best bedroom. We thought it the wisest thing to do; he was in considerable pain."

"The best bedroom? Which is the best bedroom?" said Nora. "Your room, mummy?"

"The room next to mine, darling. And just come and have a look at the drawing room, Nora."

"I will go to father first," said Nora. "Don't keep me; I can't stay."

She forgot Molly; she forgot her uncle; she even forgot her mother. In a moment she was bounding upstairs over those thick Axminster carpets—those awful carpets, into which her feet sank—down a corridor, also heavily lined with Axminster, past great velvet curtains, which seemed to stifle her as she pushed them aside, and the next instant she had burst open a door.

In the old days this room had been absolutely destitute of furniture. In the older days again it had been the spare room of Castle O'Shanaghgan. Here hospitality had reigned; here guests of every degree had found a hearty welcome, an invitation to stay as long as they pleased, and the best that the Castle could afford for their accommodation. When Nora had left O'Shanaghgan, the only thing that had remained in the old room was a huge four-poster. Even the mattress from this old bed had been removed; the curtains had been taken from the windows; the three great windows were bare of both blinds and curtains. Now a soft carpet covered the entire floor; a neat modern Albert bed stood in a recess; there were heavy curtains to the windows, and Venetian blinds, which were so arranged as to temper the light. But the light of the sunset had already faded, and it was twilight when Nora popped her wild, excited little face round the door.

In the bed lay a gaunt figure, unshaven, with a beard of a week's growth. Two great eyes looked out of caverns, then two arms were stretched out, and Nora was clasped to her father's breast.

"Ah, then, I have you again; may God be praised for all His mercies," said the Squire in a great, deep hoarse voice.

Nora lay absolutely motionless for nearly half a minute in his arms, then she raised herself.

"Ah," she said, "that was good. I hungered for it."

"And I also hungered for it, my darling," said the Squire. "Let me look at you, Light o' the Morning; get a light somehow, and let me see your bonny, bonny, sweet, sweet face."

"Ah, there's a fire in the grate," said Nora. "Are there any matches?"

"Matches, bedad!" said the Squire; "there's everything that's wanted. It's perfectly horrible. They are in a silver box, too, bedad! What do we want with it? Twist up a bit of paper, do, Nora, like a good girl, and light the glim the old way."

Nora caught at her father's humor at once. She had already flung off her hat and jacket.

"To be sure I will," she said, "and with all the heart in the world." She tore a long strip from the local paper, which was lying on a chair near by, twisted it, lit it in the fire, and then applied it to a candle.

"Only light one candle, for the love of heaven, child," said the Squire. "I don't want to see too many of the fal-lals. Now then, that's better; bring the light up to the bed. Oh, what I have suffered with curtains, and carpets, and —-"

"It's too awful, father," said Nora.

"That's it, child. That's the first cheery word I have heard for the last six weeks—too awful I should think it is. They are smothering me between them, Nora. I shall never get up and breathe the free air again; but when you came in you brought a breath of air with you."

"Let's open the window. There's a gale coming up, We'll have some air," said Nora.

"Why, then, Light o' the Morning, they say I'll get bronchitis if the window is opened."

"They! Who are they?" said Nora, with scorn.

"Why, you wouldn't believe it, but they had a doctor down from Dublin to see me. I don't believe he had a scrap of real Irish blood in him, for he said I was to be nursed and messed over, and gruels and all kinds of things brought to my bedside—I who would have liked a fine potato with a pinch of salt better than anything under the sun."

"You'll have your potato and your pinch of salt now that I am back," said Nora. "I mean to be mistress of this room."

The Squire gave a laugh.

"Isn't it lovely to hear her?" he said. "Don't it do me a sight of good? There, open the window wide, Nora, before your mother comes in. Oh, your mother is as pleased as Punch, and for her sake I'd bear a good deal; but I am a changed man. The old times are gone, never to return. Call this place Castle O'Shanaghgan. It may be suitable for an English nobleman to live in, but it's not my style; it's not fit for an Irish squire. We are free over here, and we don't go in for luxuries and smotherations."

"Ah, father, I had to go through a great deal of that in England," said Nora. "It's awful to think that sort of life has come here; but there—there's the window wide open. Do you feel a bit of a breeze, dad?"

"To be sure I do; let me breathe it in. Prop me up in bed, Nora. They said I was to lie flat on my back, but, bedad! I won't now that you have come back."

Nora pushed some pillows under her father, and sat behind him to support him, and at last she got him to sit up in bed with his face turned to the wide-open window.

The blinds were rattling, the curtains were being blown into the room, and the soft, wild sound of the sea fell on his ears.

"Ah, I'm better now," he said; "my lungs are cleared at bit. You had best shut the window before your lady-mother comes in. And put the candle so that I can't see the fal-lals too much," he continued; "but place it so that I can gaze at your bonny face."

"You must tell me how you were hurt, father, and where."

"Bedad! then, I won't—not to-night. I want to have everything as cheerful as possible to-night. My little girl has come back—the joy of my heart, the light of my eyes, the top of the morning, and I'm not going to fret about anything else."

"You needn't—you needn't," said Nora. "Oh! it is good to see you again. There never was anybody like you in all the world. And you were longing for Nora?"

"Now, don't you be fishing."

"But you were—wern't you?"

"To be sure—to be sure. Here, then, let me grip hold of your little hand. I never saw such a tiny little paw. And so they haven't made a fine English lady of you?"

"No, not they," said Nora.

"And you ran away to see your old dad? Why, then, you have the spirit of the old O'Shanaghgans in you."

"Horses would not have kept me from you," said Nora.

"I might have known as much. How I laughed when your mother brought in the telegram from your Aunt Grace this morning! And weren't they in a fuss, and wasn't your Uncle George as cross as he could be, and your mother rampaging up and down the room until I said, 'If you want to bring on the fever, you'll go on like that, Ellen; and then she went out, and I heard her talking to your uncle in the passage. Clap, clap went their tongues. I never knew anything like English people; they never talk a grain of anything amusing; that's the worst of it. Why, it's the truth I'm telling you, darling; I haven't had a hearty laugh since you left home. I'll do fine now. When they were out of the room didn't I give way! I gave two loud guffaws, that I did, when I thought of the trick you had played them. Ah, you're a true daughter of the old race!"

Nora nestled up to her father, squeezing his hand now and then, and looking into his face.

"We'll have a fine time to-morrow, and the next day, and the next day, and the next," she said. "Oh! I am determined to be near you. But isn't there one little place in the house left bare, father, where we can go and have a happy moment?"

"Never a square inch," said the Squire, looking at her solemnly. "It's too awful; even the attics have been cleared out and put in order, for the servants, forsooth! says your Uncle George."

"What do we want so many retainers for? I am sure, now, if they would take a good houseful of some of the poor villagers and plant them up in those attics, there would be some sense in it."

"Oh, Nora, couldn't we get a bit of a place just like the old place, all to ourselves?"

"I'll think it over," said Nora; "we'll manage somehow. We can't stand feather-beds for ever and ever, father."

"Hark to her," said the Squire; "you're a girl after my own heart, Light o' the Morning, and it's glad I am to see you, and to have you back again."

CHAPTER XXIX
ALTERATIONS

While Nora and her father were talking together there came a sound of a ponderous gong through the house.

"What's that?" said Nora, starting.

"You may well ask 'What's that?'" replied the Squire. "It's the dinner-gong. There's dinner now in the evening, bedad! and up to seven courses, by the same token. I sat out one or two of them; but, bless my soul! I couldn't stand too much of that sort of thing. You had best go and put on something fine. Your mother dresses in velvet and silk and jewels for dinner. She looks wonderful; she is a very fine woman indeed, is your mother. I am as proud as Punch of her; but, all the same, it is too much to endure every day. She is dressed for all the world as though she were going to a ball at the Lord-Lieutenant's in Dublin. It's past standing; but you had best go down and join 'em, Norrie."

"Not I. I am going to stay here," said Nora.

"No, no, darling pet; you had best go down, enjoy your dinner, and come back and tell me about it. It will be fun to hear your description. You mimic 'em as much as you like, Norrie; take 'em off. Now, none of your coaxing and canoodling ways; off you go. You shall come back later on, and tell me all about it. Oh, they are stiff and stately, and they'll never know you and I are laughing at 'em up our sleeves. Now, be off with you."

So, unwillingly, Nora went. In the corridor outside she met her cousin Molly.

"Why, you haven't begun to dress yet," said Molly; "and I'm going down to dinner."

"Bother dress!" said Nora. "I am home again. Mother can't expect me to dress." She rushed past her cousin. She was too excited to have any sympathy then with English Molly. She ran up to her own room, and stood with a sense of dismay on the threshold. It had always been a beautiful room, with its noble proportions and its splendid view; and it was now furnished exquisitely as well.

Mrs. O'Shanaghgan had great taste. She had taken immense pains with Nora's room; had thought it all out, and got it papered and painted after a scheme of color of her own. The furniture was of light wood—the room was fit to be the bower of a gracious and lovely maiden; there were new books in the little bookcase hanging up by the bedside. Everything was new and everything was beautiful. There was no sense of bad taste about the room; it was furnished harmoniously.

Nora stood and gazed at it, and her heart sank.

"Oh! it is kind of mother; it is beautiful," she said to herself; "but am I never, never, never to lie down in the little old bed again? Am I never to pour water out of the cracked old jug? Am I never to look at myself in the distorted glass? Oh, dear! oh, dear! how I did love looking at myself in the old glass, which made one cheek much more swollen than the other, and one eyebrow went up a quarter of an inch above the other, and my mouth was a little crooked! It is perfectly horrid to know one's self all one's life long with a swollen cheek and a crooked mouth, and then see classical features without a scrap of fun in them. Oh, dear! But I suppose I had best get ready."

So Nora washed her face and hands, and ran downstairs. The dining room looked heavy and massive, and the footman and the butler attended noiselessly; and Mr. Hartrick at the foot of the table and Mrs. O'Shanaghgan at the head looked as stately a pair as could be found in the length and breadth of the land.

Molly, nicely dressed in her dinner-frock, was quite in keeping with the elder pair; but wild Nora, still wearing her gray traveling-dress, felt herself out of place. Her cheeks were flushed with the excitement of seeing her father; her hair was wild and disarranged. Mrs. O'Shanaghgan looked at her all over with marked disapproval.

"Why, she looks scarcely pretty," thought the mother to herself. "How tired and fagged she appears! Dear, dear! if after all the trouble I have gone to, Nora disappoints me in this way, life will really not be worth living."

But Mrs. O'Shanaghgan could scarcely suppress the joy which was now filling her life. She was the mistress of a noble home; she was at the head of quite the finest establishment in the county. Already all the best county folk had called upon her several times.

It is sad to state that these great and rich people had rather neglected the lady of the Castle during the last few years; but now that she drove about behind a pair of horses, that her house was refurnished, that wealth seemed to have filled all her coffers, she was certainly worth attending to.

"Now that you have come back, Nora," said her mother in the course of the meal, "I wish to say that I have several invitations for you, and that Molly can accept too." She looked with kindness at Molly, who, if only Nora had been happy, would have thoroughly enjoyed herself.

"I must show you the drawing room after dinner, my dear," said her mother. "It is really a magnificent room. And I must also show you my morning room, and the library, and your father's smoking room."

"This is a splendid house, you know, Ellen," said Mr. Hartrick to his sister, "and pays for doing up. Why, a house like this in any habitable part of England would fetch a colossal fortune."

Nora sighed and shrugged her shoulders. Molly glanced at her, and the word "Jehoshaphat!" was almost trembling on her lips. She kept it back, however; she was wonderfully on her good behavior to-night. At last the long and dreary meal came to an end. Nora could scarcely suppress her yawns of utter weariness. She began to think of nothing but lying down, shutting her eyes, and going into a long and dreamless slumber.

Mrs. O'Shanaghgan rose from the table and sailed out of the room. A footman flung open the door for her, and Nora and Molly followed in her wake.

"I'll be with you presently in the drawing room, Ellen," said Mr. Hartrick to his sister; "but first of all I'll just go up and have a smoke with O'Shanaghgan. You found your father much better to-night, did you not, Nora?"

"I thought father looked very bad indeed," said Nora. She could not add another word; she went out into the hall.

Mrs. O'Shanaghgan took her hand, squeezing it up in a tight pressure.

"You ought not to speak in that tone to your uncle," she said; "you can never, never know all that he has done for us. He is the noblest, the most generous, the best man in the world."

"Oh, I know all that, mother; I know all that," said Nora. She did not add, "But for me he would never have done it. It was I who inserted the thin edge of the wedge." Her tone was gentle; her mother looked at her with a softening of her own face.

"Well, dear," she said, "your Uncle George has taken a great fancy to you. Notwithstanding your eccentricities, Nora—and they are considerable—he says you have the making of a fine girl. But come, we must not neglect your cousin. Come here, dear Molly; you and Nora will be interested in seeing what a beautiful place Castle O'Shanaghgan is now."

Molly took hold of Nora's other hand, and they entered the drawing room. It was lit with soft candles in many sconces; the blinds were down; across the windows were drawn curtains of Liberty silk of the palest, softest shade of rose. On the floor was a carpet of many soft colors cunningly mingled. The walls were painted a pale artistic green, large mirrors were introduced here and there, and old family portraits, all newly framed, of dead and gone O'Shanaghgans, hung on the painted walls. There were new tables, knick-knacks—all the various things which constitute the drawing room of an English lady.

Nora felt for one brief, passionate, angry moment that she was back again at The Laurels; but then, seeing the light in her mother's eyes, the pink flush of happiness on her cheeks, she restrained herself.

"It makes you happy, mummy," she said, "and——"

"But what do you think of it, my darling?"

"It is a very beautiful room."

"Ah! that is right. I thought my little wildflower would appreciate all these things when she came back again. Ah, Nora! you have been a naughty, wild imp; but your father was delighted when he heard what you had done. Of course I am terribly angry."

"No, you are not, mummy; you are pleased to see me again."

"I am glad to have you back, Nora; but as to being pleased, how could I be? However, you can stay here for a fortnight or so now that you have come; and then, when your dear uncle leaves us, you and Molly can go back with him."

Nora did not say anything; but a stubborn look came into her face which her mother knew of old.

From the drawing room they went to the library, which had also undergone complete rejuvenation. The walls were laden with standard works of different kinds; but some of the shelves were still empty.

"The old books, your uncle says, were of great value," said Mrs. O'Shanaghgan, "and he sent them all to Dublin to be rebound. They have not come back yet. They are to be bound in old calf, and will suit the rest of the room. Is it not a magnificent apartment?"

Nora said "Yes" in a somewhat dreamy voice.

They then went to her mother's morning-room, and then on to the Squire's smoking-room.

"They might at least have left this alone," thought the girl. "They might at least have left this one room, where he could retire when he felt quite choked by all the furniture in the rest of the place."

But even the Squire's smoking-room was changed into the smoking-room of an English gentleman. There were deep easy-chairs covered with leather; there were racks for pipes, and great brass dogs before the fireplace; on the floor was a thick carpet. Nora felt as if she longed to give it a savage kick.

At last the terrible ordeal of going through the—to her, utterly ruined— house was over, and she and Molly found themselves alone.

"I will go up to your father for a few minutes," said Mrs. O'Shanaghgan, nodding to Nora. "You and your cousin will like to have a chat; and then, my dears, I should recommend you both to go to bed as early as possible."

When they were back again in the big drawing room Nora gave Molly a wild look.

"Come out," she said; "at least out of doors the air is the same as of old."

Molly caught up a shawl and wrapped it round her head; but Nora went out just as she was.

"You'll catch cold," said English Molly.

"I catch cold in my native land!" replied Irish Nora. "How little you know me! Oh, come, Molly, I am going to be wild; I am going to give way."

They both stepped outside on the broad gravel sweep. The moon was up, and it was shining over everything. In the moonlight Castle O'Shanaghgan looked very much as it had done before. The moon had always glorified the old place, and it glorified it still. Nora stood and gazed around her; up to the tops of the mountains, with their dark summits clearly defined against the evening sky; across the wide breadth of the Atlantic; over the thick plantations, the fields, and the huge trees in the background.

"It's all the same," she said, with a glad laugh; "thank God it is all the same. Even your father, Molly, cannot destroy the place outside, at least."

"Oh Nora, it is such a lovely, lovely place!" said Molly. "Cannot you be happy in it with its modern dress?"

"Happy," said Nora, suddenly brought back to her sense of misery by the word. "I am thankful that my father is not so ill; but—but you must help, Molly. Promise that you will."

"I am sure I'd do anything in the world," said Molly. "I think I have been very good to-day. I have kept in my naughty words, Jehoshaphat and Moses and Elephants, and all the rest. What do you want me to do, Nora?"

"We must get him out of that room," said Nora.

"Him? You mean your father?"

"Yes; he will never recover there. I have been thinking and thinking, and I'll have my plan ready by the morning; only you must help me. I'll get Hannah Croneen to come in, and we'll do it between us if you can help me."

"But what is it?" said Molly.

"I'll tell you in the morning; you wait and see."

CHAPTER XXX
THE LION IN HIS CAGE

The Squire was better, and not better. He had received a very nasty flesh-wound in the thigh; but the bullet had been extracted. There was not the slightest clew to the identity of his would-be murderer. The Squire himself had said nothing. He had been found almost bleeding to death by the roadside; the alarm had been given, and in terror and consternation his own tenants had brought him home.

The Squire could have said a good deal, but he said nothing. The police came and asked him questions, but he kept his lips closed.

"I didn't see the man," he said after a pause. "Somebody fired, of course; but I can't tell who, for I saw no one; it was from behind the hedge. Why the scoundrel who wanted to do for me didn't shoot a little higher up puzzles me. But there, let it rest—let it rest."

And the neighbors and the country had to let it rest, for there was no evidence against anyone. Amongst those who came to inquire after the Squire was Andy Neil. He came often, and was full of commiseration, and loudly cursed the brute who had very nearly done for his old landlord. But the neighbors had suspicions with regard to Andy, for he had been turned out of his cot in the mountains, and was living in the village now. They scowled at him when he passed, and turned aside; and his own face looked more miserable than ever. Still, he came daily up to the big kitchen to inquire for the Squire.

The doctor said there was no reason whatever why Mr. O'Shanaghgan should not get quite well. He was by no means old—not more than fifty; there was not the slightest occasion for a break-down, and yet, to all appearance, a break-down there was. The Squire got morose; he hardly ever smiled; even Nora's presence scarcely drew a hearty guffaw from his lips. The doctors were puzzled.

"What can be wrong?" they said. But Nora herself knew very well what was wrong. She and her father were the only ones who did know. She knew that the old lion was dying in captivity; that he was absolutely succumbing to the close and smothered life which he was now leading. He wanted the free air of his native mountains; he wanted the old life, now gone for ever, back again.

"It is true the place is saved, Norrie," he said once to his daughter, "and I haven't a word to say. I would be the most ungrateful dog in existence if I breathed a single word of complaint. The place is saved; and though it nominally belongs now to your Uncle George, to all intents and purposes it is my place, and he gives me to understand that at my death it goes to my boy. Yes, he has done a noble deed, and of course I admire him immensely."

"And so do I, father," said Nora; but she looked thoughtful and troubled; and one day, after she had been in her father's room for some time, when she met her uncle in the avenue she spoke to him.

"Well, my dear girl," he said, "what about coming back with me to England when I go next week?"

"It is not to be thought of, Uncle George. How can I leave my father while he is ill?"

"That is true. I have been thinking about him. The doctors are a little distressed at his growing weakness. They cannot quite understand it. Tonics have been given to him and every imaginable thing has been done. He wants for nothing; his nourishment is of the best; still he makes no way. It is puzzling."

"I don't think so," said Nora.

"What do you mean, my dear girl?"

"You might do all that sort of thing for an eagle, you know," said Nora, raising her clear eyes and fixing them on her uncle's face. "You might give him everything in his prison, much more than he had when he was free; but, all the same, he would pine and—and he would die." Tears rose to the girl's eyes; she dashed them away.

"My dear little Nora, I don't in the least see the resemblance," said Mr. Hartrick, who felt, and perhaps justly, rather nettled. "You seem to imply by your words that I have done your father an injury when I secured the home of his ancestors for him."

"Oh, forgive me, Uncle George," said Nora. "I don't really mean to say anything against you, for you are just splendid."

Mr. Hartrick did not reply; he looked puzzled and thoughtful. Nora, after a moment's silence, spoke again.

"I am most grateful to you. I believe you have done what is best—at least what you think best. You have made my mother very happy, and

Terence will be so pleased; and the tenants—oh! they will get their rights now, their cabins will be repaired, the roofs mended, the windows put in fresh, the little gardens stocked for them. Oh, yes, you are behaving most generously. Anyone would suppose the place belonged to you."

"Which it does," muttered Mr. Hartrick under his breath.

"You have made a great many people happy, only somehow—somehow it is not quite the way to make my father happy, and it is not the way to make me happy. But I have nothing more to say, except that I cannot leave my father now."

"You must come to us after Christmas, then," said Mr. Hartrick. "I must go back next week, and I shall probably take Molly with me."

"Oh! leave her with me here," said Nora suddenly. "I do wish you would; the air here is so healthy. Do let her stay, and then perhaps after Christmas, when things are different, we might both go back."

"Of course things will be different," said Mr. Hartrick. "A new doctor is coming to see your father next week, and he will probably change the *régime*; he may order him fresh air, and before long we shall have him strong and well amongst us again. He has absolutely nothing wrong except——"

"Except that he has everything wrong," said Nora.

"Well, well, my dear child, I will think over your suggestion that Molly should stay with you; and in the meantime remember that we are all coming to O'Shanaghgan for Christmas."

"All of you!" said Nora in dismay.

"Yes, all of us. Your aunt has never spent a real old-fashioned Christmas in her life, and I mean her to have it this year. I shall bring over some of our English habits to this place. We will roast an ox whole, and have huge bonfires, and all kinds of things, and the tenantry shall have a right good time. There, Nora, you smile; that pleases you."

"You are so kind," she said. She clasped his hands in both of hers, and then turned away.

"There never was anyone kinder," thought the girl to herself; "but all the same he does not understand." She re-entered the house and went up to her father's room.

The Squire was lying on his back. The days were now getting short, for November had begun. There was a big fire in the grate; the Squire panted in the hot room.

"Just come in here," he said to Nora. "Don't make much noise; lock the door—will you, pet?"

Nora obeyed.

"Now fling the window wide open; let me get a breath of air."

Nora did open the window, but the air was moist and damp from the Atlantic, and even she, fearless as she was, hesitated when she heard her father's cough.

"There, child, there," he said; "it's the lungs beginning to work properly again. Now then, you can shut it up; I hear a step. For Heaven's sake, Nora, be quick, or your mother may come in, and won't she be making a fuss! There, unlock the door."

"But you are worse, father; you are worse."

"What else can you expect? They don't chain up wild animals and expect them to get well. I never lived through anything of this sort before, and it's just smothering me."

Mrs. O'Shanaghgan entered the room.

"Patrick," she said, "would you like some sweetbread and a bit of pheasant for your dinner?"

"Do you know what I'd like?" roared the Squire. "A great big mealy potato, with a pinch of salt."

Mrs. O'Shanaghgan uttered a sigh, and the color rushed into her pale cheeks.

"Upon my word," she said, "you are downright vulgar."

The Squire gave a feeble guffaw. Nora's heart beat as she noticed how feeble it was. She left the room, because she could not stay there another moment. The time had come to act. She had hesitated long, but she would hesitate no longer. She ran downstairs. The first person she saw was Molly.

"Well," said Molly, "how is he?"

"Very bad indeed," said Nora; "there's not a moment to lose. Something must be done, and quickly."

"What can be done?"

"Come out with me; I have a thought in my head."

Nora and Molly went outside. They crossed the avenue, went along the plantation at the back, and soon found themselves in the huge yard which flanked the back of the house. In a distant part of the yard was a barn, and this barn Nora now entered. It was untidy; the doors fitted badly; the floor was of clay. It was quite empty.

Nora gave a sigh of relief.

"I dreamed of this barn last night," she said. "I think it is the very place."

"For what, Nora; for what?"

"I am going to have father moved here to-day."

"Nora, what nonsense you are talking! You will kill him."

"Save his life, you mean," said Nora. "I am going to get a bedstead, a straw paillasse, and an old hard mattress, and I am going to have them put here; and we'll get a bit of tarpaulin to put on the floor, to prevent the damp coming up; and I'll put a curtain across this window so that he needn't have too much draught, the darling; and there shall be nothing else in the room except a wooden table. He shall have his potatoes and salt, and his bit of salt bacon, if he wishes, and he shall have his great big bare room. I tell you what it is, Molly, he'll never get well unless he is brought here."

"What a girl you are! But how will you do it?"

"Leave it to me. Do you mind driving with me on the outside car as far as Cronane?"

"The outside car? I have never been on it yet."

"Oh, come along; I'll introduce you to the sweetest conveyance in the world."

Nora's spirits rose at the thought of immediate action.

"Won't it surprise and delight him?" she said. She went up to one of the grooms. He was an English groom, and was somewhat surprised at the appearance of the young lady in the yard.

"What can I do for you, miss?" he said.

"I want Angus," answered Nora. "Where is he?"

Angus was one of the few old Irish servants who were still left at Castle O'Shanaghgan. He now came forward in a sheepish kind of way; but when he saw Nora his face lit up.

"Put one of the horses to the outside car at once—Black Bess if you can," said Nora.

"Yes, miss," said the man, "with all the pleasure in life."

"Don't take it round to the front door. Miss Molly and I want to drive to Cronane. You needn't come with us, Angus; just put the horse to, and I'll drive myself."

Accordingly, in less than ten minutes' time the two girls were driving in the direction of Cronane. Molly, brave as she was, had some difficulty in keeping on. She clung to the sides of the car and panted.

"Nora, as sure as Jehoshaphat and Elephants, I'll be flung out on to the highroad!" cried Molly.

"Sit easy and nothing will happen," said Nora, who was seated comfortably herself at the other side and was driving with vigor.

Presently they reached Cronane, which looked just as dilapidated as ever.

"Oh, the darling place! Isn't it a relief to see it?" said Nora. "Don't I love that gate off its hinges! It's a sight for sore eyes—that it is."

They dashed up the avenue and stopped before the hall door.

Standing on the steps—where, indeed, he spent most of his time—and indulging in the luxury of an old church-warden pipe, was Squire Murphy. He raised a shout when he saw Nora, and ran down the steps as fast as he could.

"Why, my bit of a girl, it's good to see you!" he cried. "And who is this young lady?"

"This is my cousin, Molly Hartrick. Molly, may I introduce you to Squire Murphy?"

"Have a grip of the paw, miss," said Squire Murphy, holding out his great hand and clasping Molly's.

"And now, what can I do for you, Nora alannah? 'Tis I that am glad to see you. There's Biddy in the house, and the wife; they'll give you a hearty welcome, and no mistake. You come along right in, the pair of yez; come right in."

"But I cannot," said Nora. "I want to speak to you alone and at once. Can you get one of the boys to hold the horse?"

"To be sure. Dan, you spalpeen! come forward this minute. Now then, hold Black Bess, and look alive, lad. Well, Nora, what is it?"

Molly stood on the gravel sweep, Nora and the Squire walked a few paces away.

"It's this," said Nora; "you haven't asked yet how father is."

"But he is doing fine, they tell me. I see I'm not wanted at O'Shanaghgan; and I'm the last man in the world to go there when the cold shoulder is shown to me."

"Oh! they would never mean that," said Nora, in distress.

"Oh, don't they mean it, my dear? Haven't I been up to the Castle day after day, and asking for the Squire with my heart in my mouth, and ready to sit by his side and to colleague with him about old times, and raise a laugh in him, and smoke with him; and haven't I been repelled?—the Squire not well enough to see me; madam herself not at home. Oh, I know their ways. When you were poor at O'Shanaghgan, then Squire Murphy was wanted; but now that you're rich, Squire Murphy can go his own way for aught you care."

"It is not true, Mr. Murphy," said the girl, her bright blue eyes filling with tears. "Oh!" she added, catching his hand impulsively, "don't I know it all? But it's not my father's fault; he would give the world to see you—he shall see you. Do you know why he is ill?"

"Why so, Nora? Upon my word, you're a very handsome girl, Nora."

"Oh, never mind about my looks now. My father is ill because—because of all the luxury and the riches."

"Bedad, then, I'm glad to hear it," said the Squire of Cronane. He slapped his thigh loudly. "It's the best bit of news I have heard this many a day; it surprised me how he could put up with it. And it's killing him?"

"That's about it," said Nora. "He must be rescued."

"I'll do what I can," said Squire Murphy. "Will you do this? Will you this very day get out the long cart and have an old bedstead put into it, and an old paillasse and an old mattress; and will you see that it is taken over this very afternoon to O'Shanaghgan? I'll be there, and the bedstead shall be put up in the old barn, and father shall sleep in the barn to-night, and you and I, Squire, and Hannah Croneen, and Molly, will help to move him while the rest of the family are at tea."

The Squire stared at Nora so long after she had made these remarks that she really thought he had taken leave of his senses; then he burst into a great loud laugh, clapped his hand to his side, and wrung Nora's until she thought he would wring it off. Then he turned back to the house, walking so fast that Nora had to run after him. But she knew that she had found her ally, and that her father would be saved.

CHAPTER XXXI
RELEASE OF THE CAPTIVE

All Nora's wishes were carried into effect. The long cart was got out. An old mattress was secured, also an old bedstead. The mattress happened to be well aired, for, indeed, it was one on which the Squire himself had slept the previous night; but, as he remarked, he would gladly give the bed from under him for the sake of his old friend O'Shanaghgan.

Molly helped, also Biddy and Nora, in all the preparations, and at last the three girls jumped upon the outside car and returned to O'Shanaghgan. Biddy felt that she was anything but welcome. She was certainly not looking her best. Her dress was of the shabbiest, and her turned-up nose looked more celestial than ever. Molly was gazing at her just as if she were a sort of curiosity, and finally Biddy resented this close scrutiny, and turned to Nora, grasping her by the hand.

"Tell her," said Biddy, "that it is very rude to stare in that sort of stolid way. If she were an Irish girl she would give a flashing glance and then look away again; but that way of staring full and stiff puts a body out. Tell her it is not true Irish manners."

"Oh, Jehoshaphat!" exclaimed Molly, "I hear you both whispering together. What is it all about? I am nearly wild trying to keep myself on this awful car, and I know you are saying something not in my favor."

"We are that," cried Biddy; "we are just wishing you would keep your English manners to yourself."

Molly flushed rather indignantly.

"I did not know that I was doing anything," she said.

"Why, then," cried Biddy, "is it nothing when you are bringing the blushes to my cheeks and the palpitation to my heart; and is it nothing to be, as it were, exposed to the scorn of the English? Why, then, bedad! I have got my nose from the old Irish kings, from whom I am descended, as true as true. Blue is my blood, and I am as proud of my ancestry as if I was Queen Victoria herself. I see that you have neat, straight features; but you have not got a scrap of royal blood in you—now, have you?"

"I don't think so," answered Molly, laughing in spite of herself. "Well, if it offends you, I will try not to look at you again."

The drive came to an end, and Nora entered the big, splendidly furnished hall, accompanied by Molly and Biddy. Mrs. O'Shanaghgan happened to be standing there. She came hurriedly forward.

"My dear Nora," she began, but then her eyes fell upon Biddy. Her brows went up with a satirical action; she compressed her lips and kept back a sigh of annoyance.

"How do you do, Miss Murphy?" she said.

"I am fine, thank you kindly, ma'am," replied Biddy; "and it is sorry I am that I had not time to change my dress and put on the pink one with the elegant little flounces that my aunt sent me from Dublin."

"Oh, your present dress will do very well," said Mrs. O'Shanaghgan, suppressing an internal shudder at the thought of Biddy at the renovated Castle of O'Shanaghgan in her dirty pink dress with the flounces.

"But, Miss Murphy," she continued, "I am sorry that I cannot ask you to stay. The Squire is too unwell to admit of our having friends at present."

"Oh, glory!" cried Biddy, "and how am I to get back again? Why, it was on your own outside car that I came across country, and I cannot walk all the way back to Cronane. Oh, but what a truly beautiful house! I never saw anything like it. Why, it is a sort of palace!"

Biddy's open admiration of the glories of O'Shanaghgan absolutely made the good mistress of the mansion smile. Mrs. O'Shanaghgan felt that Nora did not really care for the beautiful place—the grandly furnished rooms had brought no enthusiasm or delight to her heart. Nora had tried very hard to keep in her real feelings; but her mother was quite sharp enough to know what they were. There was little pleasure in taking a girl round rooms, corridors, and galleries when she was only forcing herself to say pretty things which she did not feel. Molly, of course, had always lived in a beautiful and well-furnished house; therefore there was nothing exciting in showing her the present magnificence of O'Shanaghgan, and half Mrs. O'Shanaghgan's pleasure was showing the place in its now regal state to her friends. Biddy's remark, therefore, was most fortunate. Even wild, unkempt, untaught Irish Biddy was better than no one.

"I tell you what it is," said the good lady, with quite a gracious expression stealing over her features, "if you will promise to walk softly, and not to make any loud remarks, I will take you through the suite of drawing rooms and the big dining room and my morning room; but you must promise to be very quiet if I give you this great pleasure."

"And it is glad I'll be, and as mum as a mouse. I'll hold my hands to my heart, and keep in everything; but, oh, Mrs. O'Shanaghgan, if I am fit to burst now and then, you will let me run to the window and give a big sigh? It is all I'll ask, to relieve myself; but mum's the word for everything else."

On these terms Mrs. O'Shanaghgan conducted her unwelcome guest through the rooms, and after a brief tour Biddy joined her companions in the yard. Nora was busy sweeping out the barn herself, and, with the aid of Hannah Croneen and Molly, was already beginning to put it to rights. Biddy was now free to join the other conspirators, and the girls quickly became friends under these conditions.

Hannah proved herself a most valuable ally. She whisked about, dashing here and there, raising a whirlwind of dust, but, in Nora's opinion, effecting wonders. Angus also was drawn into the midst of the fray. His delight and approval of Nora's scheme was almost beyond bounds.

"Ah, then," he said; "it's this will do the masther good. Oh, then, Miss Nora, it's you that has the 'cute ways."

A tarpaulin was found and laid upon the floor. From Hannah's cottage a small deal table was fetched. A washstand was given by Angus; a cracked basin and jug were further secured; and Nora gave implicit directions with regard to the boiling of the mealy potatoes and the little scrap of bacon on which the Squire was to sup.

"You will bring them in—the potatoes, I mean—in their jackets," said the Irish girl, "and have them hot as hot can be."

"They shall screech, that they shall," replied Hannah; "and the bacon, it shall be done as tasty and sweet as bacon can be. I'll give the last bit of my own little pigeen, with all the heart in the world, for the Squire's supper."

Accordingly, when the long cart arrived from Cronane, accompanied by the Squire and his factotum, Mike, the barn was ready to receive the bedstead, the straw paillasse, and the mattress. Nora managed to convey, from the depths of the Castle, sheets, blankets, pillows, and a counterpane, and everything was in apple-pie order by the time the family was supposed to assemble for afternoon tea. This was the hour that Nora had selected for having the Squire removed from his feather-bed existence to the more breezy life of the barn. It was now the fashion at O'Shanaghgan to make quite a state occasion of afternoon tea. The servants, in their grand livery, were all well to the fore. Mrs. O'Shanaghgan, dressed as became the lady of so beautiful a place, sat in her lovely drawing room to receive her guests;

and the guests came up in many conveyances—some in carriages, some on outside cars, some on dog-carts, some on foot; but, come as they would, they came, day after day, to show their respects to the lady whom now the whole country delighted to honor.

On these occasions Mr. Hartrick sat with his sister, and helped her to entertain her visitors. It had been one of the sore points between Nora and her mother that the former would not appear to afternoon tea. Nora had made her sick father her excuse. On the present occasion she took good care not even to show her face inside the house. But Molly kept watch, just behind the plantation, and soon rushed into the yard to say that the carriages were beginning to appear.

"A curious party have come just now," said Molly, "in such a droll carriage, with yellow wheels and a glass body. It looks like a sort of a Lord Mayor's coach."

"Why, it must be the coach of the O'Rorkes," cried Nora. "Fancy Madam coming to see mother! Why, Madam will scarcely pay a visit to royalty itself. There is no doubt that mother is thought a lot of now. Oh, dear, oh, dear, what a frightfully society life we shall have to lead here in future! But I have no time to think of mother and her friends just now. Squire, will you come upstairs with me to see father? Hannah, please wait down here to be ready to help? Angus, you must also come upstairs, and wait in the passage outside the Squire's room until I send for you."

Having given her directions, Nora entered the house. All was quiet and peaceful. The well trained English servants were, some of them, in the kitchen premises, and some of them attending in the hall and drawing rooms, where the guests were now arriving thick and fast. Nora had chosen her hour well. She entered her father's room, accompanied by Squire Murphy.

The old Squire was lying, half-dozing, in his luxurious bed. The fire had been recently built up. The room felt close.

"Ah, dear!" said Squire Murphy, "it is difficult to breathe here! And how's yourself, O'Shanaghgan, my man? Why, you do look drawn and pulled down. I am right glad to see ye, that I am."

The Squire of Cronane grasped the hand of the Squire of O'Shanaghgan, and the Squire of O'Shanaghgan looked up at the other man's weather-beaten face with a pathetic expression in his deep-set, hawk-like, dark eyes.

"I am bad, Murphy—very bad," said the Squire; "it's killing me they are amongst them."

"Why, then, it looks like it," said Squire Murphy. "I never was in such a smotheration of a place before. Faix, then, why don't you have the window open, and have a bit of air circulating through the room?"

"It's forbid I am," said the Squire. "Ah, Murphy! it's killing me, it's killing me."

"But it shall kill you no longer, father," said Nora. "Oh, father! Squire Murphy and I have made up such a lovely, delicious plan. What would you say to a big, bare room again, father; and a hard bed again, father; and potatoes and a pinch of salt and a little bit of bacon again, father?"

"What would I say?" cried the Squire. "I'd say, glory be to Heaven, and all the Saints be praised; but it is too good luck to be true."

"Not a bit of it," said Squire Murphy; "it is going to be true. You just do what you are bid, and you will be in the hoight of contentment."

The wonder-stricken Squire now had to listen to Nora's plan.

"We have done it," she cried, in conclusion; "the barn is ready. It makes a lovely bedroom; there are no end of draughts, and you'll get well in a jiffy."

"Then let's be quick," said the Squire, "or your lady-mother will be up and prevent me. Hurry, Nora, for Heaven's sake! For the life of me, don't give me a cup of cold water to taste, and then dash it from my lips. If we are not quick, we'll be caught and prevented from going. I am ready; wrap me up in a rug, and carry me out. I am ready and willing. Good-by to feather bed-dom. I don't want ever to see these fal-lals again."

The next few moments were ones of intense excitement; but before ten minutes had elapsed the Squire was lying in the middle of the hard bed, gazing round him with twinkling eyes and a smile on his lips. The appearance of Hannah Croneen, with a dish of steaming potatoes and a piece of boiled bacon, was the final crown to his rapture.

CHAPTER XXXII
ANDY

Are there any words in the language to describe the scene which took place at O'Shanaghgan when Mrs. O'Shanaghgan discovered what Nora had done? She called her brother to her aid; and, visiting the barn in her own august person, her company dress held neatly up so as to display her trim ankles and pretty shoes, solemnly announced that her daughter Nora was guilty of the murder of her own father, and that she, Mrs. O'Shanaghgan, washed her hands of her in the future.

"Yes, Nora," said the irate lady, "you can go your own way from this time. I have done all that a mother could do for you; but your wildness and insubordination are past bearing. This last and final act crowns all. The servants shall come into the barn, and bring your poor father back to his bedroom, and you shall see nothing of him again until the doctor gives leave. Pray, George," continued Mrs. O'Shanaghgan, "send one of the grooms at once for Doctor Talbot. I doubt if my poor husband has a chance of recovery after this mad deed; but we must take what steps we can."

"Now, look here, Ellen," said the Squire; "if you can't be aisy, be as aisy as you can. There's no sort of use in your putting on these high-falutin airs. I was born an Irishman. I opened my eyes on this world in a good, sharp draught, and, if I am to die, it's in a draught I'll leave the world; but, once for all, no more smotherations for me. I've had too much of 'em. You say this child is likely to be the death of me. Why, then, Ellen—God forgive yer ignorance, my poor wife—but it's the life of me she'll be, not the death. Isn't it in comfort I'm lying for the first time since that spalpeen behind the hedge tried to fell me to the earth? Isn't it a good meal I've just had?—potatoes in their jackets, and a taste of fat bacon; and if I can wash it down, as I mean to later on, with a drop of mountain-dew, why, it's well I'll slumber to-night. You're a very fine woman, me lady, and I'm proud as Punch of you, but you don't know how to manage a wild Irishman when he is ill. Now, Nora, bless her pretty heart, saw right through and through me—the way I was being killed by inches; the hot room and the horrid carpets and curtains; and the fire, not even made of decent turf, but those ugly black coals, and never a draught through the chamber, except when I took it unbeknownst to you.

Ah, Nora guessed that her father was dying, and there was no way of saving him but doing it on the sly. Well, I'm here, the girleen has managed it, and here I'll stay. Not all the doctors in the land, nor all the fine English grooms, shall take me back again. I'll walk back when I'm fit to walk, and I'll do my best to bear all that awful furniture; but in future this is my bedroom, and now you know the worst."

The Squire had a great color in his face as he spoke; his eyes were shining as they had not shone since his accident, and his voice was quite strong. Squire Murphy, who was standing near, clapped him on the shoulder.

"Why, Patrick," he said, "it's proud of you I am; you're like your old self again—blest if you're not."

Nora, who was kneeling by her father's bed, kept her face slightly turned away from her mother; the tears were in her eyes, but there was a well of thanksgiving in her heart. In spite of her mother's angry reproaches, she knew she had done the right thing. Her father would get well now. After all, his Irish daughter knew what he wanted, and she must bear her English mother's anger.

In an incredibly short space of time two or three of the men-servants appeared, accompanied by Dr. Talbot. They stood in the entrance to the barn, prepared to carry out orders; but now there stole past them the Irish groom, Angus, and Hannah Croneen. These two came and stood near Nora at the head of the bed. Dr. Talbot examined the patient, looked round the cheerless barn, and said, with a smile, glancing from Mrs. O'Shanaghgan to O'Shanaghgan's own face:

"This will never do; you must get back to your own comfortable room, my dear sir—that is, if I am to continue to attend you."

"Then, for God's sake, leave off attending me, Talbot," said the Squire. "You must be a rare ignoramus not to see that your treatment is killing me out and out. It's fresh air I want, and plenty of it, and no more fal-lals. Is it in my grave you'd have me in a fortnight's time? You get out of this, and leave me to Mother Nature and the nursing of my Irish colleen."

This was the final straw. Mrs. O'Shanaghgan left the barn, looking more erect and more stately even than when she had entered it. Mr. Hartrick followed her, so did the enraged Dr. Talbot, and lastly the English servants. Squire Murphy uttered the one word, "Routed!" and clapped his hand on his thigh.

The Squire, however, spoke sadly.

"I am sorry to vex your lady mother, Nora," he said; "and upon my soul, child, you must get me well as quick as possible. We must prove to her that we are in the right—that we must."

"Have a dhrop of the crayther, your honor," said Hannah, now coming forward. "It's truth I'm telling, but this is me very last bottle of potheen, which I was keeping for me funeral; but there, his honor's wilcome to every drain of it."

"Pour me out a little," said the Squire.

He drank off the spirit, which was absolutely pure and unadulterated, and smacked his lips.

"It's fine I'll be to-night," he said; "it's you that have the 'cute ways, Nora. You have saved me. But, indeed, I thank you all, my friends, for coming to my deliverance."

That night, in her smoke-begrimed cabin, Hannah Croneen described with much unction the way madam and the English doctor had been made to know their place, as she expressed it.

"'Twas himself that put them down," said Hannah. "Ah, but he is a grand man, is O'Shanaghgan."

Mrs. O'Shanaghgan spent a very unhappy night. No comfort could she derive even from Mr. Hartrick's words. Nora was an out-and-out rebel, and must be treated accordingly; and as to the Squire—well, when Nora attended his funeral her eyes might be opened. The good lady was quite certain that the Squire would have developed pneumonia by the morning; but when the reports reached her that he looked heartier and better than he had since his illness, she could scarcely believe her ears. This, however, was a fact, for Mother Nature did step in to cure the Squire; and the draughty barn, with its lack of every ordinary comfort, was so soothing to his soul that it began to have an equally good effect upon his body.

Notwithstanding that it poured rain outside, and that great eddies of wind came from under the badly-fitting doors and in at the cracks of the small windows, the Squire ate his food with appetite, and began once again to enjoy life. In the first place, he was no longer lonely. It was impossible for his old friends and retainers to visit him in the solitude of his grand bedroom; but it was perfectly easy, not only for Squire Murphy and Squire Fitzgerald, and half the other squireens of the neighborhood, to slip into the barn and have a "collogue," as they expressed it; but also the little gossoons in their ragged trousers and bare feet, and the girleens, with their curly hair, and roguish dark-blue eyes, to scuttle in also. For could they not dart under the bed like so many rabbits if madam's step was heard, and didn't the Squire, bless him! like to have them with him when madam was busy with her English friends? Then Nora herself, the darling of his heart, was scarcely ever away from him now. Didn't she sit perched like a bird on the foot of the hard bed and cause him to roar with laughter as she described the English and their ways? Molly, too, became a prime favorite with the Squire. It is sad to relate that he encouraged her in her naughty words, and she began to say "Jehoshaphat!" and "Elephants!" and "Holy Moses!" more frequently than ever.

The grand fact of all, however, was this: the Squire was getting well again.

About a week after his removal to the barn Nora was out rather late by herself. She had been visiting her favorite haunts by the seashore, and was returning laden with seaweeds and shells, when she was startled by hearing her name spoken in a low tone just behind her. The sound issued from a plantation of thick underwood. The girl paused, and her heart beat a little faster.

"Yes. What is it?" she said.

The next moment a long and skinny hand and arm were protruded, Nora's own arm was forcibly taken possession of, and she was dragged, against her will, into the underwood. Her first impulse was to cry out; but being as brave a girl as ever walked, she quickly suppressed this inclination, and turned and faced the ragged and starved-looking man whom she expected to meet.

"Yes, Andy, I knew it was you," said Nora. "What do you want with me now? How dare you speak to me?"

"How dare I! What do you mane by that, Miss Nora?"

"You know what I mean," answered the girl. "Oh, I have been patient and have not said a word; but do you think I did not know? When all the country, Andy Neil, were looking for my father's would-be murderer, I knew where I could put my hand on him. But I did not say a word. If my father had died I must—I must have spoken; but if he recovered, I felt that in me which I cannot describe as pity, but which yet prevented my giving you up to the justice you deserve. But to meet me here, to dare to waylay me—it is too much."

"Ah, when you speak like that you near madden me," replied Andy. "Look at me, Miss Nora; look well; look hard. Here's the skin tight on me arums, and stretched fit to burst over me cheek-bones; and it's empty I am, Miss Nora, for not a bite nor sup have I tasted for twenty-four hours. The neighbors, they 'as took agen me. It has got whispering abroad that it's meself handled the gun that laid the Squire on what might have been his deathbed, and they have turned agen me, and not even a pitaty can I get from 'em, and I can't get work nowhere; and the roof is took off the little bit of a cabin in which I was born, and two of the childers have died from cowld and hunger. That's my portion, Miss Nora; that's my bitter portion; and yet you ashk me, miss, why I spake to ye."

"You know why I said it," answered Nora. "There was a time when I pitied you, but not now. You have gone too far; you have done that which no daughter can overlook. Let me go—let me go; don't attempt to touch me, or I shall scream out. There are neighbors near who will come to my help."

"No, there are not," said Andy. "I 'as took good care of that. You may scream as loud as you please, but no one will hear; and if we go farther into the underwood no one will see. Come, my purty miss; it's my turn now. It's my turn at last. Come along."

Nora was strong and fearless, but she had not Andy's brute strength. With a clutch, now so fierce and desperate that she wondered her arm was not broken, the man, who was half a madman, dragged her deeper into the shade of the underwood.

"There now," said Andy, with a chuckle of triumph; "you has got to listen. You're the light o' his eyes and the darlin' o' his heart. But what o' that? Didn't my childer die of the cowld and the hunger, and the want of a roof over them, and didn't I love them? Ah! that I did. Do you remember the night I said I'd drown ye in the Banshee's pool, and didn't we make a compact that if I let ye go you'd get the Squire to lave me my bit of a cabin, and not to evict me? And how did ye kape your word? Ah, my purty, how did ye kape your word?"

"I did my best for you," said Nora.

"Yer bhest. A poor bhest when I've had to go. But now, Miss Nora, I aint waylaid you for nothin'. The masther has escaped this time, and you has escaped; but as shure as there is a God in heav'n, if you don't get Squire to consint to let me go back, there'll be mischief. There now, Miss Nora, I've spoken. You're purty, and you're swate, and 'tis you has got a tinder heart; but that won't do you no good, for I'm mad with misery. It's me bit of a cabin I want to die in, and nothing less will contint me. You may go back now, for I've said what I come to say; but it's to-morrow night I'll be here waiting for ye, and I warn ye to bring me the consint that I crave, for if you don't come, be the powers! ye'll find that you've played with fire when you neglected Andy Neil."

Having uttered these words, the miserable man dropped Nora's arm and vanished into the depths of the plantation. Nora stood still for a moment, then returned thoughtfully and slowly to the house.

CHAPTER XXXIII
THE CABIN ON THE MOUNTAIN

Nora slept little that night. She had a good deal to think of, and very anxious were her thoughts. She knew the Irishman, Andy Neil, well, and she also knew his ferocious and half-savage temperament. Added to his natural fierceness of character, he now undoubtedly was possessed by temporary insanity. This had been brought on by hunger, cold, and great misery. The man was desperate, and would think little of desperate deeds. After all, his life was of small value to him compared to his revenge. Whenever did an Irishman, at moments like the present, consider life? Revenge came first, and there was that in the man's gleaming dark eyes, in his high cheek-bones, in his wild, unkempt, starved appearance, which showed that he would, if something was not quickly done, once again attempt the Squire's life. What was she to do? Nora wondered and wondered. Her father was getting better; the open air treatment, the simple food, and the company of his friends were effecting the cure which the luxurious life in the heavily furnished chamber had failed to do. The Squire would soon be well and strong again. If he were careful, he would once again stand in health and strength on his ancestral acres.

He would get accustomed to the grandeur of the restored Castle O'Shanaghgan; he would get accustomed to his English relatives and their ways. He would have his barn to retire to and his friends to talk to, and he would still be the darling, the best-loved of all, to his daughter Nora; but at the present moment he was in danger. In the barn, too, he was in much greater danger than he had been when in the safe seclusion of the Castle. It would be possible for any one to creep up to the barn at night, to push open the somewhat frail windows or equally frail door, and to accomplish that deed which had already been attempted. Nora knew well that she must act, she must do something—what, was the puzzle. Squire O'Shanaghgan was one of the most generous, open-hearted, and affectionate of men. His generosity was proverbial; he was a prime favorite with his tenants; but he had, like many another Irishman of his type, a certain hard phase in his character—he could, on occasions, be almost cruel. He had taken a great dislike to Andy Neil and to some other tenants of his class; he had been roused to stronger feeling by their open resistance, and had declared that not all the Land Leagues in Ireland, not all the Fenians, not all the Whiteboys, were they banded together in one great insurrection, should frighten him from his purpose.

Those tenants who defied him, who refused to pay the scanty rent which he asked for their humble cabins, should go out; they should, in short, be evicted. The other men had submitted to the Squire's iron dictation. They had struggled to put their pence and shillings together, and with some difficulty had met the question of the rent; but Andy Neil either could not or would not pay; and the Squire had got the law, as he expressed it, to evict the man. There had come a day when the wild tenant of the little cabin on the side of the bare mountain had come home to find his household goods exposed to the airs of heaven, the roof off his cabin, the door removed from its hinges; the hearth, it is true, still warm with the ashes of the sods of turf which were burning there in the morning, but the whole home a ruin. The Squire had not himself witnessed this scene of desolation, but had given his stern orders, and they had been executed by his agent. When Andy saw the ruins of his home he gave one wild howl and rushed down the side of the mountain. His sick children—there were two of them in the cabin at the time—had been taken pity on by some neighbors almost as poor as himself; but the shock (or perhaps their own bad health) had caused the death of both boys, and the man was now homeless and childless. No wonder his brain gave way. He vowed vengeance. Vengeance was the one last thing left to him in life; he would revenge his wrongs or die. So, waiting his opportunity, he had crouched behind a hedge, and, with an old gun which he had stolen from a neighbor, had fired at the Squire. In the crucial moment, however, his hand shook, and the shot had lodged, not in the Squire's body, but in his leg, causing a nasty but scarcely a dangerous wound. The only one in all the world who suspected Andy was the Squire's daughter Nora; but it was easy for her to put two and two together. The man's words to her in the cave, when he threatened to drown her, returned to her memory. She suspected him; but, with an Irish girl's sympathy, she would not speak of her suspicions—that is, if her father's life was spared.

But now the man himself had come to her and threatened fresh mischief. She hated to denounce the poor, starved creature to the police, and yet she *must* protect her father. The Squire was much better; but his temper could be roused to great fury at times, and Nora dreaded to mention the subject of Andy Neil. She guessed only too well that fear would not influence the fierce old Squire to give the man back his cabin. The one thing the wretched creature now craved was to die under the shelter of the roof where he had first seen the light; but this natural request, so dear to the heart of the Squire himself, under altered circumstances, would not weigh with him under existing conditions. The mere fact that Andy still threatened him would make him more determined than ever to stick to his purpose. Nora did not dare to give her father even a hint with regard to the hand which had fired that shot; and yet, and yet—oh, God help her! she must do something, or the consequences might be too fearful to contemplate.

As she was dressing on the following morning she thought hard, and the idea came to her to take the matter into her own hands, and herself give Andy leave to go back to his cabin; but, on reflection, she found that this would be no easy matter, for the cabins from which the tenants were evicted were often guarded by men whose business it was to prevent the wretched creatures returning to them. No doubt Andy's cabin would be now inaccessible; still, she might go and look at it, and, if all other means failed, might venture to beg of her father's agent to let the man return to it; but first of all she would see the place. Somewhat cheered as this determination came to her, she ran downstairs. Mr. Hartrick was returning to England by an early train, and the carriage, which was to convey him to the station, was already at the door. Mrs. O'Shanaghgan was almost tearful at the thought of parting with her beloved brother. Molly, delighted at being allowed to stay on at the Castle, was also present; but Nora's entrance on the scene caused Mrs. O'Shanaghgan to speak fretfully.

"Late as usual, Nora," said that lady, turning and facing her daughter as she appeared. "I am glad that you condescended to appear before your uncle starts for England. I wonder that you have taken the trouble."

"Oh, do not scold her, Ellen," said Mr. Hartrick, kindly. "I begin to understand something of the nature of my Irish niece. When the Squire is well again she will, I am sure, return to England and resume her studies; but at present we can scarcely expect her to do so."

"I will come back some time, Uncle George," said Nora; "and oh!" she added, "I do thank you for all your great and real kindness. I may appear ungrateful, but indeed, indeed I am not so in my heart, and it is very good of you to allow Molly to stay; and I will promise to take great care of her, and not to let her get too wild."

"Thank you. Any message for your aunt, Nora?" said Mr. Hartrick gravely. "I should like you, my dear," he added, coming up to the girl, and laying his hand on her shoulder and looking with his kind eyes into her face, "to send your Aunt Grace a very special message; for you did try her terribly, Nora, when you not only ran away yourself, but induced Molly to accompany you."

Nora hesitated for a moment, the color flamed into her face, and her eyes grew very bright.

"Tell her, Uncle George," she said, speaking slowly and with great emphasis, "that I did what I did for *father*. Tell her that for no one else but father would I hurt her, and ask her to forgive me just because I am an Irish girl; and I love—oh! I love my father so dearly."

"I will take her your message, my dear," said Mr. Hartrick, and then he stooped and kissed his niece.

A moment later he was about to step into the carriage, when Nora rushed up to him.

"Good-by; God bless you!" she cried. "Oh, how kind you have been, and how I love you! Please, please, do not misunderstand me; I have many cares and anxieties at present or I would say more. You have done splendidly, only——"

"Only what, Nora?" said her uncle.

"Only, Uncle George," answered the girl, "you have done what you have done to please my mother, and you have done it all in the English way; and oh! the English way is very fine, and very noble, and very generous; but—but we *did* want the old bare rooms and the lack of furniture, and the place as it always has been; but we could not expect—I mean father and I could not expect—you and mother to remember that."

"It was impossible, Nora," said her uncle. "What I did I did, as you express it, my dear, in the English way. The retrograde movement, Nora, could not be expected from an Englishman; and by-and-by you, at least, will thank me for having brought civilization to O'Shanaghgan."

A moment later Mr. Hartrick went away, and Nora returned to the house. Mrs. O'Shanaghgan had left the room, and Nora found herself alone with her cousin Molly.

"What is it, Nora?" said Molly. "You look quite pale and anxious."

"I look what I feel," said Nora.

"But can I help you in any way, Nora?"

"Yes. Will you come for a drive with me this morning?"

"Of course I will. You know well that I should like nothing better."

"Then, Molly dear, run round to the yard and tell Angus put Black Bess to the outside car, and to bring it round to the corner of the plantation. I do not want any one to know, and tell Angus that I will drive Black Bess myself."

"All right," replied Molly, running off on her errand.

Nora did not stay long with her father that morning, and soon after ten o'clock she and Molly were flying through the boreens and winding roads in the direction of Slieve Nagorna. At the foot of the mountain they dismounted. Nora fastened Black Bess's reins to the trunk of a tree which stood near, and then she and Molly began to ascend the mountain. It was a glorious winter's day; the air was mild, as it generally is in the west of Ireland, and the sun shone with power. Nora and Molly walked quickly. Nora, who was accustomed to climbing from her earliest years, scaled the rocks, and jumped from one tiny projection in the ground to another; but Molly found her ascent more difficult. She was soon out of breath, and called in laughing tones to Nora to wait for her.

"Forgive me," said Nora; "I sometimes forget that you are not an Irish girl."

"You also forget that I am practically a London girl," answered Molly. "I have seldom or never climbed even a respectable hill, far less a mountain with sides like this one."

"We will reach the spot which I am aiming for before long," said Nora; "but if you are tired, do sit down, and I'll go on alone."

This, however, Molly would not hear of, and presently the girls reached a spot where once a small cabin had stood. The walls of the cabin were still there, but the thatched roof had disappeared, the doors and windows had been removed, and the blackened earth where the hearth had been alone bore evidence to the fact that fires had been burnt there for long generations. But there was no fire now on the desolate hearth.

"Oh, dear!" said Nora. "It makes me cry to look at the place. Once, long, long ago, when Terry and I were tiny children, we came up here. Andy's wife was alive then, and she gave us a hot potato each and a pinch of salt. We ate the potatoes just here, and how good they tasted! Little Mike was a baby, such a pretty little boy, and dear Kathleen was so proud of him. Oh! it was a *home* then, whereas now it is a desolation."

"A very poor sort of home I should say," answered Molly. "What a truly desolate place! If anybody ever lived here, that person must be glad to have got away. It makes me shudder even to think of any human being calling this spot a home."

"Oh!" answered Nora, "it was a very pretty home, and the one who lived in it is broken-hearted—nay, more, he is almost crazed, all and entirely because he has been driven away. He deserved it, I know; but it has gone very hard with him; it has torn out his heart; it has turned him from a man into a savage. Oh! if I had only money, would not I build up these walls, and put back the roof, and light the fire once more, and put the man who used to have this house as a home back again? He would die in peace then. Oh! if only, *only* I had money."

"How queer you look!" said Molly. "How your eyes shine! I don't understand you. I love you very much, but I confess I don't understand you. Why, this desolate spot would drive most people mad."

"But not Irish people who were born here," said Nora. "There! I have seen what I wanted to see, and we had best be going back. I want to drive to the village, and I want to see John Finnigan. I hope I shall find him at home."

"Who is John Finnigan?" asked Molly.

"The man who *does* these sort of things," said Nora, the red, angry blood rushing to her cheeks.

She turned and quickly walked down the mountain, Molly racing and stumbling after her. Black Bess was standing motionless where her mistress had placed her. Nora unfastened the reins and sprang upon the car, Molly followed her example, and they drove almost on the wings of the wind back to the village. There they were fortunate enough to find John Finnigan. Leaving Molly holding Black Bess's reins, Nora went into the house. It was a very small and shabby house, furnished in Irish style, and presided over by Mrs. Finnigan, a very stout, untidy, and typical Irishwoman, with all the good nature and *savoir-faire* of her countrywomen.

"Aw, then, Miss Nora," she said, "I am glad to see you. And how's the Squire?"

"Much better, thank you," said Nora. "Is your husband in, Mrs. Finnigan?"

"To be sure, deary. Finnigan's abed still. He was out late last night. Why, listen; you can hear him snoring; the partition is thin. He snores loud enough to be heard all over the house."

"Well, do wake him, please, Mrs. Finnigan," said Nora. "I want to see him on a most important matter at once."

"Then, that being the case, honey, you just step into the parlor while I go and get Finnigan to rise and dress himself."

Mrs. Finnigan threw open the door of a very untidy and small room. Several children were having breakfast by a table which bore traces of fish-bones, potato-peelings, and bacon-rinds. The children were untidy, like their mother, but had the bright, very dark-blue eyes and curly hair of their country. Nora knew them all, and was soon in the midst of a clamorous group, while Mrs. Finnigan went out to get her husband to rise. Finnigan himself appeared in about a quarter of an hour, and Nora went with him into his little study.

"Well, now," said that worthy, "and what can I do for you, Miss O'Shanaghgan?"

Nora looked very earnest and pleading.

"My father is better," she said, "but not well enough yet to be troubled with business. I understand that you are doing some of his business for him, Mr. Finnigan."

"Some, it is true," answered the gentleman, frowning as he spoke, "but not all, by no means all. Since that English fine gentleman, Mr. Hartrick, came over, he has put the bulk of the property into the hands of Steward of Glen Lee. Steward is a Scotchman, and why he should get work which is rightly my due is hard on me, Miss Nora—very hard on me."

"Well," said Nora restlessly, "I know nothing about the matter. I am sorry; but I am afraid I am powerless to interfere."

"Oh, Miss Nora!" said Finnigan, "you know very well that you have kissed the Blarney Stone, and that no one can resist you. If you were to say a word to the Squire he would give me my due; and now that so much money has been put into O'Shanaghgan, it would be a very fine thing for me to have the collecting of the rents. I am a poor man, Miss Nora, and this business ought not to be given over my head to a stranger."

"I will speak to father by-and-by," said Nora; "but I doubt if I can do anything. But I have come to-day to ask you to do something for me."

"And what is that, Miss Nora? I am sure I'd be proud to help such a beautiful young lady in any way."

"I dislike compliments," said Nora, coloring with annoyance. "Please listen. You know the man you evicted from the cabin on the side of Slieve Nagorna—Andy Neil?"

"Perfectly well, perfectly well," answered Finnigan,

"You had my father's orders?"

"I had that, Miss Nora."

"I want you, Mr. Finnigan, now to take my orders and to give Andy back his cabin. Put a bit of roof over it—anything, even an old tarpaulin— anything, so that he may sleep there if he likes to-night. I want you to do this for me, and allow me to take the risk of offending my father."

"What!" said Finnigan, "and risk myself all chance of getting the agency. No, no, Miss Nora. Besides, what would all the other tenants say who have been evicted in their time? The man shall get his cabin back and a fresh roof and new windows, by the same token, when he pays his rent, and not before."

"But he has no money to pay his rent."

"Then he must stay out, Miss Nora."

"I wish, I wish," said Nora, clasping her hands and speaking with passion, "that you would oblige me in this. Indeed, it is of the utmost importance."

"What!" said Finnigan, going up to her and staring into her face; "has that scoundrel threatened? Is it possible?"

"No, no, no; you are mistaken," said Nora eagerly. "I only meant that I—I—pitied him so much."

"That being the case, Miss Nora, I will say nothing further. But the fact is, I have before had my suspicions as to the hand which pulled that trigger which sent the shot into the Squire's leg, and it would be an extremely graceful act on my part to have that person arrested, and would doubtless insure the agency for me. But I will say no more; only, please understand, under *no* circumstances, except the payment of the rent, can Andy Neil get back his cabin."

CHAPTER XXXIV
A DARING DEED

Having failed to get any help from John Finnigan, Nora returned to the Castle. As she drove quickly home she was very silent. Even loquacious Molly did not care to interrupt her thoughts. As soon as they reached the Castle she turned to her cousin and spoke quickly.

"Go to the barn and look after father, Molly. Talk as many naughty words as ever you like; make him laugh; keep him occupied. After dinner I shall probably want your aid again. In the meantime you will help me best by taking father off my hands."

"And I desire nothing better," answered Molly. "I love the Squire; it is the height of entertainment, as he would call it, to talk to him."

Molly accordingly ran off. The Squire was now well enough to sit up in a great easy-chair made of straw, which had been carted over from Cronane for his special benefit, for the padded and velvet-covered chairs of the Castle would not at all have suited his inclinations. He sat back in the depths of his chair, which creaked at his every movement, and laughed long and often at Molly's stories.

"But where's Light o' the Morning herself?" he said after a pause. "Why don't she come to visit her old father? Why, it's craving for a sight of her I am."

"I think Nora is very busy to-day," answered Molly, "May I read the paper to you, Squire?"

"You read the paper to me?" answered Squire O'Shanaghgan. "Why, bless yer little heart, my pretty girleen, but I must decline with thanks. It is perfect torture to listen to your English accent when you are trying to do the rich Irish brogue. Irish papers should be read by Irish colleens, and then you get the flavor. But what did you say my colleen was after—business, is it? She's very fond of poking that little finger of hers into other people's pies. What is she after now at all, at all?"

"I cannot tell you," answered Molly, coloring slightly as she spoke.

The Squire looked annoyed and suspicious.

"You go and call her to me," he said. "Tell her to come along this blessed minute; say it's wanting her I am."

Molly ran out of the barn. She found Nora in earnest conversation with Angus, while Hannah Croneen stood close by plucking now and then at the girl's skirt, looking eagerly into her face, and uttering such ejaculations as "Oh, glory!" "Be the powers!" "Did ye ever hear the like?" "Well, well, that beats all!"

"Nora," said Molly, "will you go to your father? He wants you immediately."

"Have you let out anything?" said Nora, turning and looking anxiously at Molly.

"No; but he asked after you, and I said you were busy. The Squire said then, 'I hope she is not poking her little finger into other people's pies.'"

"Well, I will go to him," said Nora. "I'll manage him. You stay where you are, Molly."

Nora's black hair was curling in crisp waves all round her beautiful white forehead. Her dark-blue eyes were darker and more shining than ever, there was a richer bloom on her cheeks, and there were sweeter smiles on her lips than she had ever perhaps worn before as she now entered the Squire's room.

"Well, father?" she said.

Squire O'Shanaghgan, who had been sitting wrapped in thought, roused himself on her entrance, gave her a smile, and motioned her to come to his side.

"Kneel down by me, colleen," he said.

Nora knelt. The Squire took his big hand and put it under her chin; he raised her blooming face and looked into her eyes, which looked back again at him. As he did so he uttered a quick sigh.

"You're after something, mavoureen," he said. "What's up, little girl? What's fretting that tender heart of yours?"

"Something, father," said Nora then.

"And you won't tell your old dad?"

"I would rather not. Won't you trust me?"

"Trust her, is it?" cried the Squire. "I'd trust her with all I possess. I'd trust her with my hopes of heaven itself. Trust her, is it? Nora, you fret me when you talk like that."

"Then *do* trust me, father, and don't ask me any questions. I'll tell you by and by—yes, I faithfully promise, but I shall be busy to-day. I may have to be away from you for a great part of to-day, and I may want Molly to help me. Can you do without me?"

"Why, now, the conceit of the creature," said the Squire. "As if I cannot do without you, you little piece of impertinence. To be sure, and to be sure I can. Why, there is your lady mother; she'll come and sit with me for an hour or so, and let out at me all her grumbles. Nora, my heart, it is dreadful to hear her; but it's good penance too, and maybe it's too comfortable you have been making me, and I ought to have a bit of what I do not like to keep me humble. You go along now, and come back when you have done that which is filling your heart to the brim."

Nora kissed her father very gravely; she then went out of the barn, and returned to where Angus and Hannah, and also Molly, were waiting for her.

"I have thought how I can manage, Miss Nora," said Angus. "When those Englishmen—bad cess to 'em!—are at dinner I'll get the long cart out of the yard, and I'll put the white pony to it, and then it's easy to get the big tarpaulin that we have for the hayrick out of its place in the west barn. I have everything handy; and if you could come along with me, Miss Nora, and the other young lady, and if Hannah here will lend a hand, why we'll do up the place a bit, and the poor forsaken crayther can die there at least."

"Do not forget the basket of provisions, Hannah," said Nora, "the potatoes, and the bacon, and a tiny bottle of potheen; and do not forget some fagots and bits of turf to kindle up the fire again. Oh, and, Hannah, a blanket if you can manage it; and we might get a few wisps of straw to put in the bottom of the cart. The straw would make a fine bed."

"To be sure," said Hannah. "You lave it to me, me beautiful young lady."

The two servants now departed, and Nora and her cousin went into the house. The early dinner, or rather lunch, as it was now called, was served soon afterwards; and almost immediately after the meal was over Nora and Molly ran down to the bottom of the plantation, where they found Angus, Hannah, the long cart with the pony harnessed to it, and the tarpaulin, straw, basket of provisions, etc., all placed in the bottom.

"Jump in, Molly," said Nora.

Molly scrambled in as best she could; Nora followed her; and Hannah, climbing in over the left wheel, sat down at the bottom of the cart. Angus jumped on the driver's seat, and whipped up the pony. The pony was stout and very strong, and well accustomed to Irish hills. They were off. Molly had never been so rattled and bumped and shaken in the whole course of her life, but she enjoyed it, as she said, immensely. Only, what was Nora doing? The tarpaulin had been carefully hidden from view by the straw which Angus had cunningly placed over and not under it; and it was well that this was the case, as after the little party had left O'Shanaghgan a couple of miles, they were met by John Finnigan driving on his outside car.

"Why, then, Miss Nora, what are you doing now?" he said.

"Having a drive for my own pleasure," replied Nora, nodding gayly.

Finnigan looked with suspicion at the party, but as there was nothing contraband in anybody driving in a long cart, and as he could not possibly guess what they were doing, he drove on his own way without saying anything further. After less than an hour's driving they reached the foot of Slieve Nagorna, and here the real toil began, for it was quite impossible for the pony, willing as he was, to lug the cart up the mountain. Where there is a will, however, there is generally a way; and although the pony could not drag the cart up, he could go up himself, being very sure-footed and quite willing to be turned into a beast of burden for the nonce. The heavy tarpaulin, therefore, was fastened on his back, and, with Angus leading and Hannah following with the basket of provisions, and the two girls making up the rear, the little cavalcade started forward. Oh, how hot it seemed, and oh, how tired Molly got! But never mind; they were making progress. After a time they reached the site of Andy's cabin, and then Angus and Hannah developed strength which fairly took Molly's breath away, for the tarpaulin was absolutely lifted up and deposited as a sort of temporary roof over the roofless walls; and when this had been done Angus managed to cut a hole in the center to make a chimney; then the fagots were placed on the hearth and the turf put on top of them, and the remainder of the turf laid handy near by; and the straw was ready, soft and inviting, in a corner not too far away from the fire, and the blankets were spread over it; and the basket of provisions, cold boiled potatoes, cold bacon, and the little bottle of potheen were all left handy. It was indeed a miserable home, but, compared to the desolate appearance it had presented, it now looked almost comfortable. Nora laughed with pleasure. "He shall come back here. It is better than nothing. He shall stop here. I will explain things to my father by and by," said the girl; and then they all turned their steps homeward.

At the appointed hour that evening Nora went down to the shore. She fully expected to find Andy Neil waiting for her. Wild and half-insane as he was, he kept his selfmade appointments, as a rule. She wandered about, fearing that someone would notice her; for she knew that if John

Finnigan thought for a single moment that she was secretly befriending Andy, he would not leave a single stone unturned to circumvent her. He was very proud of his powers of evicting tenants, and, as he had the Squire's permission to do his worst on this occasion, would be the last man in the world to relax his iron grip. Nora, however, wandered about in vain; there was no sign of Andy. She even ventured to go to the borders of the plantation and softly call his name.

"Andy—Andy Neil," called the girl, but no Andy responded. She now felt really nervous. Why was Andy not there? What could possibly have happened? She returned slowly and thoughtfully to the house. It would not do to show any alarm, but she certainly felt the reverse of comfortable. What had happened to the man? She did not for a moment think that he could be dead; on the contrary, she pictured him alive and still more insane than the night before, still more desperate in his mind, still more darkly pursued by the grim phantom of revenge. Was Andy now so really insane that he had even forgotten his appointment with Nora? This was probably the case. But although the man was too insane to think of meeting the girl, he was probably not at all too insane to make another attempt on the Squire's life. He was perhaps so desperate now that his one idea was to carry out his revenge before he died. What was Nora to do? She thought and thought, and walked up to the house with more and more lagging footsteps. Finally she made up her mind. There was nothing whatever left for it but for her to sit up with the Squire that night; she herself must be his guardian angel, for he must not be alarmed, and yet most certainly he must be protected. Nora carefully considered this idea. She had made the little cabin quite ready for Andy's reception; he could creep into it once more, light his fire, eat his food, and lie down on the bed at least, as good as any other bed he had ever slumbered on; and if death came to him, it would find him in his old house, and perhaps God would forgive him, seeing that he was so desperate and life had been so hard. Yes, Nora felt that God was very merciful—far more merciful than man. But to-night—how was to-night to be got through? She had now reached the yard, and found herself face to face with Angus.

"Is there nothing I can do for you, miss?" said the young man, touching his hat respectfully to the girl.

"If you could be near somewhere, Angus, and if it were necessary, and we wanted the long cart to-night, could we get it?"

"You ask me, Miss Nora, what we could get and what we could not get at O'Shanaghgan," answered Angus; "and I answer ye back that what ye want, Miss Nora, ye shall have, if it is the heart out of me body. The long cart, is it? To be sure, me pretty lady, and at a moment's notice, too. Why, it's meself will slape in the bottom of the long cart this blessed night, and all you has to do is to come and pull the front lock of me hair, and I'll be up in a jiffy. You give it a sharp tug, Miss Nora, for I slapes heavy; but if you come, the long cart and the powny will be there."

"Then that's all right," answered Nora.

She went into the barn. The Squire had now contrived to renew all his old accustomed habits. On the little wooden table was a small lamp which smoked badly; the local paper was laid on the table, and the pipe which the Squire best loved lay near. He had been enjoying a good smoke, and was thinking of turning in, as he expressed it, when Nora appeared.

"Good-night, father," she said. She went up to him, and bent down over him, to give him her accustomed kiss.

"Why, then, it's sleepy I am," said the Squire. "I am thinking of turning into bed. I am getting on fine; and Angus, boy that he is, always comes and gives me a helping hand on to my bed. I cannot see your face with the smoke of that lamp, mavoureen; but things are all right—aren't they?"

"That they are, father," replied the girl; "but I am a little tired; and if Angus is coming to help you, and you do not want anything more from me, I will go to bed myself."

"Do that," said the Squire. "Your voice sounds peaky; you have been doing too much."

Nora lingered another moment or two. How thankful she felt that that smoky lamp prevented her father reading the anxiety in her eyes! She could not keep all the tiredness out of her voice, but she could at least keep anxiety from it; and the Squire bade her a hearty goodnight, and parted with her with one of his usual jokes. Nora then went into the house. The hour for late dinner was over; she herself had not been present, but Molly had managed to appear as usual. Nora ran down to the kitchen premises. The cook, a very stately English woman, stared when she saw the young lady of the Castle appear in the great kitchen.

"What is it, Miss O'Shanaghgan?" she said, gazing at Nora all over. What did this wild and eccentric girl want? How was it possible that she could demean herself by coming so freely into the servants' premises?

"I want to know, Mrs. Shaw," said Nora, "if you will oblige me?"

"Of course I will, Miss O'Shanaghgan; if I can."

"Will you pack a little basket with some cold pie, and anything else tasty and nourishing which you have got; and will you put a tiny bottle of brandy into the basket, and also a bottle of water; and can I have it at once, for I am in a great hurry?"

"Well, there is a fresh pigeon pie in the larder," answered the cook; "but why should you want it?"

"Oh! please, Mrs. Shaw," answered Nora, "will you give it to me without asking questions? I will love you for all the rest of my life if you will."

"Love me, is it?" thought the cook. "A pretty creature like that love me!"

"Your love is cheaply purchased, miss," she said aloud, and then went without a word into the larder, and soon returned with a well-filled basket, which she placed in Nora's hand. "And I added some fruit, a little cup of jelly, and a knife and fork and a spoon, and some salt; but why you, Miss Nora, should need a picnic in the middle of the night beats me."

"Remember our compact," said Nora. "You say nothing of this, and—I love you;" and then, overcome by a sudden impulse, she bent forward and laid the lightest of kisses on the astonished Mrs. Shaw's forehead.

Mrs. Shaw felt slightly overawed. "Bless her! What a beautiful young lady she is!" thought the good woman. "But the ways of the Irish beat all comprehension."

CHAPTER XXXV
THE COT WHERE HE WAS BORN

Nora avoided Molly that night. On reflection, it occurred to her that it would be best for Molly to know nothing of her design. If she were in complete ignorance, no amount of questioning could elicit the truth. Nora went into her bedroom, and changed her pretty jacket and skirt and neat sailor hat for a dark-blue skirt and blouse of the same material. Over these she put a long, old-fashioned cloak which at one time had belonged to her mother. Over her head she tied a little red handkerchief, and, having eaten a small portion of Mrs. Shaw's provisions, she left the room. It was already night-time; and Mrs. O'Shanaghgan, Molly, and the servants had gone to bed. Nora now locked her door from the outside, slipped the key into her pocket, and her basket of provisions partly hidden under the falls of her cloak, ran downstairs. The dogs generally slept in the big hall; but they knew Nora's step, and rose slowly, wagging their heavy tails. Nora patted them on their heads, gave them each an endearing word, and stooped to kiss pretty Cushla on her black forehead. She then softly unbolted one of the windows, lifted the sash, and got out. She carefully shut the window as noiselessly as she had opened it. She now found herself on the grassy sward in the neighborhood of the drawing-room. Under the old *régime* that sward was hard, and knotty tufts of weed as well as grass grew up here and there in profusion; but already, under the English government, it was beginning to assume the velvet-like appearance which a properly kept lawn ought to have.

Nora hated to feel such softness; she disliked everything which seemed to her to flavor of the English and their ways. There was a hot, rebellious feeling in her heart. Why should these things be? Why should not her Irish land and her Irish people be left in their wild freedom? She ran round to the yard. Angus had received instructions to leave the little postern door on the latch, and Nora now opened it and went softly in. The moon was beginning to rise, but was not at the full. There was, however already sufficient light for her to see each object with distinctness. She went and sat down in the shadow made by the great barn. She sat on the step to the barn, wrapping her warm cloak tightly round her, and keeping her basket of provisions by her side. Here she would sit all night, if necessary. Her vigil might have no result, but at any rate it would insure her father from danger. For now only over Nora's dead body could the wild Andy Neil approach the Squire.

"Andy shall kill me first," she thought; "and if I die, I will scream and father will awaken. Angus is on the watch; the alarm will be given; at least my father's life will be spared. But why do I think of danger of this sort? Andy will not kill me. I place my trust in God. I am doing the right thing—I know I am doing the right thing."

When Nora had let herself in at the postern door she had immediately drawn the bolt at the other side, thus preventing anyone else from entering the great yard by the same way; but she knew that, although Andy could not now enter the yard, in all probability he was already hiding there. There were no end to the ways and devices of a wild Irishman of Andy's sort. He was so thin and emaciated, too, that he could squeeze himself into the tiniest space. It lay in his power to remain motionless all night, until the moment when his revenge was ripe. Nora sat on. She heard the old clock in the ancient tower of the Castle strike the hours. That old clock had been severely animadverted on by Mrs. O'Shanaghgan on account of the cracked sound in the bell; but Nora felt relieved to find that, amongst all the modern innovations, the old clock still held its own; it had not, at least, *yet*, been removed from the tower. It struck solemnly now the hour of midnight.

"The witching hour," thought the girl. "The hour when the Banshee walks abroad. I wonder if I shall see her. I should like to see her. Did she hear me when I called to her in the cave? Would she help me if she came to my rescue now? She belongs to us; she is our own Banshee; she has belonged to our family for many, many generations."

Nora thought these thoughts; but then the feeling that *Someone* else who never fails those who trust Him was also watching her during this silent hour came to her with a sense of comfort. She could hear her father turning once or twice in the creaky old wooden bed. She was glad to feel that, unknown to him, she was his guardian angel. She began to think about the future, and almost to forget Andy and the possible and very great peril of the present, when, shortly before the hour of one, all her senses were preternaturally excited by the sound of a footfall. It was a very soft footfall—the noise made by a bare foot. Nora heard it just where the shadow was deepest. She stood up now; she knew that, from her present position, the one who was making this dead sort of heavy sound could not possibly see her. She waited, her breath coming hard and fast. For a minute, or perhaps more, there was again absolute and complete silence. The night was a breathless one; there was not a sound abroad; overhead the sky was of an inky blue-black, the stars were shining gloriously, and the moon was growing brighter and more clear, and more nearly approaching her meridian each moment. The girl stood with her hand pressed against her beating heart; she had flung aside her little red handkerchief, and her hair had fallen loose and was tumbling over her shoulders; she raised her other hand to her left ear to listen more intently— she was in the attitude of one about to spring.

Again there came the sound which she expected, and which, now that it had arrived, caused her heart to beat no longer with fear, but with a sort of wild exultation. Her suspicions had been right—the danger was real; her father's most precious life was in peril. The steps came quicker and more quick; they approached the other window of the barn. This window lay in complete shadow. Nora now stepped out of her hiding place, and, going with two or three quick strides down the yard, waited within a foot or two of the man, who now proceeded to lift himself up by the window ledge preparatory to opening the barn window. With the aid of a claspknife he could very easily push back the quaint and imperfect fastening; then it was but to push in the glass, and he could enter the barn. He sat on the window ledge with his back to Nora. His huge, gaunt form looked larger than ever, intensified now by the light of the moon. He breathed quickly; his breathing proclaimed that he himself was in physical suffering.

"Andy," said Nora in a low, very low whisper.

But this low tone was as startling to the madman on the window as though a pistol shot had been sounded in his ears.

"Be the powers!" he said, and he tumbled so quickly off the window sill that Nora herself held out her hand to help him. Then he turned fiercely and faced the girl. She saw the light of madness gleaming in his sunken eyes; his wild face looked more cadaverous than ever; his great, skinny, long hand shook. He raised it as if to fell the girl to the ground, but paused to look in her face, and then his hand hung feebly to his side.

Nora had enacted all this scene beforehand to herself; she now thrust into Andy's face, within an inch or two of his nose, a great lump of bread and a slab of cold pie.

"Before you do anything more, eat," she said; "eat quickly; make no noise."

It was as impossible for the famished man to resist the good and tempting food as it would have been impossible for a needle to resist the influence of a powerful magnet. He grasped the bread, thrust the knife into his wretched shirt, and, tearing the bread in fragments, began to stuff it into his mouth. For a couple of minutes there was no sound but that of the starved creature tearing the bread and feeding himself. When he had slightly satisfied the first cravings of his starved body Nora took his hand.

"You have not had enough yet," she said. "You have fasted long, and are very hungry; there is more where this came from."

She took his hand quite unresistingly, and led him round to the entrance of the barn.

"I am up," she said, "but no one else. No one else knows of this. You have come without a gun?"

"I have a knife instead," he said. His eye glittered strangely.

"Give me your knife," said the girl. "I will give you food in exchange for it."

The famished creature began to gibber now in the most horrible manner; he pointed to his breast and uttered a laugh.

"Laugh again, and I will call those who will soon put a stop to your wild and terrible purposes, Andy," said the girl, "Here's food—fruit, jelly, bread. You shall have them all—all, when you give me that knife."

The man looked at the food, and now his eyes softened. They became full not only of rapture, but also of laughter. He gave a low guttural sound, sank down on the ground, and held out both his hands imploringly for some of the nourishment.

"The knife," said Nora.

He thrust his hands into his bosom and held the knife out to her. It was a huge clasp knife, and Nora noticed with a shudder that it had all the appearance of having been newly sharpened. The moment she got it she put it in her pocket, and then invited the man to feed. He sat now quite humbly. Nora helped him to pie. She had already taken the precaution to hide the knife which Mrs. Shaw had supplied her with. The man ate and ate, until his consuming hunger was satisfied. Nora now gave him a very little of the brandy mixed with water. He lay back at last, exhausted and also satisfied.

"It's wake I am, it's wake I am—it's wake I am entoirely," said he. "Why are you so good to me, Miss Nora? It was to take the life of the Squire I was afther to-night."

"I knew that," said Nora, "and I thought I would prevent you. Why did you not meet me this evening down by the shore?"

The miserable creature now raised his hand and pushed back a gray lock of unkempt hair from his forehead.

"Why, then," he said, "it was bothered I was entoirely. I knew there was something I had got to do. It was waker and waker I was getting, for I did not touch bite nor sup since I saw you last, except a morsel of a cold pitatie; and there was not much of the nourishment in that; and as the night came, I could not think of anything except to keep me word and have me victory."

"Well, you have had it," said Nora.

"What do you mane now, missie?"

"You have conquered yourself; that is the best victory of all. But come, you made a bargain with me last night, and I am prepared to keep it. I went down to the shore to tell you that I would do what you wanted me to do. The cabin is ready on Slieve Nagorna; we have made it fairly comfortable for you; and I will do better—yes, I will try to do better by and by. I will speak to my father when he is strong enough. Go to Slieve Nagorna now, and you will find the old cot in which you were born. You can sleep there, and—and I—I will see that you are not interfered with."

"The old cot in which I was born," said Neil very slowly. "The old cot, and I'll see it again. Is it a-joking me you are, Miss Nora?"

"Would I joke with you just now, Andy? Would I?"

"I know it's saft you are making me. There was a lump of ice in me; but, somehow, it's melted. It's the food and your bonny face, and yer ways. But do you know that it was your *father* I wanted to kill—t'ould Squire? There, I have said it!"

"I know—and I have saved him," answered Nora. "But come, he may hear us speaking; he would wonder. I do not want him to know anything of this night. When he is stronger I will plead with him. Come, Andy, come; your home is ready for you. Go back to it."

The man tottered to his feet, and began to stagger across the barn.

"Stay! you are not strong enough," said the girl. "Come outside the yard, here; come with me."

She walked across the yard, reached the little postern gate, and opened it.

"Come out and wait," she said in a mysterious voice. "You cannot walk to Slieve Nagorna, and yet you must get there; but I will get Angus to take you."

"Angus! ay, he is a true Irish boy. Aw, I'd trust him."

"You well may; he is a broth of a boy," said Nora. "Sit there. I will soon be back with you."

She shut Andy out, bolting the little gate. The man heard the bolt being drawn, but did not move; he had not the slightest fear but that Nora would keep her word. She ran across the yard and opened the door of the barn at the farther end. Angus was already awake; he heard her light step.

"Is it me you're wanting, Miss Nora?"

"Angus, all is well," she said. "What I wanted to do I have succeeded in doing. It is Andy Neil who is without; he is broken down and is very weak. Get the long cart and take him to the foot of Slieve Nagorna, help him up the mountain, and see him into the old cot where he was born. Good-night, Angus, and God bless you."

Nora returned to her own bedroom. She unlocked the door and let herself in. Without waiting even to undress, she flung herself on the bed, curled herself up, and went off into dreamless slumber. When she woke again it was broad daylight, and Molly was standing over her.

"Why, Nora, you have lain undressed all night! What—what has happened?"

"Do not ask me," said Nora. "Do not ask me. I have done what I wanted to do, and I am thankful."

"And you won't really tell me?"

"No, I won't. I cannot ever. There is more to attend to, Molly; you and I have got to go to Slieve Nagorna immediately after breakfast."

Molly did not ask anything further.

"I brought your hot water," she said. "You do not want any of the grand English servants to see you look like this."

"What a dear old thing you are!" said Nora. "I am so grateful to you."

She got up, took off her clothes, indulged in a hot bath, and came down to breakfast looking exactly as if she had spent an ordinary night. Mrs. O'Shanaghgan was a little more fretful than ever, and told Nora that her conduct was making her mother quite ridiculous in the neighborhood.

"I met those remarkably nice people, the Setons of Seton Court," yesterday," said Mrs. O'Shanaghgan—"charming English people—and they asked me if it was really true that my husband, the owner of Castle O'Shanaghgan, was sleeping in a barn."

"And what did you answer, mother?" asked Nora, her dark-blue eyes bright with sudden fun.

"Well, my dear, I made the best of it. I could not deny such a patent fact. I said that the eccentricities of Irish squires were proverbial. But you can imagine, my dear Nora, my mortification as I had to make this admission. If this sort of thing goes on I shall ask your uncle to let the place, and allow us all to live in England."

"Oh, come, mother," said her daughter. "You ought to be thankful this morning—you ought to be. Oh, mother! do give me a loving kiss. It is so long, so long since you have done so, and somehow I am tired, mother."

"Tired!" said Mrs. O'Shanaghgan, alarmed and surprised by the new tone in Nora's voice. "You look tired. How black those shadows are under your eyes! and you have lost some of your color. There! of course I will kiss you, and I hope I am thankful, for we certainly have had wonderful mercies since your dear Uncle George came over and delivered us all. But what do you mean by special thankfulness this morning?"

"Never mind, mother," said Nora. "Only *do* be thankful, *do* thank God for His mercies; and oh, mother, do give me that kiss!"

"There, child! of course you shall have it."

Mrs. O'Shanaghgan pressed her lips lightly to Nora's cheek.

"Now eat your breakfast," she said. "These eggs are quite fresh, and the honey was bought only yesterday—you know you are fond of honey—and these hot cakes are made in a new and particularly nice way. Eat plenty, Nora, and do, my dear, try to restrain your emotions. It is quite terrible what wear and tear you give yourself over these feelings. It is really, my dear girl, unladylike; and let me tell you another thing, that when you lose your fresh wild-rose color, you will lose the greater part of your beauty. Dear me! it will not stay long with you if you excite yourself about every hand's turn in the ridiculous way you are doing."

Nora did not say any more. She sat down to the breakfast table. Was her mother right? Was she indeed exciting herself over every hand's turn, and was that thing which had happened last night—which, now that it was over, caused her heart to beat a trifle too fast, and brought that tired, that very tired feeling into her sensitive frame—was that indeed but a trifling thing? Thank God—oh, thank God—she had been in time!

Soon after breakfast Nora and Molly started once more for Slieve Nagorna. They went on the outside car this time, and Nora found her strength and courage returning as she handled the reins and urged Black Bess to speed. They presently reached their destination. Nora fastened up the horse as she had done on the previous day, and the girls began to climb the mountain.

"You must not be afraid when you see Andy," said Nora. "He was very weak last night, and will in all probability be in his house. I am going to arrange to have provisions sent to him every day. He will stay there now that he has got back again."

"But how has he got back again? You will remember you never told me what happened last night."

"And you must not ask me, Molly. What happened last night can never be told by me to any human being. Only Angus knows something of it; and Angus will not tell anyone else."

"And you were frightened? You look, Nora, as if you had gone through a great deal."

"I went through more than anyone will ever know," said Nora, "but I am very thankful."

The girls had now reached the old cabin. The tarpaulin was over the roof, but there was no smoke issuing from the hole.

"I wonder he did not light his fire," said Nora in an anxious voice. "Will you go in with me, Molly, or shall I go alone?"

"I'll go in with you," said Molly stoutly. "If you are not afraid, neither will I be."

"I afraid now?" said Nora, with a smile. "Come, Molly, I hope the poor creature is not very ill."

Both girls entered the cabin. The tarpaulin had been so contrived that a piece hung over, and formed a temporary door. Nora now pushed it aside, and they both stepped into the miserable cabin. Andy was lying on the straw; the basket of provisions had not yet been touched, nor was the fire lit. Andy lay very still and quiet on the straw. Nora went up to him; his eyes were shut, and his head was slightly turned round, so that she could not at first get a proper glimpse of his face. She went on her knees, then presently touched his forehead with her own slim hand, calling his name softly at the same time. There was no answer—there would never be an answer again, for the wild Irishman was dead.

CHAPTER XXXVI
"I'M A HAPPY MAN!"

It was just before Christmas, and the preparations for the festive season were great at Castle O'Shanaghgan. The Squire was quite well again. Once more he walked all over his estate; once more he talked to his tenants; once more he joked and laughed with the other squires of the neighborhood. To a certain extent he had grown accustomed to the grand house with its grand furniture; to the terrible late dinner, at which he stoutly declined to appear in evening dress; to the English servants who knew none of his ways. He began to bear with these things, for Light o' the Morning, as he called his beloved Nora, was always by his side, and at night he could cast off the yoke which was so burdensome, and do what he liked in the barn. At Mrs. O'Shanaghgan's earnest request this barn was now rendered a tolerably comfortable bedroom; the walls had been papered, and the worst of the draughts excluded. A huge fireplace had been built out at one end, and the Squire did not object at all to a large turf fire on a cold night; but the old bedstead from Cronane still occupied its old place of honor in the best position in the room, the little deal table was destitute of cloth or ornament of any kind, and the tarpaulin on the floor was not rendered more luxurious by the presence of rugs.

"Rugs indeed!" said the Squire, snorting almost like a wild beast when his wife ventured to suggest a few of these comforts. "It is tripping me up you'd be? Rugs indeed! I know better."

But compared to its condition when the Squire first occupied it, the barn was now a fairly comfortable bedroom, and Squire Murphy, Squire Fitzgerald, Squire Terence Malone, and the other squires of the neighborhood had many a good smoke there, and many a hearty laugh, as they said, quite "unbeknownst" to the English lady and her grand friends. And Nora, Molly, and even Biddy Murphy often shared in these festive times, laughing at the best jokes, and adding sundry witticisms on their own account.

It was now, however, Christmas Eve, and Mrs. O'Shanaghgan's nearest English relatives were coming to spend the festive season at the Castle. Mrs. Hartrick, for the first time in her life, was to find herself in Old Ireland.

Linda was also accompanying her mother, and Terence O'Shanaghgan was coming back for a brief visit to the home which one day would be his. Terence was now permanently settled in his uncle's office, and was likely to make an excellent man of business. Mr. Hartrick was glad of this, for he would much prefer the O'Shanaghgans to have money of their own in the future, rather than to depend on him to keep up the old place. Inwardly the Squire was fretting and fuming a good bit at Mr. Hartrick really owning Castle O'Shanaghgan.

"I must say, after all's said and done, the man is a gentleman," he remarked to his daughter; "but it frets me sore, Nora, that I should hold the place under him."

"It's better, surely, than not having it at all," answered Nora.

"Yes, be the powers! it is that," said the Squire; "but when I say so, it's about all. But I'll own the truth to you now, Nora: when they were smothering me up in that dreadful bedroom before you came, mavourneen, I almost wished that I had sold the place out and out."

"Oh, but, father, that time is long over," answered Nora; "and I believe that, after all, it will be good for the poor people round here that you should stay with them, and that there should be plenty of money to make their cabins comfortable, and to give them a chance in life."

"If I thought that, there'd not be another grumble out of me," said the Squire. "I declare to you, Nora, I'd even put on that abominable dinner suit which your lady mother ordered from the best Dublin tailors. My word! but it's cramped and fussed I feel in it. But I'd put it on, and do more than that, for the sake of the poor souls who have too little of this world's goods."

"Then, father, do believe that it is so," said Nora; and now she put one of her soft arms round his neck, and raised herself on tiptoe and kissed his cheek. "Believe that it is so, for this morning I went round to the people, and in every cabin there was a bit of bacon, and a half-sack of potatoes, and fagots, and a pile of turf; and in every cabin they were blessing you, father; they think that you have sent them these Christmas gifts."

"Ah, ah!" said the Squire, "it's sore to me that I have not done it; but I must say it's thoughtful of George Hartrick—very thoughtful. I am obliged to him—I cannot say more. Did you tell me the things were sent to every cabin, Nora—all over the place, alannah?"

"Every cabin, father," answered his daughter.

"Then, that being the case, I'll truss myself up tonight. I will truly. Mortal man couldn't do more."

The preparations, not only outside but inside, for the arrival of the English family were going on with vigor. Pretty suites of rooms were being put into their best holiday dress for the visitors. Huge fires blazed merrily all over the house. Hothouse flowers were in profusion; hothouse fruit graced the table. The great hall quite shone with firelight and the gleam of dark old oak. Mrs. O'Shanaghgan dressed herself in her most regal black velvet dress for this auspicious occasion; and Nora, Molly, and even Biddy Murphy, all in white, danced excitedly in the hall. For Biddy Murphy, at Nora's special suggestion, had been asked to spend Christmas at the Castle. It was truly good to see her. Notwithstanding her celestial nose and very wide mouth, it would have been difficult to have looked at a happier face than hers. And, Irish as Biddy was, she had got the knack of coming round Mrs. O'Shanaghgan. She did this by her simple and undisguised admiration.

"Oh, Mrs. O'Shanaghgan!" Biddy would cry, "it is the very most lovely thing I have ever clapped eyes on. I never saw anything so magnificent as this room. It's fairyland; the whole place is fairyland;" and as Biddy spoke her eyes would twinkle, and her big mouth would open, showing her immaculate white teeth. So much did she contrive to win over Mrs. O'Shanaghgan that that lady presented her with a soft white muslin dress for the present occasion. If Biddy was proud before, she was almost rampant with pleasure now. She twirled round, and gazed at herself in the long mirrors which had been inserted in the hall between the oak panels.

"Why, then, it's proud me ancestors, the old Irish kings, would be of me now," she was even heard to say.

But, all things being ready, the time at last approached when the tired travelers would arrive. At the eleventh hour there had come a great surprise to Nora and Molly; for Mrs. Hartrick and Linda were bringing Stephanotie with them. How this came to pass was more than either girl could possibly conjecture; but they both felt that it was the final crown of their happiness.

"Can I ever forget," said Nora, "that but for Stephanotie lending us that money I should not have been able to run away to Ireland, and my dear, dearest father might not now have been alive?"

But the sound of wheels was at last heard without.

"Come, girleens, and let's give them a proper Irish welcome," said the Squire, standing on the steps of the old house.

Nora ran to him, and he put his arm round her waist.

"Now then, Nora, as the carriage comes up, you help me with the big Irish cheer. Hip, hip, hurrah! and *Caed Mille a Faitha*. Now then, let every one who has got a drop of Irish blood in him or her raise the old cheer."

Poor gentle English Mrs. Hartrick turned quite pale when she heard these sounds; but Mr. Hartrick was already beginning to understand his Irish relatives; and as to Stephanotie, she sprang from the carriage, rushed up the steps, and thrust a huge box of bon-bons into Squire O'Shanaghgan's face.

"I am an American girl," she said; "but I guess that, whether one is Irish or American, one likes a right-down good sweetheart. Have a bon-bon, Squire O'Shanaghgan, for I guess that you are the man to enjoy it."

"Why then, my girl, I'd like one very much," said the Squire; "but don't bother me for a bit, for I have to speak to my English relatives."

"Oh, come along in, Stephanotie, do," said Molly. "I see that you are just as eccentric and as great a darling as ever."

"I guess I'm not likely to change," answered Stephanotie. "I was born with a love of bon-bons, and I'll keep it to the end of the chapter."

But now Mrs. Hartrick and Mrs. O'Shanaghgan had met. The two English ladies immediately began to understand each other. Mrs. O'Shanaghgan, without a word, slipped her hand inside her sister-in-law's arm, and they walked slowly across the magnificent hall and up the wide stairs to the palatial bedroom got ready for the traveler.

Then the fun and excitement downstairs became fast and furious. The Squire clapped his brother-in-law, George Hartrick, on the shoulder; the Squire laughed; the Squire very nearly hallooed. Terence looked round him in undisguised amazement.

"I would not have known the old place," he said, turning to Nora.

Nora gave a quick sigh.

"Where is my mother?" said the lad then.

"She has gone upstairs with Aunt Grace; but run after her, Terry, do," said his sister.

Terence gave another glance round, in which pride for the home where he was born kindled once more in his dark eyes. He then rushed up the stairs three steps at a time.

"Why, then," said the Squire, "it's cramped and bothered I am in these clothes. What possesses people to make Merry-andrews of themselves night after night beats my comprehension. In my old velveteen jacket and knee-breeches I am a man—in this tomfoolery I do not feel as good as my own footman."

"You look very well in your dinner dress all the same, O'Shanaghgan," said Mr. Hartrick. And he added, glancing from Nora to her father, "I am glad to see you quite recovered."

"Ah! it's she has done it," said the Squire, drawing Nora forward and pressing her close to his heart. "She's a little witch. She has done fine things for me, and I am a happy man to-night. Yes, I will own to it now, I'm a happy man; and perhaps there are more things in the world than we Irish people know of. Since I have my barn to sleep in I can bear the house, and I am much obliged to you, George—much obliged to you. But, all the same, it's downright I'd have hated you, when you altered this old place past knowing, had it not been for my little girl, Light o' the Morning, as I call her."